DARLING YOUNG ONE

A Visionary Tale of the Utopian 1960s

MARK S OWEN

Burning Bright Books Publishing
marksowenbooks@gmail.com

Original cover art by Rosa Tara Cortes of Bogota, Colombia

For you of undaunted courage
with the eyes that see
and the heart to be.

Part One

"No one believed us, so we did it anyway."
—The wandering hippie

"You have come here to learn a great lesson –
that you cannot die."
—Paramahansa Yogananada

Chapter 1

WHEN THE KNOCK came at our door on that sunset evening it was unexpected. Nobody visits us in our plain house on the outskirts of this laid-back town, hidden from the road by trees and an old storage shed. Late rays of sunlight slant into the room through the dusty windows partially covered in rose Indian bed spreads. We are just starting to chow into our raw vegetable and roasted grain supper when we hear the crunch of tires on the gravel drive.

Evan, my younger brother, looks at me, swallowing, the famished look of a salivating yogi in his eyes. Celibate vegetarians in their quest for cosmic-consciousness have only one pleasure they can honestly satisfy, their gnawing desire for food. All other sensual things are more or less off-limits, including lustful imagination and surreptitious jacking-off. One goes all the way into this other-world trip or one goes not a all.

"Who could that be in the driveway?" I wonder, taking a bite of the oven-toasted organic oat flakes with almonds and drizzled with local bee honey, an Oaxacan clay mug of spring water at hand. We are lean spare mystics who struggle with raging hard-ons, or at least I do, and we don't like to be disturbed while eating. The weird thing about the celibacy trip is that many girls are fascinated by it, their soft eyes glow with curiosity. Some even take a keen interest in upsetting the apple cart, so it can be tricky having female friends.

"Maybe somebody needs to get into that old shed," Evan says hopefully. But there are heavy footfalls on the porch steps, an abrupt knock on the white door. My brother walks past our improvised alter to see who's there. It could even be my probation officer from LA, who knows? But no, to our surprise, it's the eccentric reverend Sorenson, the big-bellied disciple of Parama-hansa Yogananda. He fills the door in his denim overalls, a beaming expression on his round face, his painter's cap in his hands. Torgen Sorenson lives up over the crest in Atascadero in a cave-like, metaphysical church.

"Excuse me for barging in on your dinner," he says at once, "if you had a phone I would've called ahead. But I promised to get back to you with an answer, so here I am!"

"No problem, Mr Sorenson." I give him an affable smile. "Would you like something to eat? Maybe some brown rice and wheat berries?"

"Oh no, no," he replies in his boyish way, "I didn't come here to eat. I've done all my due diligence and I've got something important to tell you fellows."

Evan flashes me a glance and we swallow our savory mouth-fuls. This strange individual has heavy-duty spiritual credentials. Torgelananda, which is our private nickname for him, looks like a barrel-chested wizard with luminous blue eyes and unkempt white tufts for eyebrows. Scraping one paint-spattered sneaker on the floorboards, he points at me and says, "I know now for sure that our meeting was no coincidence. Yogananda definitely sent you boys to me. Only through Master could you have ever found me!"

My brother and I share a flickering, intuitive glance. Yoga-nanda, the master he's talking about, has been physically dead for fifteen years. We've attended his homespun, candlelit meditations up in the boondocks, the reverend has a penchant for dramatic statements. And now Sorenson rushes ahead, his massive body dominating the small room, knowing he has our full attention. "Master came to me in a vision while I was over in Modesto painting, I almost fell off the ladder when I saw him. He told me what I'd suspected, that he sent you two boys to me for the higher purposes."

As Sorenson says "Master", his voice chokes with emotion and his eyes tear up. He gestures toward our coffee table alter adorned with the framed pictures of Yogananda, Lahiri Mahasaya, Sri Yukteswar, Jesus Christ, and the immortal Mahavatar Babaji. Then looking at me, the older, more worldly brother, burly Sorenson shouts, "Yogananda told me you and your brother are here with me now to do God's hidden work, the special things that has been prophesied. And I say again, there's no other way on earth you could have reached me except through him."

This blows our minds, food completely forgotten. Prophesied? My brother and I stare at him with astonished faces. What more can two dedicated Kriya yogins ever hope to hear from the dear ascended master? To be singled out, to feel the blessing descend? But I am no fool either, aiyee. Looking him in the eyes, I ask, "And what would that purpose be, Mister Sorenson?"

The big-bellied reverend fixes me in his bright gaze and declares, "To bring peace on this fucked-up earth, excuse my French, and to rid the world of war. To bring peace for all humankind once and for all, all nations, even the willfully ignorant ones."

I swallow hard. If you could read my mind, that would be my most fervent wish. Gesturing, I blurt, "But how, how can that be done? Isn't it obvious how much our own government loves to make war? That sounds a little far-fetched."

"It can be done," Sorenson intones evenly.

"But how? By what means?"

"By subjugating the devils themselves, and all those who would resist the high, holy power of ceremonial magic."

"What? What the fuck are you talking about? Are you making this up?"

Torgelananda gathers us up with his bulging blue eyes, insisting, "Most certainly not. Subjugate all the war-mongers, all the puppet-masters and the crooked politicians, throw them and the evil ones they serve into chains! The time has come to bring forth a new kingdom on this planet!"

My eyes flare open, I gape at this madman. I have taken over two hundred high-octane acid trips, I know madness when I encounter it and madness is beautiful. This salt-of-the-earth character in painter's overalls, a jack of all trades, who spent several years as one of Yogananda's personal disciples, declaring a new kingdom on earth? But we've been been told that Master loved this man. There's no way he would stand here and try to deceive us in Yogananda's name. Or would he?

"But what about God-consciousness?" Evan interrupts. "That's the only real reason I'm into this trip, to try and become one with God."

"Oh I realize that," reverend Sorenson says with great feeling, "and me too, that's the indispensable part Without that deep devotion the rest of it doesn't work. It all goes together and that's our protection. Because those ancient devils won't cut us any slack."

My brother blinks at him in bewilderment. "Yeah, okay, I can dig it. But what devils?"

"The devils that rule this earth. The demonic powers."

Frowning in skepticism, I say, "Mr Sorenson, you're saying

that there is a special method that can overthrow the evil bastards that enslave this world? Are you serious, for real?"

"That is exactly what I am saying," Torgelananda replies, scrapping one foot, his face bright with knowledge. "There are secret techniques that come down from Solomon and his father King David and from the Chaldean light-masters. But these disciplines are arduous and exacting, there is a purification period, this isn't for dabblers. You have to really commit. And we need to spend a lot more time together than just two meditation sessions a week. That is, if you're interested."

"That's incredible," I mutter, looking over at Evan, who's staring back at me. How many conversations have we wondered if world peace could be gained through some advanced metaphysical methods? Now this country-bumpkin yogi-wizard comes through our door and lays this amazing number on us.

"There are no coincidences," the reverend states, as if reading our thoughts.

"But we've already been purifying ourselves," Evan points out, "we've been celibate for almost a year, even longer for Jake, and our diet is totally organic. We fast every weekend, water only, and we do hours of Kriya meditation every day."

"We also do Hatha yoga asanas," I say, "and master's energization exercises every morning and night. But then I drive the laundry truck around and Evan tends the garden and gather sacks of fruit, that doesn't leave us much time."

"I know, I know that," Sorenson placates, pointing his thick blunt finger at the guru photographs. "What you boys are doing is incredible, living in self-imposed ashram conditions out here in the world. There's not one in a million who can do that. That's how I knew you showing up like you did is no accident!"

"Wait a minute, Reverend," Evan blurts, "you want us to move up into that strange building with you, the Center of Light, in Atascadero? Is that what you mean by commit?"

"Yes, you hit the nail pretty much on the head. That is what I mean," Torgie admits, beaming with satisfaction. "The ceremonial work must go on every day and night for a year or more. It's a very demanding metaphysical science."

"Whoa, man," I hold up my hand, "a year or more? We, I mean, I don't know about that. That'd be a huge change from the way we live. And we escaped LA so we could live like this."

"All right," Sorenson replies, regarding me with his somber, luminous eyes. "But you're both ready for it or Master wouldn't have sent you. And I tell you this in God's holy truth, if you will commit to this work, totally commit and follow through with me, the whole world will bow and scrape at your feet."

"Say what? Come again?"

"The whole goddamn world will kneel before you, hear what I say." Sorenson says in a fierce, impassioned tone, stabbing his finger at us. "All men will bow and grovel at your feet, all the forces of nature will do your bidding."

We stare at him in stark incredulity. Lifting one thick hand, he nods at Evan. "You will be the New Pope, the illuminating spiritual guide. All religions will come under your personal direction."

"Huh?" Evan mumbles, his mouth hangs as he gapes at the hig-bellied lunatic.

Turning his finger and bulging blur eyes on me, the reverend proclaims, "and you, Jake Acree, will be the supreme commander over all powers on earth, over all armies, you will rule the nations. You will have dominion over them all, both visible and invisible, even over Satan himself."

In shock I stare into Sorenson's fervent, demented eyes, encyclopedias flickering in my brain. "Whoa man, dig," I say. "I'm a radical conscientious objector, I hate all war. And I don't even know if Satan exists. As far as I can tell that's all part of the bullshit nonsense."

"Come up and see me for Wednesday evening meditation," Torgie says with a humble smile, "and I'll lay it out for you in better detail."

MY BROTHER AND I came up to the remote central coast this rainy spring, 1967, leaving the frenetic LA, scene in our rambling Dodge panel wagon loaded with our hodgepodge of cargo. Other than some cartons of books, a typewriter, some threads, a few sticks of furniture and camp gear. Hippie nomads don't carry much, we're running mainly on inspiration. Gone were my fast British motorcycles, gone were the fragrant bricks of Mexican weed and the amber jars of pure Lsd. In escaping to the country I abandoned all that, we shed our wild-child identities and plunged ever deeper into our yoga practices. You reach a point where there is no turning back unless you wimp out.

This sleepy town of San Luis Obispo straddles highway 101 in a verdant coastal valley at the foot of the Santa Lucia Mountains, about mid-way between Los Angeles and San Francisco, and thirteen miles inland from foggy Morro Bay. SLObispo only has 25,000 people living in it, including 5000 students at Cal Poly, an agricultural college popular with farm and ranching families. This is a radical shift in vibes from the flamboyant freak trip of LA, you get that right away. But there are open roads and green hills and wild empty seacoast wherever you roam, that's the beauty.

The day we landed in San Luis we got lucky. Stopping in a

restaurant for coffee and salad, reading the local classified ads, we see this: One bedroom house on vacant quarter acre lot. Unfurnished. Electricity, gas, water, trash included. 1-2 people only. No weirdos, no cows. $125 per month. Evan and I look each other over. We're not wearing any beads or hippie adornments, we just might qualify.

Following the directions, we take Broad Street to the outskirts of town and find the place. It's an old frame house situated behind a rambling workshop-storage shed, with a gravel driveway. The house is bordered on one side by a weedy lot, and on the other by a small farm with a fruit orchard. The door is unlocked, we walk right in to check things out. Bare wood floors, a single gas wall heater for all three rooms. There's one bedroom with an attached bathroom, tub and shower fixture. I tell Evan he can have this room for his own space. I'll throw my sleeping pallet under the windows in the front room, where we can set up our meditation area at one end. The kitchen is narrow, a four burner gas stove and little oven, rattling old fridge, linoleum floor, cracked linoleum counters and stained porcelain sink. Like the house itself, all the walls and cupboards and doors are painted white.

There's an enclosed back porch with a washer hookup, a rustic iron sink and a fold-down table, perfect for storage. But what seals the deal for us is the sprawling back lot. The backyard is wide and deep, the rough fertile ground for the organic garden that we have envisioned. A sagging clothes line runs along the back of the house. We share a gleam of a smile and nod, feeling certain that we have been guided to this secluded place. Not stain of paranoia shadows this scene.

Gauging the town's conservative vibes, I trim my longish hair back to collar length. Within a week, another stroke of luck, I score a job driving a laundry and dry-cleaning delivery truck. The job pays me $800 a month and doesn't even start for two weeks, giving us time to do the heavy work of putting our garden in the ground. It's already high spring on the central coast, where everything grows in profusion. Avocados to lemons, apples to figs, flowers to melons, broccoli to beets, everything. The afternoons are blue with benevolent sunshine, in the evenings the sea fog from Morro Bay and Los Osos rolls inland and envelops San Luis in a damp cocoon. The fog reminds me of the monsoon rains of Oaxaca's Sierra Madre, mystical and deep, a sheltering presence in our austerer meditations.

We rent a gas-powered push-tiller to break up the heavy soil, carving out a large rectangular plot about 40 by 30 feet, then spend days chopping it, raking it, and sifting it with spade, hoe and rake, blistering our hands. We get rid of the bone-crunching rocks, the tangled weedy roots, the old tin cans, mixing into the dirt big 50 pound bags of organic compost and fertilizer. We intend this to be the holy grail of vegetable gardens and spend almost two weeks preparing it. The old farmer with a thick European accent who owns the orchard next door watches over the fence, parsing out his advice. He is a burly and confident curmudgeon, skeptical of our organic presumptions. He tells us such fanciful notions will not work hereabouts.

"The ravenous birds and nasty grasshoppers will eat you alive without spraying on the pesticides", he scoffs. "Your garden will be devoured before you can even pick a squash."

We listen, but ignore his advice, telling him we are involved in a special, moon-sign gardening experiment. Waving us off, he calls out to his wife in derisive humor. The short, stout woman, busy spraying apricot trees with a hand-plunger ddt canister, pauses to look at us but does not laugh. Nodding politely, she says, "I have heard of that method and I wish you luck. But he's right, my husband. This is a bad year and you are getting a late start. All the rains caused a plague of insects. If the bugs don't get your crops the birds will eat everything. The birds are so terrible! Look at our scarecrows!"

Evan and I go on about our visionary work, intending no rudeness, permitting no interference. We consult the detailed notes on planting by astrological moon-signs that I compiled during months of library research back in Los Angeles. This will be a lunar-solar garden, protected by chants and holy spells. Using the lunar phases in fertile Taurus we plant various vegetables in sequence, keeping a precise journal. To run a comparison, we plant some crops in unfavorable moon phases to find out if there is any difference. On the drop-down back porch table, we sort out our organic seeds, gathered through my day-dreamer, mail-order garden catalogs.

We put these precious seeds into the ground one packet at a time, invoking the sacred Aum sound. Squatting, on our knees, we plant carrots and beets, zucchini and string beans, staking and running yards of cord. We put in rows of spinach and soybeans, a section of broccoli, some cucumbers, a few cauliflowers and scattered vines of mouthwatering cantaloupes. These life-giving crops will ripen in waves of 60, 90, and 120 days. You are what you eat, dig it. Finally, at the four corners of the garden, we plant giant yellow sunflowers like wands of celebration.

Truth is what it is and nothing is how it seems. Anyone who has ever tripped on a pure dose of acid can attest to that. And the reality is that my brother and I have become solitary and purely obsessed. We wade into a monastic rhythm of meditation, work, fasting, metaphysical study, along with the tedious hoeing and weeding of the talisman garden. I confess that most of this grunt work falls to Evan, who cannot seem to find a regular job and doesn't really want one. Whereas I spend my weekdays in a white Ford van with Pablo's Dry Cleaners painted in red letters on the sides, picking up and delivering laundry to the far-flung towns of SLO County. On some days I'm driving Los Osos, Morro Bay, Cayucos, Cambria and San Simeon, hitting restaurants, bars, stores and remote ranches on the spectacular, lonely coast. Other days I'm down south in Arroyo Grande, Santa Maria, and the fog-shrouded eucalyptus groves of Nipomo and Halcyon. When I get home in the late afternoon I feel pretty bushed. Bananas and peanuts and apples and affirmations will only take you so far. But after doing Yogananda's energization exercises and wolfing down a plate of our delicious yogi cuisine, my body feels restored. Then, in the drifting sundown fog, my brother and I bless our garden with ancient Sanskrit chants.

The bountiful garden flourishes like mad. Vegetables spring up in natural exuberance. The hungry insects make a run at us but we control them with a rust-colored liquid that is wholly derived from plant roots. The bugs eat the leaves not treated with this stuff, and shun the leaves sprayed with it. We buy it in gallon jugs at the local garden store, it washes right off with water, no pesticides or lethal chemicals residues. The old man across the fence mocks our efforts in his gruff voice, calling us hippie dreamers but the earth is sacred and we have read the plangent warnings in Rachel Carson's book, Silent Spring. We carry on and let our garden speak for itself.

The reality is that his own little showcase farm is being devoured by hordes of insects and marauding birds. His wife confesses it is like a Biblical plague, she has never seen a year so bad. We see the birds swarming over their peach and plum and apricot trees, feasting on the ripening fruit. The maddened woman flaps at them with brooms and blankets, they erect macabre scarecrows, they light smudge fires, but to little avail. Despite their chemical repellents, they are being robbed of their presumed harvest by chattering magpies and ravenous insects. Evan and I watch these bizarre scenes out of the corners of our eyes, keeping our mouths shut, trying not to gloat.

On our side of the fence the insects are defeated and the hungry birds leave us alone. At sunset we stand at opposite ends of the garden, in the slanting sunlight and long shadows, facing each other with hands raised at our shoulders, chanting the holy AUM vibration. We encircle our garden with natural radiance, asking for its health and blessing and protection. The old folks across the way look on in silent wonderment, not knowing what to think. The tall yellowing sunflowers rise like sentinels at the four corners, forming their budding solar blossoms. Anything that we planted according to the fertile moon signs grows in far more robust abundance than the other spare patches, an abundance that is based on old astrological crop science, not synthetic fertilizers.

"But that is all superstition," the old curmudgeon mutters, leaning on the fence, scowling at our flourishing garden, arguing with himself. Some kind of hocus-pocus is afoot, earth magic reigns, some kind of hippie hoodoo, something incomprehensible.

Chapter 2

M Y BROTHER AND I feed off of one another's zealous energy, an esoteric society of two. Other than random visits across town to our cousin Lawrence and his artist wife, we have no social life. We steep ourselves in our devout yoga lifestyle, seeking illumination sans drugs now, sans intoxicants of any kind, aiming to sublimate the feverish Kundalini that courses through our young and feral bodies.

We are up right at dawn each damp, cool morning, often in billows of fog, do 15 minutes of yoga energization exercises, then dive into deep lucid meditation using the SRF Kriya techniques for a solid hour. Cosmic Consciousness is the name of this game. We come out of it and devour a breakfast of ripe purple figs, yellow bananas, red apples, whole grain toast smeared with crunchy peanut butter and a handful of dry roasted almonds, once in a while a hard boiled egg with sea salt, and for me a mug of strong, dark-roast coffee.

Then, alert and ready, I leave our sanctuary and get into my route truck. No, not the 1948 Dodge wagon that made the trek up the coast with the busted 2nd gear, that I sold for a hundred bucks, instead the fast white Ford van with the bold red lettering on the sides. My new bosses are two Italian brothers who are kind enough to let me drive the van home at night. I take off into the foggy mornings on my rural excursions, with my fruitarian lunch sack and notebook of scribbled poetry.

My brother ventures forth, too. Evan takes a paper sack on his daily adventure of food-foraging through the back streets of San Luis Obispo. Natural fruit grows on the trees here in private yards, trees laden with ripe mission figs, peaches and apricots, dark juicy plums and lemons. Evan makes friends with the residents in his easy-going way, a strange but friendly vegan. They usually give him permission to take what he wants, otherwise it goes to the ants and the marauding birds.

Each day he comes home with his burgeoning food sack, his vital contribution. More fresh fruit than we can possibly eat, so whatever begins to rot we dump into a compost pit. For some reason regular work eludes Evan, or he dodges it, and I can dig that. I dealt pounds of weed and quarts of pure acid rather than squeeze myself into the strait-jacket of an ordinary job. He confesses to me, guiltily, that some mornings he stops and stuffs himself with glazed donuts, sabotaging our purist regime. I take perverse delight in his hang-dog face, his mournful expression, needling him about these poisonous sugar and bleached flour snacks. "Aiyee, you will die, man, your kidneys will give out. You will die wheezing and belching and horribly constipated."

But he swears off, he claims, bringing home his sacks of ripe fruit and to fill the rattling refrigerator, then does much of the dirty work in the garden, weeding and hoeing, reluctantly killing insects, so I have no complaints. He is my loyal brother and partner on this holy quest.

Meanwhile, our kitchen becomes a cornucopia of savory organic foods, a vegetarian paradise. Using the mail-order catalogs from companies like Arrowhead Mills, we order 25 pound burlap sacks of oat flakes and brown rice, peanuts in the shell, Montana red wheat berries, and 10 pound bags of millet and lentils and dry roasted almonds. We ship in wooden slats of delicious organic dates from Indio, cases of black and butternut olives, and 10 pound bolsas of dark Colombian coffee beans. On the back porch we set up a burr hand-grinder and a multi-tiered sprouter. Pure vegan food is our sensual indulgence, our new psychedelic. Most of my extra money goes into these food stocks and we drool with anticipation as the precious cargo comes in, a revolutionary act of smuggling organic contraband across the fast-food wasteland of America, for at heart, I am still a smuggler.

On the weekends we fast for a full 24 hours, from Friday sundown until Saturday sundown. We take no solid food of any kind, not even fruit juice, only spring water with a few drops of lemon. Obsessed with the purification our bloodstream and cellular bodies, we take strong herbal enemas while crouching in the cold bathtub, squatting on the toilet to purge hideous streams of putrid fecal matter. We are shitting out years of negative karma and vile substances, there can be no doubt. Trembling thin ascetics, we emerge empty and radiant with new-born faces.

But some things are weird, weirdness always lurks in the shadows. The nights turn strange and convoluted, for me, haunted by the residues of my former psychedelic excesses. The purifying processes trigger violent effects in my sympathetic nervous system. I get caught up in roaring nightmares as the trapped psychoactive particles are discharged from the cellular tissues, jolting me awake in shivering, bug-eyed sweats. But I know what is happening and I do all I can to assist the cleansing. Our bodies will completely regenerate if given the chance.

My personal studies in this science of regeneration are relentless. In fact, this becomes my intellectual specialty. I am fascinated with the Arnold Ehret mucus-less diet healing system, which I chance upon in a rare book. Doctor Ehret lived in Bavaria in the 1890's, stricken with a wasting kidney disease considered incurable. However, Ehret decided to try and heal himself by long periods of fasting and embracing a pure mono-diet. For weeks he would consume only organic grapes along with alpine spring waters while he took vigorous hikes in the Alps. He succeeded in purging all disease from his body and became effulgent with renewed health. Ehret grew a long black beard and dressed in prophet robes while he walked all over Europe with a staff preaching his mucusless rejuvenation system. Around the turn of the century he moved to southern California and lived at Mount Washington, not far from where the Self-Realization Fellowship headquarters are located. His main contention is that mucus-producing foods such as milk, cheese, red meats and processed grains are the root cause of lethal disease in the human Organism. Mucus is death.

Digging into his radical organic system, I am struck by how similar his advice is to that pioneering food evangelist old Doc Kloss of "Back To Eden" fame. People eat themselves to death out of stupidity, their piggish appetites rob them of longevity! Tribal elders in the old testament lived for hundreds of years, fathering children with hot, young wives. Arnold Ehret predicted in lectures that he himself would probably live to be 150 years old or more. Oddly enough, that was not to be, although I can't find any confirmed reports of how or even if he died. Some say a large iron safe that was being hoisted above the streets of Vienna fell on him and crushed him like a salamander. Others report that one night walking in the misty streets of Los Angeles that Ehret slipped and cracked his head on the curbstone, and never woke up. One thing is certain. No matter how brilliant, you have to stay alert or you can go kaput in an instant.

THE SUMMER FOG rolls in from Los Osos and Morro Bay, blanketing SLObispo in quietude. Around ten o'clock each evening Evan and I go into our deep nocturnal meditations. Another hour, sometimes two or more, devoted to the science of awakening to Super-Consciousness. These late night meditations can be quite tricky. First, we do a session of Yogananda's unique exercises, the intent being to drive any lethargy from the body. But it's always difficult to stay awake when you are on the cusp of your sleep cycle, and these swooning meditations give rise to bizarre and chaotic phenomena.

As the fog swirls through the trees and over the garden, we settle cross-legged on cushions facing the low makeshift alter, covered with a blue cloth and presided over by the immortals. Sandalwood incense wafts in the air, candlelight flickers, all is tranquil here on the fringes of sanity. We begin our inward Sanskrit chants, palms open in our laps, eyes closed and focused up into the nebulous effulgence of our foreheads. The photographs of the SRF master lineage gleam in the dim light, blessing and protecting. All goes well for the first thirty minutes or so, then we begin to swoop and dive through the veils of the subconscious, buffeted by confusing imagery, losing track of our Kriya tones. We come awake to find that we have pitched so far forward that our faces are only six or eight inches from the floor, drooling and mumbling, a strange and recurrent problem.

We talk it over, Evan and I, about how to overcome this ignominious swoon. To counter the phenomena, we take a page right out of Sri Yukteswar's book, Yogananda's stern guru. Yukteswar, as an aspiring yogi, would attempt to meditate on God's holy name deep into the night, only to find in dismay that his chin had dropped, his head sagged forward, nodding out over and again. To conquer this irredeemable flaw in his practice he anchored an iron ring in the roof rafter above his head, attached a rope to the wall and then ran it through the overhead ring, and tied the loose end around his long, gathered hair. Afterwards, when in meditation his chin drooped, that taut rope would snap him back into wakefulness.

Seeing our own solution in this anecdote, my brother and I rig up a smooth board supported by concrete blocks about thirty inches in front of us and the same level as the low alter table. We wrap the board in old towels for cushioning. Now, if we dip and swoon, our foreheads will come into contact with this board and jolt us back upright. This crude invention works so well that many bizarre things happen. As we dive through the subconscious curtains our foreheads smack into the board, jarring us aware! But sometimes we are so immersed in mind-wanderings that our foreheads strike the board repeatedly, like a woodpecker tapping on tree bark. Many nights what brings us around to clarity is this bizarre head-tapping resonating in our bewildered ears. We rub our foreheads, mutter ruefully, meditate some more, then fall into bed. At dawn, we arise with a subtle ringing inspiration and begin anew. The outer world is wreathed in ocean fog and I hear nothing other than my sonorous breath, the inner chant, and the early conversation of the birds.

The summer months shine in organic abundance, the after-noon skies are a vast peerless blue, then the coastal fog rolls in. The breaking of the surf on the wild coastline above Cambria ravishes my senses. Our garden comes forth in beautiful multi-hued stages, the beet greens, spinach and carrots, string beans and tomatoes, green and yellow squash, the luscious round canta-loupes and giant sunflowers bursting with edible seeds. The old griper across the fence has been devastated by bad garden karma, the birds and insects have eaten everything but his root vegetables.

He stares at our bountiful crops in grudging respect, shaking his head, talking to himself under his breath.

On our days off, our almost-guilty do-nothing days, Evan and I wander all over the place exploring. Over on the fringes of Cal Poly we discover a big unfenced grove of avocado trees bursting with ripe aguacates. The orchard keeper tells us this experimental grove contains over 200 varieties of avocados from all around the world, mostly producing trees. This blows our minds, we cannot hide our bright-eyed lust.

"Take whatever you want," he drawls with a smile, taking stock of our lean, hunter-gatherer physiques. "Pick the ripe ones off the lower branches or up off the ground, as you can see they're plentiful. Otherwise most of it just goes to waste, which is a real shame."

Ahh, what a great and unexpected bonanza! We start passing a couple times a month, filling a sack with delicious mature avocados, plump alligator pears, and the black thin-skinned ones from Mexico that you can sprinkle with sea salt and eat like an apple. Our narrow back porch overflows with natural, tree-grown food. In between our ascetic fasting and ardent meditations, we gorge like decadent vegetarian princes. We will never eat meat again and the accidental smell of frying bacon makes us want to puke.

All is good, yet the hard truth is we are feeling lonely and isolated up here on the central coast. Far from our hip friends in Los Angeles, our only socializing takes place on Sundays with our cousin Lawrence and his shy wife, Rebecca. They occupy a sagging shotgun house closer into town, living in one side, Rebecca's art studio on the other. She's a freckled red-haired woman who shows us around her blooming herb and flower garden, murmuring of the fairies that hover over each plant. She may be daft, but

Lawrence is her solid and gentle protector. He operates a Culligan water truck and hand publishes chapbooks of his earthy poetry. We know Lawrence from years ago, where in our Texas post oak childhood he taught us how to play baseball in a field of bluebells and prickly pear cactus. His thick horn-rimmed glasses slide down on his nose. He seems to be active in grass-roots politics, which to us is incomprehensible. When we visit on Sundays he mostly talks sports, either major league baseball or professional football, a TV game always droning in the background. Rebecca disappears into her studio or never even comes out. Lawrence puts out snacks but we barely nibble the greasy potato chips he favors, wishing for the giant roasted Peruvian corn kernels that I used to munch on back in my pot-smoking daze. Our cousin boils bitter black coffee on his antique gas stove, pointing out that the grinds are an excellent laxative. He sports a neatly trimmed mustache, we ramble on about American history or classical western philosophy, but Lawrence disparages my favorite existentialists Camus, Nietzsche, and the depraved Jean Genet who had a penchant for sniffing bicycle seats. He thinks Rimbaud was an arrogant fool, and other than a skeptical shrug our agnostic cousin expresses no interest whatsoever in the SRF philosophy or in our mystical aspirations. Peering over his horn rims, his demeanor lets us know that he considers our unusual lifestyle to be a passing "new-age fallacy."

Frustrated by our self-imposed seclusion, I buy a used yellow Studebaker Lark. This enables us to drive 200 miles down to Los Angeles to spend a spontaneous weekend reconnecting with our old comrades, pound the drums, drink some red wine and talk avant-garde philosophy deep into the night. On Sunday mornings, we go and meditate at the SRF Hollywood Chapel, talk to cordial brother Mokshananda, then visit the Lake Shrine and Gandhi's ashes out on Sunset before making the long trek home up the sundown coast on 101. We always make it home in time for our Sunday night devotions, obsessed with our intimate personal evolution.

These occasional trips help but they are not the answer. We feel stranded way up here in conservative San Luis Obispo valley. Our deep solitary meditations, our homegrown diet, the purging of past so-called sins is not enough. Something vital is missing.

The poetic letters I exchange with Dawn accentuates these lonely feelings. When are we going to get back together? When will it happen? She wants to know and I have no answers. The images that I paint as to how Evan and I spend our days and nights seem to put her off. She is cooling on the idea of coming out joining us with baby Tia Velina. Apparently ours is not the new-age commune that she's been dreaming of, where you roll a fat potent joint and slip into the erotic sack. Not that I blame her she needs what she needs, and I half-suspect she's found another boyfriend back there in Illinois. The world has gone mad and in our own ways we've all gone mad with it. Vietnam rages on like a dooms-day slaughterhouse, lying politicians ignore truth with their eyes wide open, and we must all find our way forward. All the attachments, the fond illusions, the fleeting emotional securities are being peeled away and we stand alone. My brother and I feel almost like strangers to ourselves in this arduous and ambiguous journey into the unknowable.

Chapter 3

THE EARLY WEEKS of Indian Summer chase away the gloomy marches of fog, bringing blue sky days and clear warm nights. The local See Canyon apple harvest comes in and our back porch fills with baskets of crisp apples—the tangy winesap, the sumptuous red and golden delicious. In this benign climate our garden keeps on producing broccoli and cauliflower late into December and we scarf like wolves to appease our feral and restless bodies. From time to time we take Instamatic snapshots of each other in yoga poses. These photos show intense young men so lean and ethereal that a translucent solitude shines right through them. Sometimes, when I look at these photos, I hardly recognize myself. What happened to that long-haired rebel on his black British motorcycle?

The reality is that strange things happen and you never know when they're coming down. And in his random foraging for late-season figs, my day-dreaming bother stumbles right into the ambush. We have feasted on so much sweet fruit this summer, those juicy purple figs, that stinging cracks irritate the corners of our mouths. We try to to air-dry some figs by dangling them on cords but the ants eat them, so Evan keeps searching for producing trees. One afternoon he ambles past a shabby house that has a rundown orchard in the deep backyard. A scatter-brained woman with unruly gray hair lives there. She never remembers Evan's name or even that they have talked before, but otherwise seems friendly enough.

"Oh of course, young man", she rasps, hacking on her stubby Chesterfield. "Help yourself to those apricots, I don't like them, it all just goes to waste."

"Well, not apricots ma'am, I mean the big old fig tree, I'd like to pick that."

"Oh, yes, the birds are fond of that tree, I call it my bird-feeder. Yes, you can take some. Are you in the movies, young man? You look like someone I saw in a movie."

"No," Evan blushes, explaining, "I've never been in a movie. I'm just a yogi fruit-picker."

"How quaint," the old lady mumbles, dismissing him with a waggle of her bony hand. "Well, help yourself to that tree. I never eat it anymore. It's disgusting, all the loose bowels. All I eat anymore are eggs and cupcakes with a little red wine."

Evan walks around to the sideyard and contorts himself into the gnarled limbs of the ancient fig, plucking the unpecked morsels and dropping them into his brown paper sack. He has the weird feeling that he is being watched. After a while he emerges from the green limbs with a full sack. He's certain that the old woman is spying on him from behind her rear screen door, he can almost make out her brooding figure. Stepping out into the yard he hoists his fruit sack and calls out, "Thanks very much, I've got all we need, I'll be going now."

Aiyee, the banshee hag comes shrieking out of her back door onto the sagging porch, something flashing in her grip as the hair goes up on my brother's neck. She leaps down the weathered steps in her faded dress, scrambling toward him with crazed white eyes.

"Nooo you nasty beggar," she shrieks, brandishing a steel butcher knife. "You are stealing my figs, the bird's figs, I said apricots, apricots!"

"What, huh no" Evan cries, trying to fend off her slashing blade with his paper bag of figs. "What the fuck, no, no, you said help yourself!"

"You nasty foreign boy," the hag babbles, flailing at him, "you're not from here!"

She slashes through the fig sack, slashes into his right hand, almost cutting off his little finger. Evan drops the sack and makes a run for it. He dashes along the side of the house and into the front yard, freaked out. A tough-looking man in a gray pickup is driving past on the street, sees Evan, and slams on his brakes. "Damn son, get in," he shouts, tossing Even a rag to staunch the wound. This nameless stranger listens to Evan's frantic story, muttering, "Well god dang, she's got to be pigeon-shit crazy," and drives him right over to the local hospital.

My brother's little finger was reattached with many stitches but tendons were severed. The finger has a permanent half-closed appearance, it's basically useless. Evan doesn't want to involve the police and talks me out of taking revenge on the crazy bitch, wreaking havoc on her doors and windows with a baseball bat. The bizarre incident only underscores how isolated we feel in remote San Luis Obispo, with no real friends or kindred souls, indeed, foreigners.

Hoping for relief, we write a letter to Self-Realization Fellowship headquarters in Los Angeles, asking if there are any SRF meditation groups up here on the central coast. Other than a few doddering theosophists and Edgar Cayce types, we haven't met any mystical aspirants around here We're not giving up on our back-to-the-country endeavor, but finding a few confidants would really help to feel more at home.

About a month later, almost forgetting about our letter, we get a response back from the friendly Brother Mokshananda, the orange-robed monk who used to talk with us at the SRF chapel on Sunset. Mokshananda writes that he has some pertinent news to share, that yes, actually, one of Master's former disciples lives not far from us. This news hits us like a thunderbolt, it seems miraculous! But friendly monk goes on to say that due to the unusual circumstances about this individual, he prefers to discuss it with us in person. He invites us down to the Christmas Eve Celebration at the Mt. Washington SRF headquarters. where we can chat face to face.

All right, dig it, we laugh, this is what we've been waiting for! Evan and I nail our plans down on the spot. The intrigue implied in the big-footed monk's cryptic message only makes it more enticing. Who is he talking about, what does he mean? We absolutely have to know.

In the meanwhile, Evan's mangled finger begins to heal. One day he holds his hand aloft, displaying the deformed, little finger. "Guess what I just found out?" he says.

"Can't imagine. This has to do with your hacked-up digit? Lay it on me."

"Right, ha ha ha. Well dig, turns out that crazy old hag did me a big favor. This finger, in its weird condition, makes me unfit for military duty. It totally disqualifies me. The army will not draft me unless the country gets physically invaded."

A sudden laugh bursts from my chest, ah, what luck! The Selective Service has been hounding my brother, looking for another young body to feed into their killing-ground of Vietnam. I've been schooling him in the conscientious objection claim that I once tried to make happen. But now, another karmic twist, just like my Mexico smuggling bust freed me from the insidious draft, the mad woman's attack on Evan has gotten him off the hook. At least now we can both flip-off the soulless war-mongers and do our own thing without interference. Fuck all war. Fuck the perpetrators of war right into the Hell of their own evil-making.

IN LATE DECEMBER we take some days off and drive on down to LA, visiting a few friends. On Christmas Eve afternoon we show up early at the SRF Mt. Washington ashram. The friendly orange-robed residents direct us to Brother Mokshananda, who's tending Yogananda's rose garden. His big square face lights up when he sees us, his shy effusive smile. After a few pleasantries, we get right into the reason for this meeting.

"I have to admit," Mokshananda confesses, "when I first read your letter asking if there was anybody up where you live with SRF ties, it gave me pause." His kind eyes search our faces, almost as if appealing for our understanding. "I had to meditate and pray about it, asking for Master's guidance. Then I went and discussed your request with Sri Daya Mata and she thought it over too. Afterwards, she gave me the go ahead to tell you what I thought to tell you in the first place."

This unusual statement brings us to full attention. The fact that Daya Mata, the matriarch of the Self Realization Fellowship, was involved in this decision enhances its allure.

"Okay then, brother Mokshananda, lay it on us. Daya Mata advised you on this? What's the story?"

Mokshananda nods and smiles, relaxing, and we relax with him. Pulling at his ear lob, he says, "One of Master's disciples in his final years was a strange man named Torgen Sorenson. Mr Sorenson, or Torgie as Master called him, tended to be stubborn and unpredictable. He would wear the orange robes when he was around the ashram, but sometimes he'd just disappear for weeks.

That was very peculiar behavior. And he didn't like to sit and meditate all that much, he preferred to be working somewhere out on the grounds."

"Far out. You mean he'd just go off like that on a whim? Yogananda let him do that?"

"Yes, he did. Master pretty much let him come and go as he pleased. Torgie was completely devoted to Paramahansa and Master loved him very much. They would raid the refrigerator late at night together and tell jokes. For some reason he tended to be lenient with Sorenson. Master used to emphasize that we brothers and sisters at the ashram should do two hours of Kriya meditation each day, but he didn't require that of him."

Mokshananda laughs a bit self-consciously, adding, "At the time it seemed a little unfair, I don't know why."

"Brother Mokshananda," Evan asks, "when did all this happen? How long ago?"

"Oh, this was a good 15 years ago, maybe more. Master dropped his body and went into mahasamadhi in 1952 after reading a poem at a public gathering."

"Have you ever seen this man Sorenson since then?"

"No, I have not. But Daya Mata has met with him personally a few times."

"Hmm, so he left the ashram?" I muse aloud. "Why do you think he was an exception?" In the back of my mind I'm wondering if maybe I'm an exception too, seeing as how I detest rules myself.

"Well, it's hard to say," Mokshananda replies, "and I don't like to speculate on such matters. Yogananda used to say that Mr Sorenson had a special work to do and for the rest of us not to be concerned. So that was good enough for me. He said that Torgie's heart was filled with true devotion to God and that's all he'd really need for his purpose in life."

"But brother, what was his purpose exactly? When he would just up and leave the ashram, what was he doing?"

"Yes, that was the big mystery," Mokshananda says in an apologetic tone. "Like I said, he would come and go and sometimes we wouldn't see him for weeks. Then he'd show up and be with us again. He liked to laugh and play jokes on people, and he used to pester Master for miracles."

"Miracles?" Evan eyes brighten with curiosity, glancing at me. "Dude, really?"

"Yes, Torgie was like a big child. He always wanted Master to show him miracles. But I have to acknowledge he was a tireless worker, always serving. When most of us were in meditation or spiritual studies, he would be out fixing something, repairing something, trying to improve something."

"Interesting," I say. "So he was like a builder?"

"You could say that. For example, he did carpentry work on the SRF chapel in Hollywood where I first met you guys. And he was one of the workers on the chapel at the Gandhi Lake Shrine out near the beach on Sunset. When he was around, he was always working on one of Master's projects. But he had some crazy idea too, like the time he wanted to cover Master's roof in concrete so it would have to be repaired again. He actually tried that and it was a disaster. The concrete was too heavy and the roof collapsed."

"Sort of a character, then," I laugh, exchanging a look with Evan. "Brother Mokshananda, it's fascinating, but is that the main thing you wanted to tell us?"

Mokshananda hesitates, then says, "No, there's more. What we want you to know is that Torgen Sorenson left the SRF ashram shortly after Yogananda passed on. All he said was that he had work to do, work that was sanctioned by Master and he had to live apart to do it. He promised to stay in touch and then moved up on the central coast to a place called Atascadero."

"Atascadero? That's only about 20 miles from where we live, up over the Cuesta Grade! So it's possible we can actually meet this guy?"

"Yes, it is, and that's what I need to know," Mokshananda says in an enigmatic tone. "Because Daya Mata says it's your decision. He's definitely a strange individual. He mixes Yogananda's teachings on Kriya Yoga and mystical Christianity with other occult-type teachings, something Master warned against. And about ten years ago he started his own meditation church called the Center of Light."

We assimilate this info, making leaps of imagination. "Yeah man, we would definitely like to meet him, definitely. We're sort of isolated up there and just his association with Master alone makes it worth it. Can you put us in touch?"

"I'd be glad to," the friendly monk smiles, obviously relieved of some misgiving. "I'll give you his post office box number in Atascadero, that's all I have. If I were you I'd write him a note saying that you'd like to meet with him and that you're SRF students, and that you spoke to me. I'm sure Sorenson will get back in touch with you soon."

"Hey that's beautiful, brother Mokshananda. Thanks, thanks, thanks."

At the Christmas Eve Christ Celebration later that evening, held in an imposing room of the 1910 Mount Washington Hotel, headquarters of the SRF, Daya Maya sits on an elevated chair facing us. We have never seen her in person before. She speaks in clear tones to a modest gathering of devotees, a small woman with honey blond hair who radiates a palpable feeling of serenity, taught by Yogananda himself. In her saffron robes, Daya Mata exemplifies his teachings on unswerving devotion to the self-realization of God-Consciousness. Many outsiders might consider those of us sitting in this room tonight to be deranged dreamers. But I don't mind being insane for the sake of cosmic illumination. She encourages us to be patient with our practice, to take it slow and steady. Living in the world makes unusual demands on the spiritual aspirant, don't be too zealous. But Evan and I are already storming the Gates of Heaven, her gentle admonitions come too late.

We all meditate together for awhile, then Daya Mata answers questions, in a maternal tone, she says, "Some of you, in your passion for natural living, might want to consider using some deodorant before coming into group satsang like this. It makes it more pleasant for others."

Aiyee, we wonder if she could be talking about us? Because although we bathe often my brother and I don't use artificial deodorant. We don't want to absorb the hideous aluminum residues and poison our bodies. At the most, we dab a little apple cider vinegar under our armpits. But I pay rapt attention to this extraordinary woman who radiates such peace. Other than a twist of fate my we might have landed in this ashram, although I don't think I'm cut out for it. In the back of my mind I'm wondering what he will be like, this renegade monk, this Torgenson.

Chapter 4

THE QUONSET HUT is one of the strangest things I have laid eyes on. Set on the outskirts of the town of Atascadero, on the arid inland plateau of the coastal range, the tin and concrete hulk faces a lonely stretch of El Camino Real within hearing distance of 101. The field rises behind the building to a faded yellow farm house and barns, and beyond that a round butte covered with oaks. On the other side of that hill is the Atascadero mental hospital, the infamous state wacky-hatch. In Spanish, Atascadero means something like *muddy spot*, and we sense that something is different here. Staring at the odd Quonset hut, getting the vibes, we are struck by two conflicting impressions— one spiritual and rather psychic, the other blood-spattered and repulsive.

"Dude, what in the world," Evan says to me in an undertone.

Fronting the gravel parking lot, the lower level of the rusting half-moon hut is a country butcher shop and meat locker. Our eyes bulge, we gape, the hairs rise on the back of our yogi necks. We read in revulsion the bold-lettered sign over the door, "Farm Fresh-Kill Country Butcher."

There are a few windows like peepholes above this abattoir on the upper floor, under the curving metal roof. Is that The Center of Light? I have run into some stark paradoxes before, but this one is a doozy.

"Man," Evan mumbles nervously, "what kind of place is this?"

"Weird vibes, yeah, truly weird," I nod in agreement. "I mean, how can a disciple of Yogananda live above a fucking slaughter house?"

We park my faded yellow Studebaker on the left side of the Quonset hut, per the instructions Torgen Sorenson wrote to us. Weathered board stairs lead up the side of the hut to a plywood platform, where a white house door set into the cinder-block wall. We go up, our hands feeling the unpainted, splintered railing. The plywood platform flexes under our feet but feels solid enough. A planked catwalk leads around the sloping metal roof of the old building to some unseen place. The house door is inset with several panes of glass, flaking with white paint. There's a round black button on the door frame, electrical wire runs through a hole drilled into the wall. Evan pushes the button twice, and we hear a loud clanging from inside the shadowed interior.

After a moment, a loud thumping gait approaches us from somewhere inside. Reverend Sorenson appears in the glass door panes, beaming like a giant cherubim. He's dressed in a black minister's suit with a white priest collar, his gray hair slicked back over his thinning pate. Yanking the door open, he exclaims, "Come in, hello! I'm glad you fellows came up early, it gives us a chance to talk! Welcome, welcome!"

We say our smiling hellos, not sure what to make of his theatrical appearance. Sorenson stands over six feet tall, a barrel-chested, big-bellied man with a large round head. He's squeezed into his black outfit, which looks to be at least one size too small. He ushers us into the dim interior, under the overhead slope of the metal roof. We are enveloped by an airy corridor leading back into the building. At once our ears are assailed by the intense din of racketing machinery, screeching fan belts and chain link drives. Huge old compressors shudder and shake on reinforced platforms under the sun-struck roof, pumping cool air into hellish meat lockers below. There's a sturdy plywood walkway laid out on the rafters, and overhead a rusted conveyor belt strung with ominous hooks. This metal belt rises out of a square chute and tracks away down the corridor. Torgen Sorenson leads us through this dim realm toward a naked light bulb on a far wall. Disoriented and intrigued, my brother and I follow after him.

The plywood walkway tee's into a wall that seems to bisect the Quonset hut's half-moon roof. The antiquated compressors shudder to a screeching stop, their rubber belts slipping. On our left, there's a large, heavy-duty locker door with a padlocked handle. The conveyor belt with dangling hooks angles toward that door and vanishes through a slot above it. To our right, the catwalk leads to a few wooden steps rising to another glass-pane door through which light shines. Sorenson leads on in a jovial fashion, showing us the narrow bathroom beside the steps – a battered door, plywood floors, an old toilet, tiny washbasin, and a cramped tin shower stall. Evan stands close behind me, taking in this glorified outhouse.

"Far out," he murmurs, realizing that wherever we are, we are on the fringes.

"Interesting," I say in a friendly tone. "Did you do this work yourself, Mr Sorenson?"

"Yes it is, and yep, I did most of it," Sorenson replies, opening the interior door. "It used to be just a rough attic. And it gets kind of noisy here at times, as you can tell. But come in, come in, I'll explain how it all works around here."

We step up into a shoe-box kitchen with a small window looking down at the gravel parking lot, a tube skylight ported in from the ceiling. There's an old fridge, a 4-burner stovetop, narrow counter space and hanging cupboards, plus an industrial-type sink. The reverend takes us through a beaded curtain into another room tucked under the curving metal roof. We see a sturdy platform bed, an oak swivel rocker, some odd milk cans that have been converted into padded stools, and an array of mystical pictures and symbols attached to the walls and book-shelves—the mahavatar Babaji, a Golden Dawn pentagram, the Rosicrucian cross, one of the ascended masters, maybe Count St. Germain. A L-shaped desk occupies the interior wall, Sorenson's office space, a vintage typewriter, and several shelves packed with arcane books. Against the rear wall, partitioned from his office-bedroom space by more of the milk can stools upholstered in blue and white naugahyde, we see a horseshoe meditation chapel dominated by an imposing alter. This antechamber is dim and windowless, a dreamlike scene out of an occultist's trance. There are some pictures on the wall, although I can't make them out.

The shelves and stacks of books and esoteric publications immediately catch my eye. "Wow, some library," I say, "dig it, Evan." I stare at the burned and smudged bindings, trying to make out the blackened titles. Books from the fringes of meta-physics and mysticism—The Ceremonial Magic of Solomon, The Ancient Lost Chaldean Conjurations, The Invocation of Azaroth, My First Two Thousand Years, Nada-Bindu Yoga. I'm not altogether sure what I'm looking at and it's plain that many of these books have been through a fire. Noticing my intense curiosity, Sorenson snatches a large open tome off his desk, shoves it onto the shelf, and abruptly draws a red satin curtain across the entire face of the library, curtains smudged by fire and soot. The reverend's round face flushes with concern and his blue eyes bulge like luminous orbs.

"That's not for your eyes just yet," he says in a cryptic tone, "first things first."

"What's the big deal?" Evan laughs. "We're into unusual and mystical books."

"For certain," I put in, backing him up, "We don't mean to snoop, Mr Sorenson, but just so you know, we're pretty well-versed in metaphysics."

"I know, I know that you are," the burly Sorenson huffs, "but first we need to get to know each other better. Those are not just any books." Turning his unblinking blue gaze on Evan, he adds, "Some of these here are not your regular spiritual teachings and it's important you understand that. There's secrets in these books that can split your brain open."

Stifling a laugh, having already had my brain opened by starburst psychedelics, I nod in feigned agreement. A cockroach scuttles from behind the book curtain and across the desk. Sorenson smashes it with the flat of his palm. grunting with satisfaction. He reaches for a roll of paper towels and wipes his hand off. All around are boxes of occult magazines, stacks of newspapers, obscure pamphlets, and sheaves of typed and scribbled notes. Something unusual is going on here.

Sneezing, Torgelananda reaches up above his head and turns on a reel to reel tape recorder with hanging speakers. Some kind of religious music comes on, praise-God hymns arising from a sonorous choir, for all we know the chorus of the asylum right over the hill. But it reminds me of music our mother used to listen to, and I squirm on my milk can stool. The only music I listen to is some radio rock and roll in my delivery van or the sitar and sarod ragas on 33 rpms at home. Torgie holds up the album cover for us to see: The Mormon Tabernacle Choir. In the most private sense I consider such music a pervasive kind of orthodox brainwashing. You are a groveling sinner, I am your almighty Lord. Obey me or be doomed, O hapless ones. Fuck that.

The reverend goes into the kitchen and comes back with a large can of Tree Sweet grapefruit juice, offering us a glass. As a rule we abhor canned fruit juice and I don't like drinking out of plastic tumblers, there is something unholy about plastic. But the label this stuff contains no added sugar, so we accept out of courtesy. It has a notably tart, acidic flavor.

"This beverage is very good for you," Sorenson points out. "It's about the most cleansing thing going when you're on a long fast. One time I fasted for 28 straight days on nothing but grapefruit juice and glazed donuts."

"What," I laugh, "glazed donuts? Glazed donuts? But why? That sounds insane."

"Well, the donuts are only for the first week or ten days to smooth out the hunger pangs. After that, you start to forget all about food. That's when extra-sensory things start to happen."

"Okay, then 21 pure days," Evan says, his eyes shining with expectation. "Like what, what happened? Did you see anything? We've fasted for a day or two but nothing like that."

"Yes I did, I had some powerful visions, if that's what you mean. But that's not exactly why I use it. I get out on the other side fairly easily now and fasting helps me stay out of my body for prolonged periods." Nodding, Sorenson slurps a red tumbler of the bitter-sweet juice. He wriggles his shaggy eyebrows. "This Tree Sweet's the best you can get. I buy it by the case when I go on a fast and starting yesterday, I just went back on the big fast. Time to clean out and lose some of this blubber I'm carrying around. Once I want on a thirty day binge when I ate nothing but sugar-glazed donuts and coffee with a splash of milk. I ate hundreds of them."

"But why? I don't understand, for Christ's sake. Why would you do that to your body?"

"Oh, I've done a number of unusual dietary experiments," Sorenson tells me. "I wanted to see if it would physically weaken me. But it didn't. I went right ahead and did my regular painting and carpentry work without any problems. To be honest, I did have some indigestion and I gobbled tums for that. One think about eating so many donuts, though, they make you fat as a hog."

I glance over at my brother Even, who has a secret proclivity for glazed donuts. To my ear, this story rings of sheer lunacy. To treat your body like that seems like some kind of flagellation.

The reverend breaks off talking to hack spasmodically then spits a wad of phlegm into a cardboard box that serves as the trash receptacle. He turns back to us with a boyish smile.

"So, Mr Sorenson," I press, digging for more, "fasting is a method you use to astral project? But also to physically rejuvenate?"

The huge monk chuckles, patting his immense belly that strains against the black minister suit. His jowls bulge around the white priest collar. "Yeah, to clean out and to take off this big fat gut. All this fat keeps creeping up on me and it's the shits as you get older. The main thing is that prolonged fasting makes it much easier to step out of the body. But it's not the most important thing. There are special inner techniques."

"You mean consciously getting free of the body, knowing that you are?"

"Sure, wide awake, of course. If you're not doing it consciously you're just pretending. Oh, I had a dream and I did such and such is just a load of hooie. Pretending is for the birds."

He beams at us with self-amused delight, a cherubim face with eyes of disarming blue clarity. Blinking, Torgelananda lifts one side of his broad ass and rips off a loud fart.

"Well, excuse me," he blushes, fanning his nose. "I was trying to sneak that one."

Wrinkling my eyes and nose, I say, "De nada. But let me ask you, does that sinus congestion ever bother you? I've got hay fever that's been bothering the hell out of me, don't know what's causing it. I've been eating ground raw horse radish with lemon juice to cleanse out the mucus."

"Nope, it's not hay fever with me, it's this infernal blubber." Sorenson mumbles, hacking another wad of snot into the box. "And mucus is bad. Mucus is one of a yogi's worst enemies. But to get rid of it I need to get rid of this fat, that's why I'm back on the big fast. If I can just stay on it for a couple of weeks and do my regular work, I'll start dropping quite a ton of weight. Hell, man, I weigh 360 pounds, all this flab's got to go."

Evan and I share a complicit glance, several questions pushing into our thoughts. Some of what he's saying dovetails with my own esoteric researches.

Glancing at the wall clock, the reverend announces, "I hope you don't mind me getting the meditation chapel set up for the service. We can carry on this private talk later. But the other folks will be up here in just a few minutes."

He hefts himself up and goes into the dim chamber under the curving metal roof, turning on a three brass floor lamps. The lamps illumine the horseshoe-shaped chapel with its linen-covered alter set against the windowless back wall. Several pictures of SRF saints and masters are arrayed there, with several large free-standing candles and brass censures, a tall gold cross, and other religious artifacts. The reverend busies himself with lighting incense and white candles while we survey the womb-like chapel. A cluster of milk canisters padded in blue and white naugahyde are arranged in a semi-circle in front of the alter. These stools are low-chair height, without backs, designed for meditation with a upright spines, as Yogananda recommends. A faded oriental rug covers the floor, a vacuum cleaner and cardboard boxes covered with sheets stand in the corner. But the most striking thing about this sanctuary is the large, imposing lithograph of master Yogananda himself, his lustrous black hair, his face and eyes glowing, gazing down at us from above the alter. This picture is a good four feet high by three feet wide, and incredibly life-like.

Noticing our quiet awe, Sorenson remarks, "Some of those were made back in the 40's when he was still around. Quite magnificent, isn't it?"

"Yeah, man, for sure," Evan says, "it's like he's almost here with us."

"Oh he is, he always is. That's exactly so," Torgen Sorenson murmurs.

The reverend's plaintive words underscores the aura of this inner sanctum, a place of profound devotion above a country butcher shop. He asks us to sit in silence for a few minutes while he attends to a few things. He goes back his office and we hear him going though loose papers or notes, talking to himself, looking for something.

A few minutes pass and we hear footsteps in the outer corridor. Reverend Sorenson turns off the religious music and goes to meet whoever it is. There are some murmured greetings, he asks if the machinery is switched off, there is a mumbled affirmative. Then he returns to the sanctuary with three curious people in tow, a Norman Rockwell illustration of country-bumpkin metaphysics. An older man and wife, Mr and Mrs Mallet, owners of the Quonset hut, the meat business downstairs, and the fertile forty acres and farm house on the land behind it. Old man Mallet is a stout, robust man of around sixty dressed in scruffy overalls and a flannel shirt, clomping around in field boots. Like Sorenson, he's balding with thin hair gray at the temples and a face that looks like a weathered tree bole. Mallet gives us a gap-toothed smile, set off by gray scrutinizing eyes.

"Howdy," he says, offering his thick calloused hand. "It's real nice to have you fellows come up and socialize with us."

Shaking hands with Mallet, I notice that his right hand is missing the index and middle fingers. We greet his thin, smiling wife, a sprite of a lady several inches shorter than us. Mrs Mallet's dressed in a calico dress with a hand-knitted shawl around her shoulders. High blue socks cover her skinny shanks. Her brown eyes dance with enthusiasm and we don't realize that she's deaf until she begins to speak. Her speech is a trifle slurred, yet carefully enunciated and intelligible. She has been stone deaf since birth and for many years taught English to dumb and deaf children at a Texas prairie school. We find this out in dribs and drabs, and she's obviously delighted that we are here.

"So good to meet you boys," she enthuses, "the reverend told us you were coming up to meditation service! We need some new blood in this group!"

"Yes mamm," I reply, wanting some space, "we're glad to be here. We just found out about your existence a few weeks ago. The Center of Light, I mean."

Mrs Mallet nods with rapt attention as I speak, her lips moving as she reads my lips. "Oh yes, yes," she murmurs in thick, wet words, "I am glad too, you're so welcome."

The third visitor is another big-bodied man, but with hunched shoulders, flabby paunch, and nervous hands. He has a red face and his hands shake like he has palsy or badly needs a shot of booze. This man's name is Ramspack and he greets us in a frank and open way. He's wearing some kind of uniform shirt and strapped to his hip is a worn .44 Smith & Wesson service revolver.

Men with guns always tend to put me on edge. I've been shot at, had pistols stuck in my face, been threatened and ripped off, although I don't let any discomfort show in my face.

"Ram is the private security patrol for most of Atascadero," Sorenson points out. "But he takes time out to come over for our Wednesday and Sunday services."

"And we're so glad he does," Mrs Mallet enunciates, "but I do wish you would take that gun off your belt when you come to meditation."

"Oh I know, and I'm sorry," Ramspack says in a flustered tone. "It's just so much a part of my wardrobe that I forget I'm even wearing it."

This jittery lawman has a strong nicotine odor and I suspect he's itching for a smoke. Appraising us, Ramspack asks, "How is it you two fellows come to know about Paramahansa Yogananda's teachings? I'd been studying the Rosicrucian philosophy when I met reverend Sorenson here and he talked me into attending these meetings. I'm a bit of a newcomer myself."

It's a tricky question, considering our notorious recent history. Evan and I explain our SRF connections in Los Angeles, taking turns, and our interest in transcendental states of awareness. But we avoid any mention of our psychedelic quests, because, obviously, this guy is a cop. Mrs. Mallet listens to our scant details with unabashed interest, reading our lips. Old man Mallet feigns a kind of disinterest, slumped on a blue and white milk canister. But his gray eyes betray an inherent skepticism and you sense that he doesn't miss much. My brother and I play the situation by intuition, strangers in this unknown place.

And sure enough lawman Ramspack blurts out, "well, I'll tell you what right now. I'm goddamned sick and tired of seeing these long-haired, unkempt hippies wander through our town. Some of those bums are even staying here now. So it's a pleasure to meet two young men like you, clean-cut and obviously responsible. I hope this isn't your only visit to the Center of Light."

Aiyee, Evan and I grimace and nod, cloaked in our disguise. Change can be strange—only last year I was smuggling weed out of Mexico and dealing pure acid by the quart from the saddle of a British bike, a vile provocateur in the eyes of any law-and-order fanatic. Ramspack hitches his gun belt around on his hips and sits down on a milk can stool, letting out a raspy cough. Always play your cards close to your chest until you know what's happening, I remind myself again.

Reverend Sorenson clears his throat and asks that we all quiet down for the Sunday service. Old man Mallet makes a move to dim the lamps and we all compose ourselves on our padded milk cans. Almost as a humorless afterthought, Ramspack mutters, "mind you, it's not the long hair that bothers me," nodding at the long flowing hair of Yogananda in the super-real lithograph. "No, it's just the habits of those thieving, doped-up freaks and their anti-American attitudes."

Mallet bubbles with sardonic laughter, shaking his balding pate from side to side, as his wife looks down at her folded hands like a tiny bird with her head cocked. Evan glances over at me, a glint of dark amusement in his eyes. And for real, what kind of a bizarre side-show have we wandered into? Brother Mokshananda warned us that Sorenson was unusual person. For all we know he and his friends might be demented lunatics teetering on the brink, but no matter.

Sorenson sits cross from me, at the other end of the alter. He settles his bulk behind a scorched portable harmonium, on a bench about three times the size of the stools, also padded in blue and white naugahyde. He bows his massive forehead into his hands for a moment, propping his elbows on the organ, then spreads his hands on either side of his head, palms facing out. He becomes Torgelananda and launches into an impassioned invocation. His eyes are closed in the candlelight, his round childlike face tilts upward. He invokes the Heavenly Father, Jesus Christ, Yogananadaji, Divine Mother, Yogananda's master Yukteswar, Babaji, Saint Francis of Assisi and all true saints, asking for their blessing and holy presence. The waxen candles flicker in the claustrophobic chapel, the incense burners waft smoke, not sandalwood, maybe myrrh or frankincense.

"Now, let's do the Aum chant seven times together," the reverend instructs. "Please lift your hands and send out the healing vibrations of Light to whoever or whatever needs it."

We all do as he says. Like some strange band of worshiping bears, we lift our paws in the air and intone a resonant series of Aums. But the incense fumes bother old man Mallet. His nose begins to twitch and snort, he breaks into a loud, convulsive spasm of sneezes. The reverend lifts his cumbrous body from the bench and steps nimbly around the harmonium to snuff out the censures. He winks at me with blue, twinkling eyes. Mrs Mallet gazes at my brother Evan in a maternal way, a trifle embarrassed.

"Sometimes the incense drives my husband a little crazy," she says in her soft, slurry voice. "I hope it doesn't bother you boys."

Oh no, no problemo, we assure her, nothing bothers us. Mallet coughs and wheezes a few more times, scuffing at the worn rug with his boots as if to calm himself. Ramspack appears to ignore it all, lost in his own thoughts.

Reverend Sorenson settles back down on his bench and says, "all right, now Mrs Mallet will read for us the Sunday lesson because she can't hear so good. These are little booklets that Master specially prepared for meditation services. Some of the material might seem new to you, because, the home discourses got kind of watered down after his passing. And just so you know, all he materials from the Center of Light are based on Yogananada's teachings and the mystical works of Jesus the Christ."

"What did you just say, Reverend?" Mrs Mallet queries. He looks over at her with patient affection, repeating what he just said word for word, only more slowly. "All right," she pipes, "I will do so with pleasure! Please pass me the lesson!"

Rubbing his hands together, Torgelananda says, "After that, we'll all chant together, then sit in the silence and meditate for awhile."

Mrs. Mallet does her slurred and careful reading of these scriptures, picking her way through the words with obvious relish. When done reading these notes of divine inspiration, she looks up at the perspiring reverend. Torgie flips open the harmonium and attempts to play and sing one of Yogananda's hymns, but bungling certain chords and phrases. From the way old man Mallet ogles Sorenson, I get the sense this performance is especially for us newcomers. The reverend cuts off the organ abruptly, seemingly disappointed that no one sang along with him, but who else knows these rare songs? He lifts up his calloused hands and leads us in three choruses of the vibratory Aum chant. The mood in the hollow chapel deepens, the chant trails off, the reverence wells up in the candlelight. People shuffle around, adjusting themselves, then become quiet.

Fascinated, I watch through slit eyelids. Sorenson appears to go into a deep swoon over the harmonium, hunched forward, his face buried in his hands. His breath becomes heavy and slow, like a bellows. Evan and I go into meditation in our usual, classic way, posture erect, heads balanced, taking rhythmic diaphragm breaths while focusing on our Sanskrit tones. But with a surreptitious glance around, I see that these redneck aspirants have bizarrely divergent styles.

The old farmer in his denim overalls slumps entirely un-yoga-like on his stool, and about ten minutes into the silence he begins to snore and drool. His wife sits next to him, her face scrunched up. Will she nudge him awake, I wonder, but then remember she is stone deaf. She sits quite upright on her milk can, her thin body showing a lot of tension in her effort to concentrate. Her hands are clinched, and every few minutes she vents a little sigh, then goes valiantly on. But at least she is conscious, not nodding and slobbering on her chest.

The ex-sheriff sits a couple of stools away from the heavily breathing bulk of Sorenson. Ramspack is twitchy. He passes minutes of inward focus, then sudden bursts of agitated foot tapping, snuffling, wheezing coughs. His bulbous nose is veined red. Again, he strikes me as a man in need of some whiskey. I cast a sideways glance at my brother, who is in a desperate struggle to keep his eyes closed and suppress his irreverent guffaws, his shoulders shaking. A ragged laugh breaks from my own lips, but I swallow it. I make myself go within, to ignore these oddball manifestations and delve into the spiritual aura of this unusual chapel.

About twenty minutes or so drift by and we're aroused by the sound of Mallet clearing his sinuses. Peering from under my eyelids at the dim wall clock, I see that we've been in meditation for about half an hour, our asses numb on the padded milk cans. Sorenson is still in deep reverie, his pose unchanged, only his breathing more quiet. Even Ramspack has calmed down, while Mrs Mallet has assumed a posture not unlike Rodin's thinking statue, eyes still closed, oblivious to the distractions around her. Her husband clears his throat again, peering at the reverend, trying to bring him out of his trance. Mallet shifts about on his stool and stabs at the floor with his boot heels. Ramspack gives an abrupt shudder and comes awake with a dry, harsh wheeze. He looks quite mad, squinting, red-faced, like a man about to burst.

Old man Mallet croaks, "Torgie, Torgie, we're going past the time!"

The big monk comes to with a start, instantly awake, his face clear as a new born child. He shuffles his feet under the harmonium and glances over at the clock. "Oh, excuse me! I didn't mean to run so far over!"

Sorenson concludes the meeting with a brief prayer of thanks, and everyone stands up to stretch. He wants to know if anyone would like cookies and coffee, milk or tea? Earlier I noticed a few boxes of sugary flour cookies stacked in the kitchen, revolting processed treats—and with mucus-forming milk? Egad, no way, no gracias, just a mug of strong black coffee for me.

Taciturn Mallet lets everyone know he has to "get going," he has farm work to do. He grins at us, shakes our hands, then clumps on out. As he goes down the outer corridor he hits a switch and the ancient machinery kicks back on with cacophonous, rattling screech.

Evan brushes past me, his eyes laughing, muttering low, "incredible, dude, incredible." He goes for the sugar cookies and to rub elbows with reverend monk Sorenson.

"That's the best meditation I've had in weeks," Mrs Mallet tells me in her slushy voice. "I'm sure the presence of two fine young students of swami Yogananda improved the vibrations here!" She invites us all up to her house, for a treat of home-grown carrot cake and organic watermelon juice frozen from last summer's crop.

"That sounds good," I tell her. "We're vegetarians and love

food like that." I speak precisely into her upturned face so she can interpret my lips.

Ramspack begs off, he has to make his Sunday rounds and take care of other business. He pumps my hand, promising to be back again on Wednesday night, then leaves fishing a pack of Lucky Strikes out of his pocket to calm his jagged nerves.

"It's a blessing having you boys here," Mrs Mallet says in her cordial tones, gazing at me as if charmed, which makes me vaguely uncomfortable.

"Please keep coming to our services, we need new blood here," she reiterates. "And the good news is that life is always what you make it. You can make a mud pie or bake an angel food cake."

"All right," I say with a wry smile, "I get your drift, and that's really quite true, isn't it?"

Chapter 5

I N SORENSON'S KITCHEN, I find my brother munching a sugar cookie, with an aloof, guiltless attitude. After all, those illicit cookies are a gift from Yogananda's own personal disciple. The reverend greets me with his beaming, jocular face, slurping from a quart jar of what looks like red wine. But I figure it to be some kind of herbal tonic for his impending fast.

"Mr Sorenson," I say, "you mind if I ask you a few questions?"

"Oh hell no," Torgie says in anticipation, "ask away! Let's all go sit down." We move through the bead curtain into his office space and sit facing each other, the reverend in his oak desk rocker, me and Evan on the wobbly milk cans. We talk for awhile, a coherent picture begins to form in my mind. Old man Mallet has owned the land and buildings for almost 40 years. Mallet built the Quonset hut by himself with the help of his son, using only a tractor and a barnyard set of pulleys. But the son had been killed in an auto accident ten years ago, leaving he and his wife permanently heart-sick. Sorenson says that the old farmer has an innate knack for mechanical engineering.

"Now he mainly just likes to plant corn and grow watermelons and collect junk. He leases out that butcher shop and fiddles with all his old machinery," Torgie confides in an amused tone. "He plants his crops every year and trades in all kinds of broken-down equipment, burned-out refrigerators and stoves, old tractors and obsolete implements that other people don't want. Right out back you'll see a fenced area where he keeps everything. That's his boneyard treasure trove."

Sorenson pauses to honk his nose, chuckling. "When we walk up to the house I'll show you what I'm talking about, it's the damnedest thing you ever saw. He's more obsessed with that crap than anything else in the world. He's so attached he'll probably reincarnate just to get his hands on it again."

Puzzled, Evan says, "but why does he hang on to all that worn out stuff? What's the point? My brother and I like to travel light. Hoarding stuff just ties your feet to the ground."

"Oh, he's convinced it'll all be worth a bunch of money some day and he's gonna make a killing. Don't mention this to him because he refuses to believe it, but Mallet was King Solomon in one of his past lives. Because of that, he's still strongly attached to carnal sex and believes that all his junk is worth a fortune."

"What? You mean King Solomon from the Bible?"

"Yes, that's what I mean. King Solomon, David's father."

Sharing an double-take with my brother, I quip, "Aiyee, reverend, Solomon had 700 wives and 300 concubines, ha ha ha. That sounds like heavy addiction to me, all the lascivious attention."

"That's it, and that's why he won't listen to me about celibacy. She will, but he's still an old goat and she's pretty much at his mercy. They're sort of an Old Testament couple, if you know what I mean. It took me a long time to convince him to come to meditations and he still doesn't get the importance of it." The reverend hawks another repulsive wad of mucus into a paper towel, tosses it into the box. "Like you saw today, if it goes even a little past thirty minutes he starts getting bent out of shape."

"Does he take the Yogananda discourses? Does she?"

"She does, yes, but he won't do more than glance at them. He keeps wanting to have visions, so because he doesn't have any visions he says it ain't working. I tell him he's got to make it work through devotion but he shrugs that off. But the real reason it doesn't work for him is because he's addicted to his pecker pleasures. Funny thing is that he's had lots of visions but just doesn't remember. He can't get his mind off of fucking, that's mainly what he thinks about, and that wipes out the deeper memories."

"The deeper memories? You mean like past lives?"

"Yes, that too. The subtle memories, the visions."

Sorenson looks around as if someone else is present, his lips silently moving. Then he confides, his blue eyes beaming at us, "look, I can tell you boys are taking these yoga teachings very seriously, I can see it in your auras. And I'm willing to bet that you've made a commitment to go deeper, am I right?"

We affirm that what he saying is true, that were into the SRF teachings hard-core.

"And that's why I can talk to you in this way," Sorenson continues, lifting one hand in the air. "I can tell because I've been celibate for 23 years now, no jacking off, no screwing around, no fucking or sucking, nothing. I've devotedly followed Master's celibacy rules."

"That's really far out," Evan remarks. "We know how hard that is. But how about the wet dreams, how do you handle the wet dreams?"

"Oh, I'm way past the wet dreams. Hell, after all this time, my prick's shrunk to the size of a little child's. I just use it to pee nowadays."

"Yeah, well, those wet dreams can be tricky," I admit, slightly uncomfortable, "I've had some real geysers. And we understand the esoteric reasons. Although sometimes you wonder why the hell am I doing all this, you know?"

"Man, let me tell you, that's the road to real power," Sorenson states, "the royal road." He peers at us, then drops his voice a notch lower. "We'll get more into that as we go along. Master taught me all about this secret science and if you fellows want to learn, maybe I can help you. It's about power, man, true power, and you have to be pure in your purposes. But I want you to remember one thing – don't repeat anything that we talk about to anyone around here. These are private conversations meant for just us three, and only us. Old Mallet would resent it and so would the ex-sheriff. All of their brain power's dribbling right out the end of their feverish peckers."

Flabbergasted, we burst into laughter and Torgie joins right in, his big belly heaving. "That's all I can say about that now," he says, dabbling at his eyes, "just so you're both in the know."

We sit around and talk for awhile, before walking up to the yellow farmhouse for lunch. Evan and I are out of our usual Sunday routine and enjoying it. Sorenson relates that before moving into the Quonset hut he was living in a house in nearby Santa Margarita that he had inherited. He used that house for special religious ceremonies, until one day he went into town and left some candles burning. When he got back the county fire department was putting out a blaze that torched his entire home. That's' where the scorched curtains and burnt books at the Center of Light came from, all the artifacts singed by fire.

"I never leave candles burning anymore, you can bet on that," he says with chagrin. "It was a bitter and costly lesson, I dropped my vigilance. There are malicious spirits around who oppose the higher work and they burned me to the ground that day."

This sounds like deranged rambling to my ear, but I let it slide. Instead, I say, "Mr Sorenson, tell me, why did you pull the curtain across your books earlier today? I doubt that anything on your shelves would in any way shock us."

"It's not just that," Sorenson replies. "Like I said earlier, there are writings up there that are extremely rare and powerful. Those studies can lead to abnormal powers, don't even doubt it, and I don't know whether you're supposed to see them yet or not. But if you are, you're both going to need some advanced training in order to handle the power. It can't just be handed out freely."

"What do you mean by advanced training?" I ask, thinking of the siddhis of Patanjali's Yoga Sutras.

"That's beyond our present conversation. But you can find out about that right here, if everything checks out," he replies curtly, glancing away.

I hesitate as our talk maunders, trying to decide whether to tell this eccentric monk about my outlaw past. I ask him if he's interested in knowing some personal things, my attitude being put your cards on the table right up front so there are no regrets later.

"You can tell me anything in complete confidence," Sorenson says. "To be honest, I wanted to ask but I didn't want to seem nosy. Because I noticed some unique patterns in your auras that I've been trying to figure out. So yes, yes indeed, go right ahead."

So straightaway I confess my adventures and misadventures of the past few years, my immersion in the psychedelic counter-culture, my journey deep into Oaxaca to the magic mushroom cult, my pot-smuggling bust at the Tecate border and bad news trial – all of this followed by our plunge into metaphysics from Gurdjieff to Meher Baba to Yogananda. I hit the highpoints with some lurid detail, mentioning that I am also on three year federal probation. I hold nothing back.

Torgelananda listens to my every phrase and nuance with the utmost attention. He interrupts now and then with brief questions, clearly intrigued with my narrative. I don't embellish much;

I just describe what actually happened. "I want you to know these things," I tell him, "because it's possible that I might not fit in here. I mean, all things considered. This seems to be a pretty conservative bunch."

"And we're still hippies at heart," Evan chimes in, "we into those communal ideals."

"Fit in?" Sorenson grunts, "I don't see why in the hell not. I was no saint when I first came to Yogananda, believe you me. Neither of you are using those drugs anymore, correct?"

"No, not at all, not even weed. We're both following Yoga-nanda's path of initiation right to the letter."

"Then don't even worry about it. I mean, I wouldn't go into all those details about Lsd and smuggling pot if I were you, 'cause some might not understand what you were trying to do. But I think that's a fantastic story, it shows me you've got real guts! Master always said to bite off a bigger bite than you normally chew and chew it, and you sure as hell tend to do that."

"All right then, cool. That's reassuring."

Nodding at us, Sorenson adds, "By the way, when you making that confession, quite a few relevant things opened up."

"Relevant things? How do you mean?"

"Well, for instance, I saw your brain patterns opening up. Over everyone's head there's a kind of spectrum of light that's called a brain pattern, and I'm able to read both of yours. The purity of your intentions are of a high degree and the discipline you've achieved is quite unusual, considering how you've been going at this on your own. Those long hours of meditation, the fastings, and your effort to stay celibate all count. There's not one person in one hundred thousand who tries to do what you fellows are striving for. And like I said, I was no saint when I first came to Master. I had been in all kinds of crap, as bad or worst than you, and it took me a helluva a fight to get straightened around. So, it's not so important what you've done. No, that's over with. It's what you're doing right now that counts and where you're head with it."

Feeling appeased, I say, "I think we can both dig what you're saying. We don't buy into all the hell and damnation bullshit. We're aiming for a whole new dimension of awareness, into pure self-realization. But it feels like we're at some kind of impasse, like a psychic block?"

"Yeah, that's exactly it," says Evan, "we're trying to feel our way ahead. I've even wondered about joining the SRF brother-hood, wearing the orange robe, you know, if that would help"

Hearing my brother's words, I squirm on my milk can. I don't like identifying myself as a monk, even though I live like one. The secret world of lust still has a delicious taste to me.

Sorenson bobs his massive head, moving his bushy eyebrows in a peculiar way. "Let me be honest with you both," he says, "you're going to need some special personal instruction. If you boys keep pushing it the way you have been you could wind up in trouble. But no, you don't have to join the SRF monkhood, that's the sheltered way. You can learn it right out here in the world, if you have the right methods and the right guidance."

For a moment I stare at him, wondering what he's trying to lay on us. How can we get in trouble in deep yoga meditation? Frowning, I say, "I don't understand what you're getting at."

"Very simple," Torgie states, lifting his wizard's brows. "You're starting to deal with power that you only know a smidgen about. You're both pushing it to the extremes, I can see that. And if you keep it up on your own there will be certain points that you'll reach that are quite confusing. You can lose your balance. Worse yet, you make wrong decisions at those stages it can kill you. Involuntary reincarnation time."

"Huh, what?" My brother's mouth drops open and he goggles at the bi-bellied monk.

"How can that be?" I retort, rubbing my forehead. "We're talking about meditation and fasting, not going out in the hills and eating wild Datura."

"I'm being on the level with you," Sorenson frowns. "When the demons leap out at you better know what you're doing or else they'll put your brains in a shoebox. I've seen one person squashed like a chicken, and a couple others land in mental hospitals because they tried to do too much on their own. You boys are tapping into vast power, it's in your auras, and without guidance that can be highly dangerous."

This stark declaration triggers a flood of demanding questions, but Sorenson waves us off. It's not the right time to talk about these things, he tells us. First, he has to get clearance from the Light Masters to take us on, whatever that means. In the meanwhile go slower, he advises, don't try to force things to happen. There is a bombastic quality to Torgen Sorenson that really annoys me, but I listen with respect. He has the indisputable Yogananda credentials, and I've experimented enough in metaphysical states to know they can be dangerous. People can go too far and wig-out, get lost in their own psyche and not be able to find their way back. The weak-willed can go raving mad.

"All right," I concede, "but let me get one thing straight. Let's suppose you do get permission and we end up working in some way together. What would this relationship be? Are you our teacher, are you some kind of sorcerer? I mean, exactly what are you?"

"No." Torgen Sorenson shakes his head. In a reverent tone, he says, "Master's your guru, he's your true teacher. I would only be your mentor. You're always meant to follow him, just as I do." He gazes over at the glowing lithograph of Yogananda above the alter, our eyes follow his gaze. "But I'll tell you this much for sure," he adds, "if you are to work with me in this Center of Light endeavor, you'll be under his protection. There's no way you could have reached me except through his guidance. He had to give the say-so else you wouldn't even be here. *He's* your guru, and mine too, forever."

This emotional statement brings our thoughts to a stop. A palpable shimmer of energy floods the room under the hollow roof, a presence that we feel. Sudden tears well up in Torgie's eyes and pour down his cheeks. He lifts his hands, chokes on his next words, then turns away and sobs for a long moment. Evan and I share an amazed glance, deeply affected by such intense feeling, so spontaneous and inexplicable. After a minute or so Sorenson turns back toward us, snorting into a paper towel.

"Excuse me," he says with a self-conscious blush. "Sometimes he sends a wave of energy through here that pulls the rug right out from under you. You guys feel that?"

"Yeah, we definitely did. We felt something completely different, something sacred."

"That's right, that was just master saying hello," Sorenson murmurs. "And just so you both know, I'm working as closely with Yogananda as I ever have, nothing's changed, he's always with me. The Mallets don't really get it, but they haven't steeped themselves in the teachings like you fellows have, and that's why I know ... "

His voice trails off, his large blue eyes luminous and aqueous. He just continues to gaze at us, from one face to the other, until we all begin to fidget.

"Mr Sorenson, look, I'd like to know something," Evan says,

getting to his feet, taking a breath. "And I'd just like to get a simple straight answer, if that's okay."

"Alright, shoot," Torgie says, looking up in a childlike way. And this is what strikes me about him—nothing is feigned, his responses and facial expressions come across as utterly candid and sincere, like an overgrown boy.

"Okay then, dig, you say you need clearance for you to know, to find out about us? How much time will you need to find out if we can work together on the self-realization techniques?"

The reverend studies us calmly, then asks, "are you absolutely interested?"

"Hell yes, I mean I think so, yes," Evan replies, glancing at me. Both he and Torgie regard me, a question in their faces, wondering about my own thoughts.

Thinking fast and clear, hedging my bets, I say, "Yeah, of course I'm interested. I just need to know more about what's going on here at the Center of Light. You mentioned a special work, you mentioned unusual powers? I need to know more before I can truly commit."

"That's a fair enough place to begin," Sorenson nods, staring at a place above my head with his unblinking eyes. Beads of sweat appear on his broad forehead, his lips appear to be moving slightly, like he's talking to someone invisible yet present. I wonder for a moment if he's lost his wits.

Feeling nervous, Evan says, "Okay then, okay, how long would you say, reverend Sorenson? Until you know for sure?"

"Oh, not too long," Sorenson murmurs sensibly, as if recovering from an absent-minded flight. "I just have to go over to Modesto and paint a house and I'll be back in about a week. I'll know by then. I can pray on it while I paint. When I get back I'll come visit you fellows."

We lean forward together and shake hands, why I'm not quite sure. The big monk's face screws up in a preposterous way as he rips another sputtering fart. "Oh, excuse me," he flusters, going red-faced, and we all break into ridiculous laughter, fanning off the stench.

The reverend leads us outside the Quonset hut and around the weathered upper catwalk. Big as he is, he seems to walk quite nimbly. Gesturing down at a fenced half-acre of Mallet's coveted junk machinery, he observes, "there it all is, what did I tell you? King Solomon's lost treasures."

The weedy compound is filled with burned-out refrigerators and stoves, rusting ac units, old tireless truck, a few decrepit cars from the 30's and 40's, an antique tractor and broken-down thrasher. The hideaway looks like a forgotten movie set, like a neglected afterthought. We trudge on to the wooden farmhouse and eat Mrs Mallet's home baked carrot cake and drink delicious organic watermelon juice, grown and frozen the previous summer. Afterwards, we tour the 40 plus acres with old man Mallet, observing the once lordly Solomon slop three rooting and doomed hogs. Strewn around the property are old but working farm machines, including a vintage green John Deere tractor. The farm seems caught in a time warp, like the Center of Light itself, its sloping fields dreaming of their annual crops of organic melons, squash, and tall green corn. And if that is so, I ask myself, what then are we doing here?

Mallet talks as we stroll around, his hands hitched in his over-all suspenders. "The trick is," he points out, "you have to rotate your crops. I use the west twenty acres one year, and the east 20 the next year. The extra acres I just use for storage. That way the ground always recovers and stays healthy. I go by the moon sins. Never used a pound of artificial fertilizer in my life."

Evan and I listen to this earth-wisdom with considerable interest. I ask him, "what do you use to nourish the soil?"

"Just cow and pig manure and compost scraps," Mallet grins, gap-toothed. "it's all you ever need. Maybe some good river bottom soil now and then if it starts getting thin. It's just a matter of common sense, which almost nobody has much of anymore."

On our way back to the Quonset hut Torgie nods at the fenced compound of rusting machinery, saying, "Probably the biggest junk pile on the central coast, but as you can tell, that old man is no fool."

He encourages us to come upstairs and meditate with him in private, and we say sure. Back in the horseshoe chapel, we try to select milk-can stools that are easier on our asses.

"Just a minute, I've got to get out of this religious monkey suit!" Sorenson goes into his curtained bed chamber, huffs and grunts, then reappears in denim coveralls and a tee shirt. He has taken off his shoes and his toenails are an grisly sight. The yellowish nails are jagged and dirty, obviously ignored a long time. He seems blissfully unconcerned with his bizarre impression on us. This man spent several years in Yogananda's private entourage and has practiced celibate yoga for over twenty years, what can we say? Still, Sorenson is so peculiar that I am about to bust a gut and so is Evan.

Torgelananda folds his sweating bulk behind his harmonium and beams at us. "Okay, what say we meditate together for about an hour? We'll go deep this time, without worrying about interruptions. Let's really tap in."

We nod our consent, curious and already intrigued. "And when we start getting deep," he adds, "don't mind me if I go over there and flop my carcass on the bed. It's easier for me to leave my body that way. After awhile you boys can go whenever you want to. I'll be out on the Astral, so don't mind me. Please shut both doors on your way out, the outer one will lock by itself."

The big reverend monk goes into his prayerful invocation, we chant the resonant Aum together seven times, then lapse into silence. The room acquires that serene quality of deepening meditation, our breathing turns inward. Some time passes, Torgelananda rises abruptly up off his organ bench and pads across the chamber to collapse on his bed face up. He flops on his mattress like a giant fish. We try to ignore this, going deeper within ourselves. The antique belt-driven motors out in the tunnel start cranking up for another refrigeration cycle. The ear-splitting racket is awful, we struggle to maintain our composure. Hideous images of squalling, slaughtered animals come to mind, making us jerk and flinch. It's hard to imagine spending much time in this strange, cacophonous place.

The reverend calls out like a man in a trance, spitting his words around his dentures, "Ignore all that noise. You've got to overcome every distraction. Go deep, go deep ... concentrate ... like Milarepa did over in Tibet." All at once he lapses into deep, resonant snores. My brother and I squint at each other, squinting at paradoxes, shaking with bottled-up laughter.

We know, or we think we know, that great yogis don't fall asleep in their trances. Or is it only his bloated body that snores? We close our eyes and go back within, using our mantra, doing our best to shut out the mechanical pandemonium. After awhile we resurface at the same intuitive moment, figuring we have acquitted ourselves well enough. We get up quietly and stretch, signaling our intention to go. Torgie has fallen into some weird state punctuated by snorting and unintelligible sputters, then a spell where he does not breath at all, only broken by an erratic snore. As we pad by his bedchamber, he unleashes a loud, cracking fart that seems to hover in the air above his round blissful face. We duck out.

We make our way down the noisy corridor convulsed with spasmodic laughter. This is one of the strangest days we have spent in awhile. As we reach the daylight of the glass-pane door, we hear a rush up the walkway behind us and a booming voice that brings us up short. Sorenson comes thumping out of the gloom, pasted in a sweaty tee shirt and tent-like boxer shorts. His face is bright and cherubic. "Hey now, did you enjoy yourselves?" he says. "Did you have a good time?"

"Uh yeah, Mr Sorenson, sure did, most unusual." We regard him with lopsided grins.

"That's good, good, glad to hear it," the reverend responds, opening the door for us pumping our hands. As we file down the steep plank steps to the parking lot, he calls out, "don't forget, I'll be out of town for about a week. When I get back I'll come see you, or if I don't, come see me at Wednesday meditation! I'll have that answer for us!"

We wave up at the big bizarre meta physician, standing in his underwear in the doorway, signaling our interest in the next step – if there is a next step. Sorenson waves and closes the door, makes sure it's locked, then his pale bulk disappears. Muttering with amusement, my brother and I get into the yellow Lark and drive across that rural valley in the rain shadow of the coastal range, then sail down the long 101 hill into San Luis Obispo, sharing our thoughts, comparing notes.

Evan says to me, "Either that guy is the real thing and into something incredible, or he's got one of the most outrageous lines of bullshit going. You think he's on the level?"

I look at my brother, nodding. "You never know, you know? and I don't know yet. But I agree, man – is this scene real or bogus? I think we need to find out."

Indeed, we need to find out if Torgen Sorenson is for real or not. For in spite of the weird aspects, there's something about this Center of Light that whispers significance. We feel like we're closer to something that we can't even name yet, like it's almost in our hands.

Chapter 6

WHEN WE RETURN the next Wednesday evening to that strange inner sanctum, we come with an almost reckless humor. This is new-age California in its flowering. There are no acknowledged limits and the previously agreed-upon rules are being tossed out. Anything seems possible. The counter-culture is ablaze with revolutionary passion. Up in Berkeley students are in the streets, our radical friends are on fire for justice, the foundations are being shook, psychedelic rock lights the way, and deep into the mystical night my brother and I burn bright. It's hard to conceive that people live in any other way. We climb the weathered stairs to the white door of the Quonset sanctuary, knowing that something unusual is bound to happen here.

We bring with us an offering of fresh fruit and wildflowers to the rustic Center of Light. Sorenson digs it, saying it reminds him of his days in the SRF ashram. The same homespun crew is present. Ramspack makes a jittery but friendly remark, shoulders hunched, six-shooter on his hip, smelling of stale cigs. Old man Mallet shakes our hands and squints at our offering with a humorous grunt. His charming wife is all smiles, saying how the wildflowers remind her of the bluebells back in her home state of Texas. She does the lesson reading in her slurry voice, then we dip into meditation. This time everybody becomes still, no one moves fidgets too much. Swashes of purple light come and go behind my eyelids, I forget about the milk can stool under my thin ass.

Afterwards, we snack on some fresh pears and Mrs Mallet's homemade brownies, making awkward small talk. Then Evan and I find ourselves alone with the occult-minded reverend, for an encounter that seems inevitable.

Sorenson sits back down at the harmonium and rubs his forehead with the heels of both hands. He's sweating, he looks as if he's about to split his black minister's suit with his rounded slabs of fat. Abruptly, he lifts his head and fixes us with a luminous, eye-bulging stare. No one says a word. I hold myself in restraint, holding my thoughts, holding his remarkable eyes with my own. A force of will sees rise up between us, challenging, but not offensive. Then Torgelananda lifts one hand and jabs his blunt finger across the horseshoe chapel at me.

"You can change the course of the whole goddamn country if you put your will to it! You've got the inherent power, I saw this in a vision!" he pauses, regarding me as though were old friends, then says gently, "can you deny it?"

Can I deny what? His highly charged statement rivets me. Intimate dreams flash through my head, wishes of such intensity that I've put them aside out of sheer exasperation. One cannot live in imaginary states, you have to be present now. But Sorenson has touched on an invisible nerve, somehow penetrating to the veiled core of my thoughts, to the beloved dream that is my violent America.

"I'm not sure I get what you're talking about," I say in a guarded tone.

"Can you deny that what you want, and what you always wanted, is to stop the whorish betrayal of this country? Answer me that."

Swallowing, I reply, "no, I cannot deny that. But I'd rather deal in reality than in daydreams."

"Aha well, there you are," Sorenson nods in apparent agreement.

All I can do is stare at him, in wonder, as tears of empathy well up in his blue eyes. He blinks them back, not taking his attention from my face, as I meet his smile with my own.

"But what difference does that make?" I retort with feeling. "When they've stacked the deck against us in such ridiculous ways? Conform, submit, obey, fuck it. There is no more frontier. We have to make our own world now."

"I know, that's true," Torgie says, wiping his tears with his fingers. "You are seeing the same things. I see the three of us being consecrated to bring about immense change."

These are secrets that I keep deep inside, but he has hit a hidden chord. I glance over at my brother, who has stayed quiet during this awkward exchange. Evan gives me a piercing look.

"Mr Sorenson," Evan says, "what you just said about my brother Jake, it's true. That's his private trip, he doesn't show that pure, patriotic side of himself to others very often. It's kind of incredible that you perceive that."

"Maybe that's so, but I've pretty much let it go," I say with a tinge of sarcasm. "That's one reason I'm on this transcendental path. It seems impossible, the political trip, no one can get along. They all have their piece of the action, haranguing for more. They shove war and obedience and stupidity down your throat – be like us, not like them—and make outcasts of free-thinkers. No, this country has been lied to and seduced by television. The people are starting to want security more than their freedom, in fact, some of the can't even tell the difference anymore. Keep me safe, oh please keep us safe! Meanwhile, Vietnam is a runaway disaster and our environment is getting raped. What the fuck is the point of cooperation? When I look around, it sickens me. This is my country? No, my country has been usurped. So for me the choice has become simple – become an anarchist, right? or transcend the whole perverted scene."

Feeling the passion rise in my throat, I wave the conversation off. I don't want to talk about it. Let the immaculate core of rage inside me be enough. Scowling, I look past Sorenson and Evan into clear inner space. My heart beats strong and steady. I will not permit anything to confuse or confine me, I will not be a captive of false values. This natural earth is my living body, the rivers my blood, the sky my consciousness and all true tribes my brethren. I am all but convinced that an alien species has taken control of our beloved planet.

Torgie wags his big perspiring head from side to side, his white hair sticking out in tufts. He takes a breath and says to me, "but you can't turn away, too many others are depending on what you do. You are one of them who can get things back on the right track!"

"What the hell are you talking about? Don't talk nonsensical bullshit, please."

Sorenson knits his brows up, jabbing his finger at me. "You have no damn right to give up on America—not you. Of all people, not you!"

"I haven't given up on anything," I just think we're losing the game to the faceless soulless bastards who control it. And don't give that shit that everybody's got a soul, I don't buy it. And I don't think we can regain control of this country short of a total revolution or a radical shift of consciousness And what are the chances of that? Everyone's plugged into their brainwashing TV."

Torgie stares at me with a fierce affection, unsettling me further. "And that's precisely why you are here, both of you. You could just as well write it on the wall."

Then he swivels his chair toward Evan, whose pupils are bigger than usual, and says serenely, "and you, my young friend. What you want more than anything in this world is God. You just want to get to God and be done with all the rest."

Evan sits and stares at Sorenson, wondering how he could know that stuff. For the truth is, I've sometimes thought that my brother might be some kind of saint in the making. Whereas for myself, I don't have any such pristine expectations.

Evan sniffs, absorbing reverend's bright gaze, then perceptively says, "so you want us to move in here with you, is that it? Move into the Center of Light, into this weird ashram, so we can all work together. Am I right?"

The idea jolts me. "I am not moving in here," I say. "It's too tight and it's too cramped, we'd all be living on top of each other. I'm willing to work with you, reverend, if that jives. But I need a certain amount of privacy and space in my life. That's just the way I am."

The big monk holds up one placating, confident hand. "There's no need to get ahead of ourselves. We can study on the best ways to accomplish these things. But for me to get the green light, the unconditional go-ahead, I need to know if you boys are willing to commit to the work involved here. No holding back."

"But that's just it, damn it," I say, "what exactly is the work invoked? You haven't told us much of anything. I need to know more details before I can commit on anything."

"Yeah, I'm with my brother Jake on that," Evan affirms. "I mean, what's the big secret? Are you trying to overthrow the United States government or something?"

Torgelananda laughs, bobbing his dome-like head. "Okay, okay, you got me there, But tell me first, are you willing to take some preparatory steps? There's highly advanced initiations involved that come down from Yogananda and Babaji. We must use those initiations to manifest the powerful attributes of ceremonial magic to work for the highest good. And it may be the only chance we get to avoid a long slide back into intense darkness."

"Say again? Man, I have no intention of sliding back into darkness."

"I'm referring to society in general, here in America and the world. There are those who are intent on plunging us all back into a primitive feudal state."

Studying him, I say wryly, "that's pretty far out, reverend, you realize how insane that sounds? What happened to the Age of Aquarius?"

"Aquarius-smarius," Torgie says, sweat glistening on his heavy jowls. "I'm talking facts, not fantasy. Of course I realize it sounds crazy. That doesn't make it any less true." He places his hands on his knees, facing me. "The real question is, are you ready to take the first step?"

For a moment I'm silent, feeling that I'm being boxed in. Then I reply, "I'm always ready to take a new step. But like I said, sir, I need to know more about what's going on. I'm speaking for myself here, Evan's got his own mind. But if I'm going to move ahead with you in some kind of esoteric work, show me the map."

"All right, fair enough," Sorenson says in a nonchalant tone. "And that allow s me to do some more meditating on it too. How would it be if I come and visit you fellows in a few days?"

My brother and I nod in agreement. This seems to be tremendously important, although I can't say why. "Okay, Mr Sorenson, that sounds good. That will work for us."

AFTER MY RECKLESS smuggling bust on the border a couple years back, I don't want to make any false steps. All those trips on high-octane psychedelics brought me certain unforgettable insights into the nature of appearances. All things that look alike are not the same. In fact, what appears to be may not even be real. The world is a cosmic carnival ride, a uniquely subjective and intimate experience, anything can pop out of the door at any time. Reality is primordial awareness which may have nothing to do with what you imagine to be real. People confuse their thoughts with reality, the self-deluded ego believes it can control the world through its thinking, but reality is non-controllable. At some point you realize that notion is laughably absurd, nothing more than your false expectations. Our choice is how we observe and engage, because we cannot evade. One's conscious existence is a risky experiment, an adventure into what ever is happening. The anxiety *what about me* usually leaves you dangling out on a limb.

The root question becomes who am I, what am I, and why am I here? Or are you merely a semi-conscious drone pollinating plants? I remember Gurdjieff saying that mankind in its sleep-walking state was fodder for the moon, which is a cosmic organism fed by the unconscious stupidity of humans. This is a sobering point of view, no? Do I possess real being or am I only imaginary? And who is this "I" always claiming to be "me"?

The other main question for Even and I, in the cross-hairs of now, is who is Torgen Sorenson in relation to our own self-determined path? Is he real or is he some kind of impostor?

Sorenson's almost nonchalant insights into our psychology baffle us. His own devotional and bombastic personality only adds to the intrigue of the situation. When we try to verbalize it, we end up scrambling for clear ideas. There are too many contradictions at play. When Torgie shows up at our door a few days later in his painter's garb, spouting his outrageous declaration that "all men will bow and scrape at your feet, Master has sent you!"—it's like gasoline thrown on the fire. Nothing that we're doing comes close to matching such potent intrigue, and the solitary celibate yogi hungers for more.

Week by week, the occult conversation with the mad reverend-monk Sorenson deepens. We visit him for the Sunday morning and Wednesday evening meditations, followed by our compelling talks. Evan wants to hear the extraordinary Yogananda stories that Torgie delights in telling. I probe him for clues to the secret work that supposedly goes on in this ramshackle Quonset hut on the outskirts of a one-horse town scattered along highway 101 half-way between LA and San Francisco. The Pacific lies over the hills twenty miles away, but its balmy coastal breezes seldom reach Atascadero. During the summers you swelter and in the winters you shiver your ass off.

The occult Quonset hut becomes our new refuge. Leaning forward on my milk can stool, elbows on my knees, I ask him, "when you say ceremonial magic work performed for the highest purposes, what do you mean? And who's involved in this ceremonial work, Mr Sorenson? Are the Mallet's included in any of these rituals?"

"No, heavens no, none of them have an inkling a about what's going on," Torgie replies. "They're just here for the meditations, they're not ready for the rigors of the higher work. This is not child's play, it's not like telling fortunes."

"But then what are we talking about? We need something other than vague images."

"It means," the reverend says, scratching his massive stomach, appraising me with his luminous eyes, "that with the help of evolved individuals as serious as you two brothers are, this Center of Light can vanquish the evil ones that are trying to subjugate the world under a Satanic tyranny. And no, I'm not talking about communists or Nazis or any of the cunning bad actors of that sort, they're just tools in the game. These evil forces are much more powerful than those clowns. I've been researching this for over twenty years and today I know all I need to know. What I've been asking for, what I've prayed for night after night are a few strong individuals who would dedicate themselves to the accomplishment of this work. And then you two boys show up out of the blue with Master's blessing."

His voice has an air of finality, as if his conviction is all the proof one needs. His round, imposing face is uncluttered by doubt, his large hands are splayed palms down on his knees. He looks from me to my brother Evan, then back, brimming with calm expectation.

Clearing my throat, I venture, "are you claiming that Yogananda knew, or has known all along, about this metaphysical work of yours? And that he sanctions it?"

"You're damn tooting I am," affirms Sorenson. I would never have gone forward without his blessing. He knew and he's always known. Why do you think he would let me get away with so much when I was living at the Fellowship? I'd pretty much come and go as I pleased. He wouldn't let others do that and when they'd bitch about it, well, he'd just say, "let Torgie alone. He's got his work to do and there's many ways to serve God.""

Pushing his nose, Evan murmurs, "far out. That's really far out. So, Yogananda was in on it?"

"Well, not in the sense for from A to Z, because his work was liberating souls from Maya. But yeah, he understood and he totally approved."

Noticing the rapport growing between him and Evan, I say,

"So Yogananda was aware of these evil doers, these ... these hidden manipulators that you speak of?"

"Yes, he was and he is. And that's a good phrase for them— evil manipulators, an ancient society, extremely cunning and powerful. Oh hell yes, Master knows." Sorenson enunciates his words as if weighing them, nodding his balding sagacious head. "And yes, God the Father knows. But this is the mess created by those of us down here on earth. If its going to be straightened out and cleaned up, we've got to do it, that's all. There won't be any sort of divine intervention, even though a lot of people keep praying for it. Nope, no one's coming back to bail us out. It's totally our responsibility."

"Wait a minute," Even says, "I want to understand something. You're saying that it's up to this Center of Light, to your esoteric network, whatever you call it, to bring down these evil assholes?"

"Evil co-conspirators," Torgie says flatly, "and their inhuman overlords. Yep, that's hitting the nail on the head. You got it."

"A metaphysical holy war to bring down the Machiavellian evil of this world?" I cannot refrain from a twisted smile. "Excuse me, but reverend, that sounds like something right out of a science fiction comic book."

"Yes, I am aware of that," Sorenson says with a lofty air. "And isn't it fascinating that some of those stories penetrate right into the hidden core of things."

Evan again pushes his nose with his index finger, gives me a quizzical look. "To tell the truth, doesn't that remind you of some of the stuff that Gurdjieff talked about?"

"Yeah, it does, it definitely does. But who is saying what to whom?"

"Well, you have heard it straight from my mouth, and I'm sworn to Master to never lie," Sorenson says, lifting one palm. "I

DARLING YOUNG ONE 75

have to assume you're supposed to hear it, and I have to think that you probably already know. Yes, that is what my work is all about and you're not here by accident. I'm at a point where I've got to have some personal help or bag it all."

"Okay, but let me be clear on something," Evan insists, agitated. "Can we do this work, this, I don't know what to call it, this interfering in the global politics and conspiracies and still reach liberation from the law of karma? Because, man, I'm fucking sick of karma, I want to be done with it and not be coming back here."

"Yes, yes you can," Sorenson states with magisterial calmness. "It all depends on the attitude you're working with. Your attitude is more important than the actions themselves. If you can do what needs to be done without guilt or shame you stay pretty much free of stains. The bottom line is, are we working in God's name or for the glorification of our own egos? That's the clincher."

I study Torgie for a moment, semi-revolted by his naked religiosity yet fascinated, then lock eyes with Evan. I've been asserting for awhile that guilt is a snare of the frightened mind, nothing more than a conditioning factor. Through guilt you're easily controlled, through buying into guilt one can be enslaved. Do what you do free and clear or don't do it at all?

Blinking me off, my brother says to him, "so alright, what you're telling us is that we've been directed here, to you, through Yogananda, to decide whether we want to help in straightening all this shit out? Or do we even have a choice?"

"Don't be ridiculous," I retort. "Did Moses write your name on a stone?"

"Yes, yes, that's it," Sorenson enthuses, ignoring me. "Master without a doubt directed you here, and sure, you always have a choice because nothing can be forced on you. If you decide, you can rule the world. And as far as your ultimate liberation goes, it doesn't make any difference one way or the other. Once you're enlightened the karma involved doesn't amount to a hill of beans."

My brother and I look at each other with an imperceptible shiver, like men transfixed between shadow and light – Aiyee, here is the treacherous world, here the immaculate sun and stars, of what would you partake? And what if this character is some kind of deranged bullshit artist?

"Fucking incredible," I mutter half to myself.

The fat, muscular monk laughs, saying, "yes, if you'll pardon my French, it is fucking incredible. And the table is all set for us."

"But dude, pardon my slang, this is the proverbial path of power, right?"

"That is absolutely correct."

"But pure yogis are taught not to seek the path of power," I point out, "because it deceives. Like you said, the danger is in ego-glorification. So how does that all work together, with attaining God-consciousness in this lifetime? Because we don't want to get trapped on a lesser path."

Sorenson shakes his head. "You won't, as long as you're work-ing with Yogananda and the Christ-power, there's no way that will happen. But this does have to be done just so or we'll fall into their snares. And if we fall, we'll fall hard. This involves an ancient ceremonial science and yes, it's like walking a tight rope. The rules have to be followed exactly. We have to be stronger and purer than the satanic malefactors or else we'll be kaput."

"Satanic malefactors? Kaput? Hey," Evan snorts, "I don't like the sound of that."

"Well, let's all slow down," Torgie says. "We're getting ahead of ourselves again. The demons must be thrown into chains and that is our job. But I can't talk about that just yet."

"Whoa," I say, "are we talking about flesh and blood beings or disembodied spirits?"

"Both. We'll be dealing with both types. And only through complete devotion to God and Master and the Christ can we succeed. But their protection is perfect and I think you know they are all one. Only by being pure in our intentions can we overthrow the demonic forces that's running things behind the scenes. Only with clean hands and pure hearts, there is no other way, because the temptations that come with power are too great, power corrupts absolutely if you're weak. Lucifer will seize our egos and make us his slaves. Yes, Lucifer himself, these agents of evil are total Luciferians, he is their king and lord."

"Aiyee man, Mr Sorenson, that's really far out and sounds like whacked-out Catholic dogma, you dig?"

"I know, but it's my responsibility to tell you the truth. How else an you make an honest decision? You boys have done days and nights and hundreds of hours of meditation, prayers and fastings. Weren't you asking to be shown the way, is that not so?"

My brother and I share a flickering glance, unable to deny it. "So now then," the reverend says, "I'm authorized to tell you that this is one of your two choices. You can come into the Center of Light and work with me for the good of all humanity and when we win out, when we're finished, we'll all ascend into the light of the Supreme Lord together, into the holy of holies! Those are their words, not mine!" Torgelananda pivots in his oak rocker, pointing at the pictures of the saints and masters on the long alter. "The other choice that might open up is that you would be able to join the SRF Fellowship as novitiate monks and put on the orange robes."

Hunching forward on my padded milk can, my hands clasped and brow furrowed, I'm trying to make sense of his astonishing ramble. Certain things cross my mind almost simultaneously. Who is making up these rules? Who says that I only have two choices going forward in my mystical way? There's a pretty good chance that Torgen Sorenson is an erstwhile madman, and besides, I'm not much of a joiner and never have been. I don't conform well with groups and I offer no apologies for being myself. But those saffron robes have a certain allure for my gentle brother, whereas the idea of acquiring godlike power does appeals to me. I won't deny that I would love to kick the asses of some evil-doers although not at the cost of my own freedom. I am nobody's witless and obedient slave, no, if anything I am a lion of God.

Looking into the Torgie's boyish face, I say, "and what if I decide to get another motorcycle, ride off into Mexico and forget all about this stuff? That strikes me as another worthwhile choice."

"All right, you could," he acknowledges with a taken-aback expression, "you could always do that, but for you that would be a giant cop-out on your destiny."

"A cop-out on my destiny, how so?"

Pointing at my heart, Sorenson declares, "because I've seen your Akashic records. I've seen you dump Satan in a wheelbarrow and roll him right out of here and throw him in irons, that's why! If you have the courage to reach for it, that's your destiny. But you have to choose."

My jaw goes slack. I find myself staring into his luminous, bulging eyes. What does one say to such an outrageous statement? Nothing. His blue eyes are lit with a prescient gleam.

Gathering my thoughts, I reply, "and you could be crazy as a madcap loon. I have no direct knowledge of any of that and I'm not even sure Satan exists. I know that evil exists because I've run into it head-on. But Satan, who is Satan? Is he some shadowy figure kicking up red dust on a country road or a suave con-man in a government tuxedo? Seems to me that humanity does a phenomenal job of fucking-up all on its own."

"Sooner or later you will know," Sorenson says with odd satisfaction, as if he has won some invisible point, "and you will gain total mastery over your mind. If you come into the inner workings of the Center of Light, both of you will, it's yours for the taking."

"Sounds awfully far-fetched to me," says Evan in a placating tone, "although I'm not putting it down. You seem to know what you're talking about, but personally, I don't want to play games with Lucifer's demons. I just want to take the high road out of here."

"And you will, oh you will," Torgie affirms with a childlike smile. "You're already on your way. All you have to do is hold the protective mantle of light for your brother and me."

Flashing on how bizarre this conversation is, annoyed and amused, I say, "Reverend Sorenson, let me ask you again, do any of these local folks have any inkling of this occult scheme of yours? Are they involved in some weird way?"

"Oh hell no," Torgie huffs, "it would blow their minds. Master's teachings are about their limit. I've tried to explain a few things to Mallet because he was a great magician in his Solomon lifetime, but I don't dare tell him too much. He can't handle the power, he dribbles all his life-force out the end of his degenerate pecker. One of our goals will be to help him get stabilized and into the inner circle with us. But to answer your question, no, there are only ten other people in the entire country who know what I'm doing, and you and your brother make eleven and twelve. You're the final keys we've been waiting for."

"Waiting for? To do what? To start some kind of world revolution?"

"No, for heaven's sake, no. We're not anarchists. What is needed is the establishment of a higher order. The three of us have to initiate the ceremonial power inside the holy pentagram and magical circle, then throw the infernal ones into bondage. This has to be done in extreme secrecy and you boys have to hold these rituals in the strictest confidence. Otherwise all the power will deflate and it'll all be for naught. This is why it's important that we're all living close together. If not living here in the Quonset hut, then living somewhere nearby in Atascadero or Santa Margarita."

Thick arms folded across his chest, Sorenson bends sideways and hawks a lugie into his trash box. "There's a lot of metaphysical work that goes on late into the night," he explains, "sometimes all day and all night. You need to be within a few miles of me and in living strictly celibate conditions, just as you are now. No hanky-panky and no beating the meat."

Evan and I sit quietly with hooded, inscrutable eyes. Putting my hand on top of my head, I give my brother a meaningful look. He picks up on it, then says to the big man, "One more thing, Mr Sorenson, if I can ask. Do you have god-consciousness now? I mean, the way that Yogananda describes it?"

"Nope, not yet," Sorenson replies candidly, "although I have taken a few major steps in that direction. I've gotten to the point where I can leave my body at will and I'm able to consciously explore up into the high astral regions. And I can help you boys attain these same abilities. But in other ways I'm still working at it, I'm still limited, just like you."

"Limited in what ways, reverend Sorenson?"

In childlike candor, Sorenson says to me, "I'm not one with God yet, as Master was. And I don't have the intellectual ability that you have, which is important, because the work to be done will require some powerful writings. As for your brother, he's so naturally devotional and single-minded that he'll act as a spiritual balancing force in our bid for supernatural power. There are others we will need to draw in as we go along, 12 men and 12 women, just like Jesus did, in order to form a perfectly harmonious group."

"You honestly believe you can do this work and still achieve cosmic-consciousness," Evan prods. "No bullshit?"

"Yes, I honestly do," reverend Sorenson nods. "We have His blessing, and we have the grace of the Christ consciousness." Glancing over at the alter, at Yogananda's imposing image and the other portraits of the SRF saints, he adds, "and it's my hope and prayer that when we finish this holy work we enter divine illumination together. By then one of you might be pulling me up because I've still got my own flaws. And remember, Master's always the leader, not me."

Chapter 7

"*A LL WILL BOW and scrape before you, the mighty will grovel at your feet!*"

With those mad words ringing in our ears, which I record in my journal, we move up to Atascadero to get more deeply involved. We figure we have more to gain than to lose, and though the reverend might be a lunatic that doesn't mean he can't be right. Crazy people have scored huge in this world. Call me an ex-acidhead still resonating on the wild-child vibes if you like, but you don't find out what is what by just reading books or gawking at television. You have to bite deeply into the apple to know its particular reality.

My brother and I do not intend to live at the claustrophobic Quonset hut and deal daily with Torgelananda's imposing presence. We want to maintain some degree of independence. We start making weekend forays through the winding, oak-lined roads of Atascadero, and once again, we get lucky. Not far from the Center of Light about a quarter mile off highway 101, we come across a green farmhouse set back in a stand of trees, a for-rent sign on the dirt driveway mail box. Turns out the two-story house itself is not for rent, there's an absentee owner. What's for rent is the caretaker's cottage under the black walnut trees, a basic three room hovel even more rustic than our San Luis digs. But the cottage sits well off the road in serene privacy, with ten acres of trees and fields, including a modest vineyard of purple Concord grapes. It's a verdant camp, a hippie dream. All we have to do is look after the place and make sure the green yard and flowering shrubs get water in the heat. There's plenty of room for another organic garden with no one hanging over the fence with wise-ass remarks. One hundred dollars a month including utilities. We rent the vineyard farm the same day that we inspect it.

Did I mention the withering summer heat? Indeed, the biggest trade-off from our cozy San Luis pad to this charming old farm is the prevailing micro-climate. Atascadero sits north of the high Cuesta Grande on a plateau that gives rise to the Salinas River flowing north to Monterrey. But this valley plateau is sheltered by the Santa Lucia Mountains that run up into Big Sur, that form a massive barrier to the cool breezes that pour in from the ocean only 20 miles away. This natural air-conditioning gets funneled into the long Morro Bay to San Luis Obispo valley running in from the coast. Because of this air-current deflection, during summertime Atascadero swelters like a panting dog. Once in a while a towering plume of fog rolls over the top of the ridge and spills onto the valley at night, but it makes little difference. The towns of Atascadero, Templeton and Paso Robles broil under the relentless sun, good for the red wine vineyards but hard on humans and beasts. Ambient temps hereabouts hover in the 90's for months, often exceeding 100 degrees. Balmy San Luis and roasting Atascadero are only 20 road miles apart but the temperature can vary by 25 degrees Fahrenheit. Sundown doesn't make much difference, unless you are fortunate enough to live on the coastal ridge that fronts the nocturnal fog.

We don't realize these purgatorial consequences right away, no. We move up over the Cuesta Grande in springtime, when the warmer daytime feels quite pleasant. We walk around in short sleeves and cut-offs, no shivering fog or nippy breezes for a skinny vegetarian to endure. The neglected farm seems like another slice of central coast paradise. When I get home in the late afternoons from my truck route, I spread my blanket on the patch of green grass and do my hatha yoga all but naked. This rustic scene is enclosed in privacy, although there are a few discordant vibes. Route 101 is just within earshot, and the coughing pipes of the passing semis rattles our meditations. But we dig in and deal with it. These highway noises and the alien machinery over at the Center of Light seem to be a challenge we are meant to overcome.

Next, we discover that the weedy soil on this farm is riddled with thousands of stones, so rocky that we decide against the hard work of putting a garden into the ground. We plant a few squash vines and cantaloupes, but that's it. We are laid-back yogis, man, not field laborers. But no organic garden means a crisis in our pure food supply. Organic produce is not plentiful around here, at least not like it was in San Luis Obispo. This forces us to make some revolting compromises with local supermarket stuff, most of it sprayed with hideous chemicals. But the deep well water that comes out of the stony ground is cool and delicious, so we figure to make do one way or another.

The loquacious reverend-monk Sorenson complicates our search for pure food with his own deranged dietary exhortations. He insists that we need more strength and endurance to go into the ceremonies and master the forces of Lucifer. The practices are demanding and rigorous.

"It's not just about spiritual purity," he tells us. "Some of these rituals last 12 hours or longer, you need to be physically able to deal with it. That vegetable-fruitarian diet you're on won't be enough. You will be contending with powerful infernal spirits, your job will be to subdue them."

The implications of these preposterous statements are daunting enough, but now he's criticizing our organic immortality diets. The fat monk is already starting to get under my nerves. He insists we need to learn to eat *occult power foods,* special foods that tend to repulse ordinary people.

Frowning at such gobbledygook, I say, "get off it. We're following the sacred Hunza diet. That all sounds like a bunch of deranged nonsense."

"Which only makes my point," Sorenson says with an amused air. "What sounds deranged is often quite right for us, and believe me, you're going to need more raw animal strength and protein. You're both skinny as rails."

"Animal strength?" Evan mutters, wrinkling his nose. "You mean like meat? We don't eat meat, reverend, we're not cannibals."

"Yeah, dig man. We don't eat things that have faces."

Reverend Sorenson smiles nonchalantly, remarking, "it wouldn't hurt you to start eating tuna and chicken salad, even some chunks of beef during the week. You're both healthy and should be able to digest it. You'll grow stronger and you're going to need all your strength, trust me."

"Hey no way," my brother retorts, "that's doesn't jive. That's against all the yoga dietary rules."

"Yeah, that's sacrilegious bullshit," I counter. "Those foods are tamasic and have lower vibrations of energy. Butchered meats are saturated with the terror of the animals being slaughtered. There's no way I'm going back to eating that garbage." Yet even as I protest, I remember Gurdjieff's words about the pathetic weaknesses of civilized man—that if man were in his natural state he would be able to eat and digest anything, even bones. Sorenson looks at me in a prescient way, as if reading my thoughts, thoughts which I don't voice.

"Look," I say instead, "doesn't Yogananda himself advise against animal protein except for maybe a few eggs? He recommends eating only pure fruit and vegetables and natural juices, he said that raw nuts and avocados were a good source of protein. And I've read that he even assigned spiritual qualities to fruits, like tranquility to bananas and joy to cherries, isn't that right?"

"That's true, he did," Torgie admits, putting his palms on his knees. "But that was mainly to cool the sensual heat of the brothers and sisters in the ashram, so they wouldn't be tempted to any shenanigans instead of learning to meditate."

"Okay then, so I'll eat more beans," Evan says, "but I'm not gonna start eating animal flesh. Just the idea totally sickens me."

"Beans are okay," the reverend chuckles, "but by themselves not nearly sufficient. Besides, you'd have to eat so many beans you'd fill up the chapel with ripe farts."

Glancing over at the Yogananda lithograph hanging above the alter, I say, "eating tamasic foods leads to corruption of the body and the mind. It's in all the teachings, the Vedas, Upanishads, and Vedanta scriptures. You are what you eat physically and psychologically."

"Not necessarily. Those injunctions are for the ashrams, for the novitiates. It doesn't make much difference for those who are advanced in their disciplines, they can eat whatever they want. The real hangup is getting over your shame and fear."

"Where do you get this stuff, reverend? Nothing in Yogananda's discourses says that's allowed. Are these just your own ideas or what?"

"Master did not go into magical alchemy," Sorenson replies, rubbing his pate "or talk about occult power foods. His mission on earth was to teach self-soul-realization and how to escape the wheel of incarnation. He didn't concern himself with anything else. But that doesn't mean that we're forbidden to make use of such things."

"Use what," I say, "occult power foods? You keep using that weird phrase. Power foods to do what?"

"Well, take yo, u for example. Because of your blood type and ability to concentrate, you can digest slabs of almost raw meat and transmute it into elemental force."

"Elemental force? By eating slaughtered animals? I'm not sure we're even on the same wavelength. We're peacemakers, Mr Sorenson. We're not into making war or manipulating life for our own egotistic advantage." Scowling, I add, "and what do you mean by blood type? Where are you getting this kind of knowledge?"

"From the Spirit," Torgie says evasively, folding his thick muscular arms. "The Center of Light works with ascended spiritual master guardians, they're our shield. And they would like to see you build more power into your bodies. You're both just too ethereal. These ceremonial rituals are demanding. You have to gain strength before we can proceed."

"Build power how?" Evan asks, opening his hands. "I thought that's what we're doing with our practices."

"You are, yes, but only as an inner spiritual foundation. You need to make it more physical. To prepare for the advanced work you fellows should start eating a T-bone steak twice a week, with salt and cayenne pepper and dripping with bloody juices. That will give you some unruly erections to be sure, but you'll learn to transmute that primal energy. That is prime power food and you'll become masters of your own bodies."

"Good God man, that's deranged," I laugh in protest. "I'm not going to start gorging on rare meat to conquer lust. It's wrong, murdering animals just to eat them. No, no way, fuck all that."

"Me neither, count me out, dude," my brother mutters, shaking his head. "Animals have been some of my best friends."

Taking us in with an unruffled gaze, Torgie says, "you need to learn to detach yourselves from all types of limited thinking. Any hangups you have about anything, the infernal powers will use against you. If you're going to walk the path of higher power you have to get over your desires and your aversions. You can eat meat, including raw meat, even rotten meat, to the spirit it simply makes no difference."

"No, that's insane, I don't believe it, you must be mad," I tell him, my eyes boring into his own. He is mad, for only a madman would utter such demented nonsense and I have to make my stand.

"Why insane?" he asks me, shifting his dentures around in his mouth.

"Because obviously it's cruel, and it's against the Ayurvedic teachings for pure health."

"Look, I'm a vegetarian to the core," Evan pleads. "I mean, I might nibble a little tuna fish or egg salad, but I'm not eating any bloody animal meat, no way, that's not gonna happen."

"Then you should learn to eat select vegetables that are old and moldering," Sorenson says in his philosophical tone. "Rotting vegetables are much more potent than the young fresh garden greens."

"Huh, man, say what?" I laugh, as my brother begins to snort. "Hey reverend, that sounds like some ludicrous joke, you know? No offense but it sounds really crazy. We are vegetarian purists. Are you saying we have to sacrifice that in order to work with you?"

"No, I'm not laying any kind of rules out, so let's all calm down a bit. I'm just pointing to a few things. I am saying you're going to need more physical and psychic strength before we go into the holy pentagram, otherwise you might just pass out from the power of the spells."

"Pass out? I don't pass out, man. I've ridden motorcycles over a 110 miles per hour and dropped up to 1000 mics of pure acid at a time. Ever do that and stay conscious? It's like riding the slipstream of a comet. No, I never pass out. What are you talking about?"

Sorenson regards me with an intrigued expression, then says, "which is why you are uniquely qualified for the confrontation with the demon archetypes. You move through fear like it isn't there. But this isn't child's play, my friends. We need to get serious to make sure nobody gets soul-snatched. Trust me, you need to think about what I'm saying."

SOUL-SNATCHED? THE CALENDAR on the wall says August, 1967, imprinted with the logo of the Atascadero lumber company But it's obvious that the Center of Light abides in its own bizarre time-warp. Salubrious gorging on raw and rotten meat, snacking on moldering vegetables? These wild assertions of Torgelananda put me on edge, making me question my own take on reality. Alone, my brother and I giggle hysterically as we recount these talks that smack of occult buffoonery. Who is this brash meta physician to make such lunatic claims, which he often punctuates with odious farts. It's little wonder that he never really fit in at the SRF ashrams, although I don't hold that against him, I never really fit in anywhere either.

Eccentricities aside, though, one thing Sorenson has are the bonafide Yogananda credentials and he is never boring. As crude as he tends to be, a former merchant seaman in his younger days, the reverend is a strong-minded and persuasive individual. I feel myself being drawn into a compelling duel of will and wits with him, strange conundrum, one that attracts and puts me off at the same time.

But the die is cast and the karmic wheels set in motion. We are meeting four or five times a week now, for meditation and special metaphysical exercises, I'm able to maintain my space by taking my free time at our vineyard farm. I do yoga asanas in the shade of the black walnut trees, scribble my intense ideas and poems into my journal to ward off the lonely moods. I wander the meandering back roads of the coastal hills, hiking up into the secluded oak groves to write. Everything seems intimate and vast in these secluded spots, overlooking the distant sea, and I love the vastness. During the week my truck route keeps me busy, so my time with the shaman reverend Sorenson is limited. I don't make excuses for sometimes not being around. But my curious brother is a different story. He wants a more personal connection and does not have my natural wariness.

Another thing, Evan can't wander around Atascadero foraging for tree fruit like he did in SLO. The town is too spread out, too redneck, and too suspicious of unknown folks. He might be mistaken for an escapee from the mental wacky-hatch over the hill or arrested as a shiftless vagrant. And since work is all but non-existent is this one-horse town, he spends most of his time hanging around the Quonset hut when Sorenson is there. They talk about miracles, saints, Torgie has a slew of vivid Yogananda stories. If he's away on a house painting job, Even burrows into the black walnut shade pouring through the scorched books Sorenson lays on us. Rare books from India, the science of Kundalini, of Nada-Bindu Yoga, describing secret breathing and tonal techniques. Mystical Christianity, the Aquarian Gospel of

Jesus Christ by Levi, the biographies of famous Catholic saints like St. Therese and St Ignatius of Loyola with whom reverend Sorenson seems to identify. Yes, Torgie might be insane I've accepted this as probable, so I take everything in stride. I want to find out for myself what works and what doesn't. I delve into the amazing history of Milerepa, the shaman saint of Tibet, I study the history of The Golden Dawn and ascended masters of The Great White Brotherhood, a plethora of the magical arts from Solomon to St Germaine—it's like a Pandora's Box of forbidden knowledge, our minds are churning like windmills. But reverend-monk Torgelananda tells us it's only preparation for the real work, mere signs on a highway that is concealed from the common sight of doom-struck man.

When I come home in the afternoons my inspired brother clues me into the more provocative secrets, like the mystical dances and chants that Jesus taught to his 12 male and 12 female disciples, sacred Tantra dances, who knows what has been left out of the scrubbed official story? I take it all in large bites, leaving some for the magpies of doubt to quibble over. I am correlating and comparing this esoteric material to what I feel I already know. And what else can you do? To doubt yourself and your own intelligence is noting but a moron's game. We have entered a zone of shadows, spirits and powers, reflections resonant, opaque and mystifying. At the end of a long hall stands a mirror draped in curtains the color of smoke-burnt wine, beckoning, look in, look in, look in.

Chapter 8

A T EVERY STEP taken with the eccentric Torgen Sorenson, I'm aware that I can turn and walk away. I don't because the "carrot of power" he keeps dangling in our faces is too compelling to ignore. My brother and I want to see what happens next, even though the adventure seems like a maze of contradictions. On the practical side, I figure that Sorenson and his Center of Light and my laundry truck route are good signs for my Los Angeles probation officer. Camilo will be visiting soon enough and I want him to feel reassured that I'm on the right track. He doesn't need to know all the fantastic details. I can present cordial reverend as my new benefactor, my spiritual adviser. I want my arrest record expunged, I want that pot smuggling erased, so it doesn't haunt me later.

After Sunday service, one in which a fog of farts so dense fills the airless horseshoe chapel that not even frankincense can mask it, Torgie drops a loaded question on us. His bright face is rubescent and his eyes are luminous blue. "We need to go into the next phase of consciousness training," he says, swiveling toward us in his office rocker. "There's a place we need to get to and you boys are close. The spirit is asking us to step it up, but that involves some hard work. I need to know is if you're ready to take that step with me?"

"What kind of step?" I ask warily, sensing this will cut into my privacy. "What are we talking about?"

"Yeah, lay it on us," says Evan, salivating over a plump sugar doughnut with a slight glaze of guilt. The reverend feeds him sweet pastries on Sundays, knowing that he can't resist.

"All right, we are talking about a significant step to where we need to go. The spirit wants us to go into some power ceremonies that involves fasting and prolonged meditations, and it will entail sacrifices from each of us."

"Hmm, what kind of sacrifices? We're not into any old testament Abraham trip."

Torgie stares at me with a weird grin. He has a penchant for wisecracks himself, so he lets me make them. "Mainly your time and energy and attention," he says, "your weekends, to be blunt."

"Our whole weekends? But we already spend most of Sunday over here."

"True, but that's not going to cut it. Starting at sundown on Friday until sundowns on Sunday we'll be on a strict grapefruit juice fast, no solid foods of any kind, plus we'll be in Kriya meditation for 10 to 12 hours a day. You'll need to bring your sleeping bags because you won't be leaving till Sunday night. That is, assuming you accept the spiritual challenge."

My brother and I exchange a sobering glance, thinking of how we like to gorge on Sundays, and our thin aching asses on the milk can stools. "That sounds pretty intense," murmurs Evan. "Daya Mata was just saying last Christmas not to over do it."

"Perhaps so, but that doesn't apply to us ones here. We need to do this in order to push open the upper astral door. This ceremony will be for four straight weekends of ashram conditions, no backing once we start, no slacking, and no whacking-off in the bathroom."

At this off-the-wall comment we both snicker, because it is plainly absurd. We don't beat off, we are devoted to Yogananda's strict celibate methods. Sorenson joins in with a big-bellied guffaw, then asks friendly-wise, "well, what do you boys say? Are you ready for this or not?"

Of course we can't really say "no", not at this point. We have dealt ourselves into the game. We've asked to behind the curtain and eccentric Sorenson is ready to deliver. Evan and I have talked over this kind of experiment, to push ourselves further, but slyly avoided doing it. We've avoided it because we are already doing a 24 hour fast from Friday evening to Saturday evening, Sunday is our day of sensual indulgence. On Sundays we gorge our yogin bodies with rich delicious foods, our consolation for the lonely hours of meditation, prayer and fasting. Aiyee, you have to cut yourself some slack! The life of a celibate aspirant is not easy, the bleak austerities, the sticky dreams with some ethereal Lolita! One by one your favorite pleasures are stripped away, like a once-free hawk being plucked of its plumage. Except that I am neither that bird nor a dreamy-eyed bleater, those shoes don't fit. I am a skeptical mystic seeking the truth and I will go as deep into this enigma as I must to find what works for me. You have to do so for yourself, no one can do it for you, at some moment there comes a revelation. And if not, if I need to turn and walk away, I want to be able to do so sans regrets.

Almost in unison, arising from our musings, we look at Torgen Sorenson and say, "Right on, reverend. Count us in. We're gonna do this thing with you."

WE DIVE INTO the Spartan regime with dauntless enthusiasm and naked ambition. Whereas I did lose a gable on the Mexican border a couple years back, it's not my nature to doubt myself. Friday afternoon I scarf a double sandwich and at 6 pm that evening our meditation marathon begins. Torgie says to drink the good water that comes from Mallet's well if our bellies feel empty, and if feeling weak, sip a cup of the tin can grapefruit juice that he stocks by the case. He offers this advice in a kindly way, already knowing that this trip can get dicey.

"We're gonna go deep, die deep," he says with a rosy glow, quaffing the tart, pale yellow juice. "This won't be amateur hour. Your mind does crazy things at times, so just do your best. Keep meditating, keep praying, use the sacred tones, the Aum and Hawng-Sah. Ignore the temptations and believe me, they'll come around. Keep putting your concentration back in the third eye, on Master and the Christ, just keep doing that."

"All right. How long do we go tonight?"

The reverend smiles, peering over his reading glasses. "We'll start at seven and go till around midnight. Then you can sleep, but if you wake up meditate some more. If you wake up do the night-watch. The aim is to saturate your consciousness in the light of the third eye, don't wander off. If you drop your attention into the throat you'll fall right to sleep."

"Okay, I think we got it. Don't let anything interrupt the current of meditation. But what about our asses going nub? I'm not sure how long we can stand these damned milk cans."

"Well, use those padded stools for awhile, then go cross-legged on your sleeping bags. After awhile get back on the stools, You can lie down if you want but the point is to stay alert. Don't drift off into fantasies. I'll start out over at the harmonium but before long I'm gonna go and flop my carcass on the bed. Most of what I do happens on the other side, in special ceremonies."

Ethereal ceremonies? I listen with the attitude of a yogi-warrior, brushing aside any misgivings. You've got to bite into the orange to know, you've got to eat the whole fruit. Evan pushes his nose, saying, "what about if we need to take a leak, is that allowed?"

"Oh, hell yes, if you need to take a dump or pee just go, that's just nature calling. But don't dawdle out there. Try to keep your mind on God and remember, no playing with your randy pecker. Master used to run these meditation sessions at Mt Washington and you'd be amazed at the whimpering and whining that went on, me included. Some people would use any excuse to flake out before we were halfway done."

"What would Yogananda say to that?"

He'd say, "Some people want full-time wages for only part-time work."

Resolving to not be like that, I ask, "And what happens tomorrow, Mr Sorenson?"

"Tomorrow comes the real nitty-gritty, tonight is just a warm-up session. Because tomorrow and Sunday we go longer, it's more intense, and we start at dawn. But don't worry, we'll take a break every four hours or so and if your bodies start to ache, do your yoga stretches. It's like being thrown in the deep end, so just do the best you can and see what happens."

Right on, one never knows until one goes. So with that taut advice we begin our immersion into the shape-shifting whirlpools and ambiguous booby-traps of the mind. The rebellious egoic-mind doesn't want to oblige, it wants to do its own thing and go where it wants, not do as it's told. *The mind is a wild horse that cannot be tethered for long.* Somewhere I've come across that Zen saying, we're about to find out the sheer and mocking truth.

There is a shaft of madness invoked here, I acknowledge that. It's Friday evening. When most of the world gathers for some cold beers and heady reefers and convivial laughs with their friends, we hunker down in the hot metal shell of the Quonset hut to engage in metaphysical experiments. Reverend Sorenson beams upon us like long-sought and cherished-specimens. The reverend has been alone too long in his salutary quest for world domination. We spread our yoga pallets on the floor, turn on the feeble window fan to help exhaust the interior, take a ceremonial cup of the bitter juice, then make our descent through the trap doors of the subconscious.

Torgie positions his sweating bulk at the harmonium, clad in his giant jockey shorts and sweat-stained tee, and plays a few desultory chords. His large placid face seems unusually rosy and shiny. He lifts his calloused hands and invokes the SRF saints, the masters, the Light of God, that we be protected and blessed with strength and revelation. The candles are flickering, the altar gleams in the countenances of the revered God-men, subtle sandalwood wafts through the space. Breathing our tones, invoking the holy presence, Evan and I go within, ignoring the complaints of our feverish, young bodies. After about thirty minutes Torgie hefts himself off his bench and pads over to his bed chamber. He guzzles a red tumbler of the tin-can grapefruit juice, burps in contentment, then flops onto his bunk with his huge belly up.

Our intention is to meditate until midnight, a tough five hour run, but only a prelude to the grind that starts tomorrow. The first couple of hours are no big deal, we are used to it; after awhile, to ease our asses we shift from the torturous milk cans to a cross-legged position on our sleeping bags, then, to relieve our aching knees we get back on the stools. To be able to move around even a little is a blessing. The body usually dictates how long you can go in meditation, one's body is the hindrance, or so you tell yourself until you fall into the maelstrom of cavorting thought.

Oh, we meditate and pray, consciously breathing and silently chanting, vowing to stay awake, train the mind, persevere. We are raja yoga initiates, we can handle this. But in those shadow spaces of the cerebellum a distressing obscurity sets in. I can't tell if I'm asleep or awake, with a visceral jolt I wonder if I am doing anything at all? Am I just pretending to meditate while only meandering off somewhere? What is real and what is not? Who in this inner "I" who's supposedly in charge?

A twisted delirium sets in. I find myself in fragmentary conversations with people I do not know, yet somehow do know, conversations ripe with meaning but which evaporate before I can glean it. My brother Evan is swooning nearby, drooling, his head down between his skinny shanks. I remind myself of what we're supposed to be doing, vaguely aware of Sorenson's mumbling snores. He grunts himself awake, pads off to go pee, returns, gulps down more of his favorite juice, watching and, saying, "stay awake, stay awake, you're breaking the shell." Then collapses back onto his mattress with a loud belch.

Under the sweltering metal roof of this strange shrine, the atmosphere is claustrophobic. We roast like chickens. The old air compressors for the butcher shop go on an off with a mind-bending racket. I wonder if sleep is even possible in this mystical hidey-hole. My consciousness goes into warp as it swoops into spaces behind thought, racing through vivid landscapes, dark beguiling caverns, or crawling like a desperate refugee though the bone yard of startling, hard-edged memories. Where did all this garbage come from? The confusion becomes so murky that my mantra slips from my focus and I am floundering, mumbling nonsensical sounds I've never heard, latch back onto my sacred tone and parrot it inside my besieged brain, a sword, a shield, a life raft. The moments becomes a torment, you wish only to escape, but to where? It is like beating your forehead against something massive, unyielding, drool falls from your lips, remembering why, why am I doing, what, boring onward like a soldier into the implacable heart of light.

Eventually, at some point, the cherub-faced reverend stands over us, beaming with approval. "Okay, okay," he says, "that's enough for tonight, you guys are troopers, it's after one o'clock. I'll tell you what, the aura around you is tremendous. But let's get some sleep, your bodies need to recuperate. Tomorrow comes early enough and that's when we start scooping into the marrows of karma. Time to rest, time to recharge."

Scooping into the marrows of karma? Much too dazed to make any sense of that comment, I give him a lopsided nod and amble off to take a piss. When I return Torgie and Evan are in animated conversation, Evan saying, "but I kept seeing it, feeling it, man, it freaked me out."

"Don't worry about that," Sorenson tells him, "it's just psychic debris from your past. The river is getting cleansed, dross is being removed. That's what these long meditations accomplish, they kick the old shit loose so it can dissipate."

They are putting out the hand-made altar candles one by one, snuffing them out, because the reverend is adamant about never blowing candles out. "The spirit doesn't like to see a sanctified candle get blown out," he insists. "It's an insult to the deva of the flame and a misuse of prana."

The seven large candlesticks are smudged out. Sorensons's face is rubescent and jocular in the bronze lamplight, as though he has been at some astral party. Amazing, how he can look so childlike and rejuvenated after these sessions, bathed in the energy of heaven. Thinking about the aphorisms of Patanjali, I go to my sleeping mat and lay my lean body down. The reverend's been at this a long time, who knows what he can do? I whisper a little prayer, then go out like a candle myself.

Chapter 9

O N SATURDAY, THE meditation marathon kicks in at 7:00 am, running until the noon break for hatha stretches, the bathroom shuffle, another cup of the purgatorial grapefruit piss, then retreat into the chamber where our minds merge with the flickering horseshoe atmosphere itself, inside-outside blurring into the self-inflicted masochism until sundown, another precious interlude, only to plunge again into the bottomless rabbit hole that hides beneath our ever-rambling thoughts. The trick is to stay attentive, but the real key to that is to remember what the fuck one is doing.

And why? That question rattles around in my brain. I don't know why, I've lost track of plausible reasoning. I only know it must be done. It has become an inner war between me and something not me, that wants to subjugate me. I'm not backing out and neither is Evan. My poor brother mumbles and swoons, almost passing out, only to pull himself erect to stare into the face of his own psychic chaos. He takes a ragged sigh, casts a glance at me, his stoic companion, then carries on. The padded milk cans are agonizing, once or twice we fall off these wobbly perches onto the hard floor. It is like mucking through a tar pit, I must confess, torturous, humbled by the helter-skelter of the mind rampant with psychotic symbols and demented images. I realize now that most meditators barely scratch the surface even as we are sucked into the primeval vortex, our tortured bodies pleading to be anywhere but here, doing anything but tied to this mental whipping post.

After awhile one sees, wordlessly understands, this all comes down to you and *It*. Battered about in this wild confusion the idea of God becomes rather meaningless. It is just about you and *It*, whatever *It* is, and whoever am I, whatever am I, in this excruciating passage of mind-body-person. Our chants, our Sanskrit tones, our skittering prayers are little twig sailboats of tattooed words in this dark and violent vortex of consciousness. You find yourself on the floor pleading to Sri Yogananda, Jesus Christ, mysterious Gurdjieff, all the saints, any saint, mumbo-jumbo, any benign being who will listen to your piteous wheedling for mercy. Diabolical images and magnificent vistas, strange sounds flash through the oceanic darkness, a darkness that swallows up everything including your name.

In the shivering intervals of clarity, you asking yourself, telling yourself, if I am not the source itself then what? Who am I supposed to be supplicating? Why have I given this whatever authority over my life and very being? What is it that I lack or imagine that I lack? For if you give something authority over yourself never for a single moment can you be free. You are a captive.

Ah well. The long night slowly passes, leaving us whipped and dazed by torrents of self-effacing conflict. Reminiscent of my former psychedelic experiments, it's hard to say what is real and not. But after the brutal pick and shovel work, things ease up a bit. We actually feel suffused with a kind of elemental peace. There is the Sunday morning interlude of group meditation to take refuge in, a cakewalk, with five more hours to the finish line. Not that these last hours are less intense, you don't fade into aimless daydreams, you do the work, only now we feel a tide of exaltation.

No one has to remind us that we're in for three more weekends of this grueling, hair-shirt flagellation.

One thing I am wrestling with in this Jacob-like paradox, along with the galloping psychic dementia, is what part of me is real and trustworthy and what part is treacherous? Because if you can't discern that, then how can you get anywhere? Then, there is the problem I am having with Torgelananda himself. There is something about the gordito reverend that seems concealed, sly and ambiguous, and how can you depend on what you cannot fathom?

I admit my annoyance with Sorenson only inwardly, keeping it to myself. But I am irritated by his lofty assumptions and how he flops his body belly-up on his bunk and swoons into hours of snoring and mumbling, which he blandly claims to be his technique of "astral traveling" to higher dimensions while we suffer like staked goats on the hideous milk cans.

"Once you learn to get out of the body and stay awake," he tells us with guileless enthusiasm, "there is no restriction. You're free to do whatever you want."

That sounds like metaphysical snake oil to my ears, how does one validate such claims? The answer always is, of course – only by doing it yourself. I remind myself that in this transcendent quest you have to keep taking leaps of faith, just as I did with the "sacred mushrooms" in the Sierra Madre of Oaxaca. Only now there are no mushrooms nor any visions you can count on.

Acutely aware now of my aching joints, I try to not resent where I am. I made my decision to take this ride and we're not skimming the surface like so many of the frivolous new-age workshops. But what confounds me is how Sorenson always bounds back up from these intense sessions in a beaming and jovial mood. He sticks his tongue for us to see, its baby-pink, indicating his corpulent body is apparently free of toxins. His fresh boyish face is rosy pink too, his eyes a shining blue. If I didn't know better I'd swear the dude's dropping liquid mescaline. He wants to know want we saw, what we heard, did we have any ethereal encounters? Fuck yeah, fragmentary glimpses of madness and leering lunatics on the run, I almost retort, but I don't, I restrain my sardonic wit. Torgie has been on his back snoring and sputtering doing deep rhythmic belly-breathing for hours. He claims that he's using secret techniques and resurfaces revitalized as if plugged into some invisible, cosmic current. He guzzles his red tumbler of the Tree Piss grapefruit juice, smacking his lips with relish. We watch the glug-glug gusto of his thirsty jowls. Then he pours himself another half-glass and goes off to the bathroom. During these interludes, Torgie passes out chlorophyll breath mints to neutralize the halitosis that fasting causes. He seems to keep one eye peeled on us, the other eye on a mission all his own.

Deep in the surreal hours of the third weekend, I stumble into the corridor for a leak, dazed yet alert. We have been meditating forever, I've lost track of time, I'm only aware that it's nighttime. The machinery goes off again like a rusty banshee, piercing my ears in the dim latrine. Then my eye catches the gleam of something anomalous. On the eye-level shelf, in a stack of towels, a bulbous glassy object. Shaking the last drops off my fervid yogi dick, I flick on the overhead light and my eyes go wide. Holy Caramba, right there under the towel is a bottle of vodka, a whole fifth, except when I slosh the contents I see it's better than half-empty. I inspect the label—Takka Vodka, New Orleans Finest—then tuck the guilty flagon back under the towels and snap the light off. My pulse quickens, I retreat to the meditation chamber. Being a notorious former pot and acid head, I know a hidden stash when I find one.

Now, as I furrow into the glittering dark spaces on the arrows of my mantras, I keep one ear tuned to Sorenson's maneuvers. Indeed, about once every hour he gets up from his sagging bed and goes off into the kitchen or bathroom. He comes back about five minutes later, flopping back down with a sigh. Then, right around midnight, I hear him making noises in the kitchen, opening another can of the grapefruit piss, murmuring to himself. I get to my feet, ignoring the ache in my shoulders, noting Evan's slumped figure on his own milk stool. Going stealthily into the kitchen, peering through the bead curtain, my eyes flare! I see Torgie in three-quarter profile, pouring into his tall tumbler straight from the Takka bottle, except this is a pint bottle, not the bathroom fifth. Sorenson doesn't see me at first, flushed, perspiring, his giant white jockies and tee shirt glued to his flesh with sweat. He tips the red tumbler up and gulps lustily, his Adam's apple abob, his big shiny face a Rudolph red.

"Aha, you boozer," I hiss in wicked delight, "so that's your fucking secret!"

Torgelananda spies me out of the corner of his eye, almost chokes. "Holy crap," he sputters like a guilty oaf, "dammit, you caught me! I was hoping you wouldn't catch me so soon!"

"Yeah, man, I found your bathroom stash," I whisper with a knowing leer. "I wasn't snooping but there it was. You're drinking rot-gut, reverend."

"Well shit, yes, I'll fess up," Torgie blurts like a spanked child, "it's my method for staying out on the astral for long periods. Vodka for me is like a metaphysical medicine."

"Say again? Ah reverend, what load of bull you trying to lay on me? Do I look dumb to you? I'm an ex-acid freak and my old man was a famous boozer. You can't trick me, man."

"No, no tricks," Sorenson protests, lifting one palm. "I admit I've gotten lazy, I have, but I only use it for special purposes. The clown sauce helps me get out of this bloated body and keeps me out. All I can say is that it helps me do my work."

Between a guffaw and a leer, I retort, "clown sauce? Hah ha ha, that's a good one! We're in there suffering like whipped dogs and you're out here having a private party?"

Fidgeting, Torgie says, "you got me cold, I admit it. I've been using it as a crutch. I know I've got to get past it and my works cut out for me. But not yet, that's the next phase coming up. Once we're done with this marathon we'll all come together and purify ourselves. We have to do that before we even set foot in the consecrated circle of conjuration."

"Conjuration of what? The gods of booze?"

"Hold on now, that's not a joking matter. I mean the holy pentagram. Where we conjure the invisible spirits to manifest before us and do our sanctified bidding."

I stare at the reverend in silence, considering what I now know, then I ask him, "Mr Sorenson, tell me straight. You addicted to that hooch?"

"Oh hell no," he scoffs in a huff, "But I admit I got a taste for it, I like it more than I should." He holds the pint of swill out toward me, saying, "here, you want a swig?"

I shake my head. "No," I scowl, "I don't like the taste of hard liquor. At the most I'll drink a few cervezas, but that's it. I haven't even touched alcohol in well over a year. I dropped it about the same time I swore off weed and psychedelics and made the deeper yoga commitment."

Torgie shrugs, then slurps from his tumbler, watching me over the rim. And what am I to make of this vodka-chugging Yogananda occultist? His countenance is sincere and his eyes seem guileless. So what if he has some bad habits, like I myself do? In peculiar ways he seems to make his bad habits work for him or so he claims. And who is to judge anyway, who gets to say what is right or wrong? We always tend to set up some omniscient authority outside of ourselves, beyond ourselves, then try to live up to those ridiculous paradoxes.

For a moment we take each other in, Torgie and me, his remarkably innocent, boyish face. He takes another slug from his glass, then sticks the nearly empty bottle back in a drawer. "Go ahead," he mumbles, wiping his mouth with the back of his fingers, "spit it out. I can handle it. I'll come clean, already you've become my conscience."

"Then dig" I say. "I'm going to ask you to put that stuff aside. You know it and I know it. It's a bad trip, It's interfering with what we're supposed to be doing here. Yogananda wouldn't like that, so I'm asking you. If we're going to do this thing together let's do it right."

Sorenson ogles me, moving his lips, fighting back tears. "Alright, I will," he say somberly. "You nailed me fair and square and I know it's high time. Let me just say you are who I thought you were, you have a knack. But I'd appreciate it if we could keep this just between us."

"No problem. I'm not holding anything over your head. Let's just forget about it and move on."

"Forget about what?" yawns Evan, standing in the beaded curtain like a dazed waif. His lean face is pale and hollow-eyed, as though something has frightened him.

"Oh, your eagle-eyed brother here caught me nipping the vodka," Sorenson confesses, "it's a bad habit of mine. I use it now and then to ease the pain in my lower back and to step out on the astral, but not anymore. I'm gonna cold-turkey the sauce. Starting next weekend I'll be going into our meditation clean, just like you boys. This is all part of Master's master plan."

Sorenson's voice chokes up, he wipes tears from his eyes. My brother stares at him in bewilderment. "You're an alchie? That's totally weird, dude. I was wondering how come you're always so happy."

Scrutinizing Evan's spooked demeanor, I say, "Hey, what's the matter with you? You look like something just freaked you out."

"Fucking-A, man," Evan says, "I had this dream, no, like a horrible vision, a vision that really gave me the creeps."

"What did you see?" Torgie demands. "Describe it to me, it could be important."

"Aggh it was disgusting, it made my skin crawl. These hideous snake-like chicks were all around me in this dark place, down underneath me, hissing, except they had the heads of beautiful women. They were writhing all over me and sucking on my body, trying to suck my soul out. Jesus, it was horrible."

"Bingo," the reverend exclaims, "those were succubus from the lower astral. They really can't hurt a celibate yogi but they can test you, they're allowed to tempt you."

"No, reverend, I don't want any part of that," Evan protests. "It was like being pulled into a sticky dark pit. They were whispering and hissing and sucking on my fingers, on my dick, my knees, even my asshole. And it was hideous, it felt like I was gonna be enslaved."

"You did good, you did fine," Torgie reassures him, "you fought them off, you resisted."

Whoa, what the fuck? Listening to this twisted exchange, I experience a flash of jealousy. I had no idea my brother was experiencing such lascivious and lunatic hallucinations, nor did I know he was so prudish. Astral houris sucking on his balls and prick and he fights them off? But why, why resist? Nothing nearly so vivid or entrancing was happening to me.

"Why are you looking at me like that?" Evan says in a defensive tone. "What's your story?"

Shaking my head, I grin. "Nothing like that, man. I've been spending hours traversing a glittering void of black energy, I don't know how else to describe it. Sometimes an arcane symbol flashes past my eyes. It's like some kind of intense vortex I can't seem to get through."

Sorenson points his finger at my chest, saying, "that is a zone of great power. On the other side of that dark space you come to the cosmic mirror, where you see your own divine face. That's where you find out who you truly are."

"For real? Wow man, I've never heard that before. How long does it usually take?"

"There's no telling. Sometimes it can take a thousand lifetimes. But you're both beginning to eat up time and karma rapidly."

Chapter 10

O N THE FINAL cross-eyed Sunday of our meditation endurance trip, Torgelananda calls an end a few hours early. It's mid afternoon, we arise from our stools dazed and grateful. The reverend is all smiles, he shakes our hands and claps us on the shoulders. We have made the long haul into the cosmic wind, showed what we're made of, for-real yoga adepts.

"This calls for a celebration," Torgie says jovially as we all crowd into the narrow kitchen. This time he's not serving another glass of the tart grapefruit juice, no. Instead he bends over, his tee-shirted belly hanging like a sack of lard, fiddles with a combination lock, then pulls from the lower cupboard a jug of dark red vino. The gallon glass jug has no label, just a thick finger-loop near the spout.

Suddenly interested, I quip, "hmm, that looks pretty righteous, reverend."

"Wait, you gotta be kidding," Evan says, half-laughing. "We haven't eaten in two days. You trying to bomb us?"

"No kidding intended," Sorenson responds, beaming like a cherub. "This is some of the best wine you'll ever drink. It's from the local Rotta Winery, where the old woman takes you into the barn and fills these jugs right from a huge wooden barrel. She calls it 'the doctor's burgundy' and I use it for ceremonial purposes."

He sets the big jug on the Formica counter for us to admire. The deep red, almost opaque wine has a beguiling appearance. I swallow, licking my lips. "You really don't expect us to drink all that? And why does she call it the doctor's burgundy?"

"Because once a month there's a doctor who drives up from LA and fills the trunk of his Cadillac with these jugs. And hell yes, I'm inviting you to take at least a cup or two with me! You just passed a major test and we're gonna have a graduation ceremony! Besides, the spirit approves of red wine. Two skinny young men like you fellows, it'll be good for your blood."

Torgelananda, the mystic boozer, pours strong portions of the blood-booster into empty pickle jars. Evan asks him to go easy but to no avail, he just chuckles. As for me, it won't be the first time I've gulped local spirits. I've stood all day and drank corn lightning with the Mazatecas in mountain Oaxaca, I figure I can handle this vino. Torgie beckons us to pick up one of the country carafes; I take a curious sip, then a swig. The burgundy has the taste of old shoe leather dried in the sun, strong and lip-puckering.

"Holy Moses," I say with a wrinkle of my nose, "how much do you pay for this stuff?"

"Believe it or not, only $2.00 per gallon straight from the cask. Plus, she charges you a one dollar deposit for each glass jug on your first visit. After that, you just exchange jugs with her, bring the empties back, she fills up new ones. You can't beat that deal!"

The shoe-leather wine is potent, a dark red devil that hits our empty stomachs like a jolt of prana. Within minutes my brother and I are lit up like Christmas trees, joining Torgie in a laughing drunk. The reverend begins to babble in tongue-twisting spooner-isms, which is a kind of idiotic gibberish, but insanely funny.

"Once," Sorenson relates, wiping gleeful tears from his cheeks, "once at the Mount Washington ashram, Master called a group of us together out on the lawn. This was in the time right before he dropped dead on that stage at the Biltmore, when he was a little hobbled up with a cane. He always had this beautiful serene face, he was in divine bliss, nothing could shake his peace."

"But why?" Evan asks. "Why does someone like that die of a heart attack at such an early age? How can that be?"

"Yeah," I say, "how does a God-realized master even get sick, let alone croak?"

Blinking his luminous eyes, Torgie shrugs. "Because he had a human body just like you and me, and that body had its own karma. When his moment came, he just dropped his body and ascended. Only Babaji has the immortal light body for this dispensation. But I think it was also because Master was picking up so much karma from the rest of us. He was taking lifetimes of karma off us disciples and working it out through his own body. It aged him quite a bit."

"Man, that's really far out," Evan murmurs, in a sense of awe. "I can't think of anything better than having a God-realized sage lifting karma off your back."

"Yeah, for real," I say "what a blessing that would be. Talk about boosting your trip."

"Oh, it's for real alright," Sorenson declares. "Paramahansa did so much for us. But that day at the ashram, only a few months before he dropped his body, that day Master showed me a miracle. He showed me the most fantastic thing."

"A honest-to-God miracle? Like what," my brother says "what did he show you?"

"Yeah, come on reverend," I laugh, feeling the heady wine, "don't hold out on us."

"Well, okay then. He called a group of us together there on the grass, where he told us his time was short, and that we were not to grieve for him. He said he would go home to God when he heard the celestial flute inside him, but hat his spirit would be in the SRF teachings and that he would always be present for anyone who asked for him in meditation."

"Wow, it's true," Evan says softly, "I have felt him, we both have, more than once."

"I know, I know that," the reverend snuffles, beaming at us with unabashed fondness. "Anyways, that afternoon on the lawn he had a personal message for each one of us. He made me wait till last, then he says, Torgie, walk with me around to the back of the building. I've got something to say to you in private."

"Hey brother, far out," I laugh, my attention primed by the shoe-leather wine, listening intently.

"You bet, and of course I did what he said," Sorenson goes on, red-faced. "I walk him around out of sight of the others, I'm thinking I'm about to get a good scolding because of my lackadaisical meditation attitude, but then he says to me, "okay, stop here Torgie. Now come around and stand in front of me. So I did as he said, I stood in front of him about the same distance between you and me, and I swear to you, all right I swear—"

Sudden tears flood down Sorenson's round cheeks and he laughs right through them, reliving the moment that sealed his destiny—"He says to me, Master does, Torgie, in other lives you were always willing to fight for me, and here is what you always wanted to see. And I swear, I'm looking at this old man in an orange robe with his long black hair and a serene face, then, in the blink of an eye, he's facing me and he's this beautiful young man you see in the photographs, strong and clear, his shining eyes, and I just gawked. I think my jaw must have hit the ground!"

Sorenson breaks into sobs of laughter, rocking against the counter, shaking his balding head. "And he says to me, Master says, "behold now, isn't this what you wanted to see? Look! This body of ours is nothing but the illusion of matter, don't ever forget that."

"Holy fuck," Evan blurts, "for how long? How long did he stay like that?"

"Oh I don't know," Torgie says, "for a good thirty seconds I guess. I just stared at him with my mouth open. Then he just turned back into his older man self and tells me, now walk me back and don't you breathe a word of this to the others."

I nod in mute wonder, overwhelmed by the flood of emotion pouring from Sorenson. This is the raw stuff you can't ever make up.

"And I never have," he murmurs, wiping his eyes, "I've never spoken of it to anyone, not until now. You boys are the only ones I've ever told."

Ducking his head, Torgie takes a block of cheddar cheese from the fridge and puts it on a plate, then dumps a box of yellow round crackers all around the luscious cheese. We are half-crocked on the earthy wine and our stomachs are growling for something to eat. But purist that I am, I haven't eaten cheese for months. Cheese comes from cows, it's mucus-forming, and mucus is death.

So all we do is eyeball the cheese, slurping the wine. Squirming, his eyes transfixed, whether from hunger or inspiration, Evan mumbles, "did you have any other experiences like that with Master? Did he ever show you anything else?"

"Yes, oh heavens yes, there was several times over the years," Torgie affirms, baiting his hooks. "But that's all I want to confide for now. For me these are very special things, but as we go along, I'll tell more." He guzzles his pint jar of wine, regarding us with his bright blue eyes. "But whatever Master wants me to talk about, I'll share gladly."

He proceeds to saw off thick wedges of the orange cheddar with a knife, stacking the round crackers, then shoves the plate over to us. Without further quibbling, we gobble this offering like drunken young wolves. It's sinful food, full of toxic and lethal mucus, but fuck it. Evan declines more wine, but not me. I nod with approval as Torgie refills my jar with several robust glugs from the loop-handled jug. I wash the delicious cheese down with copious swigs of the leathery wine, getting drunk as a lord. Lordy lord, I am lit, I am high, I haven't felt a buzz like this in awhile. Do I feel even a tinge of guilt? No, not a bit.

Flooded with emotion, I confess out loud – "okay, I finally had this vision, something like, this amazing vision early this morning. But it was so fucking brief that it almost made me cry."

"Aha," Torgelananda cries, "I thought I saw something unusual in your aura. Tell us, it's show and tell time."

"Yeah man, come out with it," Evan laughs, "remember, no secrets."

"No problem," I reply, sipping some wine, "although nothing nearly as lascivious as yours." My brother snickers, stuffing his let cheek with more cheese.

"There are celestial epiphanies that appear out of nowhere," Sorenson says, letting his voice trail off.

"Yeah, like that, except it was so damned fleeting I almost felt robbed."

"Were you here or someplace else? We're you taken somewhere?"

"In a sense I was taken away, or more like I was suddenly *there*. All at once I was sitting in vast platforms of shining clouds, overlooking immense vistas, like worlds spread out below me. It was incredible. And the amazing thing is that I was holding a sitar in my lap and somehow knew how to play it. In that moment I was about to play it."

"Wow, man, a sitar?" Evan says, his pupils dilated and scoping me. "A Ravi Shankar sitar?" He's imbibing wine through a long straw from the glass gallon jug, but where did he get that straw?

"Yes, like that," I say, "or at least an instrument very similar, with the round gourds and all the strings, beautiful and exotic."

"But how did you know how to play it?"

"Hah, that's the incredible thing. I don't know how to play one here, but I knew how to play it there. This instrument I was holding felt so natural to me, and when I struck it the most amazing tones came forth, like pure sound blossoming from the well of creation, glorious sounds. I struck it three or four times and the sound waves went rolling through me and out into the worlds around me, like those tones were creating existence itself. It felt indescribable. It felt like I was on the cusp of some tremendous revelation about to blow open. And just as I started to dive into the raga and make a universe, it was like an invisible hand reached in and plucked me right out. It was over before I could even blink."

"Whoa Jake, dude," my brother exclaims, "that is outta sight. But what a bummer!"

"Yeah, a real fucking bummer. It was like being shocked right back into this grungy hole, no offense, Mr Sorenson."

"No, not a bummer," Torgie observes calmly. "The Holy Spirit had to yank you out of there for your own good."

"What's that supposed to mean?"

"If you'd spent even a few more seconds in that vision, the bliss would've been so overwhelming you would've been ruined for the work you've got to do in this life."

"Come again' reverend? That makes no sense at all. It gets dreary when you meditate all those hours for promises you need a pay-off now and then. Either the method works or it doesn't, right? And I have to say that was the beautiful thing about pure psychedelics. They'd give you a real pay-off, every time."

"No, forget about psychedelics, that's child's play. They just squander your reserves. You have to build unflagging strength and peace of the Spirit so you don't shy away from the work. That's how you get into real transcendental reality."

"Hold on, I'm with him," says Evan, tripping on the potent wine. "That seems like a total rip-off if we can't have episodes of cosmic bliss. I mean, dig, we're not signing on to be masochists."

"That's right, right on," I laugh. "The carrot on a stick might work for the dullards, but that ain't us."

"All right now, I recognize that," Sorenson grins, ducking his shiny head. "And you will have many such moments without a doubt. But trust me, you have to exercise patience as you're building power. If the psychic forces come too early they can knock your legs right out from under you. You'll end up moping around somewhere drooling on yourself."

Evan and I glance at each other, wondering about all this metaphysical doublespeak. I am skeptical of the inner hierarchy report, the unassailable authority, the hand held over the forbidden door. Fuck all that coercion designed for gullible sheep. Sheep are meek and sheep get eaten. I'm not interested in joining any kind of flock of obedient, starry-eyed followers. Every single thing has to be tested right to the core, either it works or it's just a fanciful story.

Almost as if reading my thoughts, Torgie announces, "come with me, it's time I showed you fellows something." He goes barreling past us in his fat man's underwear, through the beaded curtain and into his office, crying, "come on, come on, come and see!"

Wine jar in hand, with an intrigued shrug, we follow Torge-lananda back into his chamber. He sits in his oak swivel chair and twirls the dial on a iron safe under his plywood desk. Opening it, he takes out a black telephone and what looks to be a mimeo-graphed booklet held together with paper clips and thick rubber bands.

"You have a phone in here," I say, surprised. "Why do you keep it locked up?"

"Yes, I do, I keep it for emergencies. But certain personages were coming when I was gone and abusing the long-distance privileges, so I stuck it in my safe. But now I have this special padlock for the rotary dial so I'm gonna put it back on the shelf."

The burly reverend-monk shuffles through his papers, my brother and I wait with mad humor dancing in our eyes. I take another swig of the doctor's burgundy, swishing it around my teeth and gums.

"Here, both you men," Sorenson says, "take a look at this manuscript. This is one of our first important projects. The Spirit wants me to get this into publication and spread it around far and wide. But I admit that it needs some work, so kindly take a look."

I lean forward beside him, Evan on his other shoulder. He spreads several pages of the booklet in a row, with black and white photos attached. The title page boldly proclaims, "The Hidden Science of Cosmic Consciousness, The Lost Art, And How You Can Attain It," copyright, Center of Light, Atascadero, California, 1967.

On the next page the introduction begins, a long-winded, rambling soliloquy about mysticism, promises of exalted initiation into ancient Raja and Kundalini Yoga Techniques that will open your third eye and illuminate your cerebellum. But the prose is god-awful, beyond embarrassing, I read it with a squint. These awkward paragraphs are the obsessed mutterings of a lunatic trying to compose an intellectual-sounding manuscript. It's so bad that I know this gimcrack brochure must never see the light of day in this form. If it does, the Center of Light will become the laughing stock of new-age California.

"Umm, interesting," I say, swallowing my incredulity. "But as you mention, it needs some work before you hand it over to the printer."

"Yes, I acknowledge that," Torgie nods, shuffling his feet, "and that is where you come in. You have a flair for language, you can write and I can't. Hell, I dropped out of high school early and went into the merchant marine. But you can see for yourselves how powerful this material is, it's an esoteric lightening rod. We are going to publish a series of 13 of these higher lessons, initiating people into the science of cosmic power and brain-illumination."

Evan grunts. "You mean like discourses, like Yogananda's home discourses? You serious?"

"Yes, similar, but more hard-hitting and dealing with lost techniques of activating total brain power. We need to light up their lethargic brains. Master had to purposely water-down some of his discourses so as not to be too controversial." Sorenson takes a lusty swig of wine, face glistening, then adds, "But we don't have to do that and these booklets are not for everyone. We're looking to gather a select group of occult light-warriors. We're gonna go for the jugular and that's where these photos come in. These photos are meant to drive the key points home in an inescapable way."

"These photos? Really?"

"They don't beat around the bush, as you can see."

Already I am surveying the black and white photos, trying to smother the irreverent laughter rising in my mind. These pictures are of Torgelananda in his black and white minister's garb, posing in various ways. Here's a photo of him with his big ham hands out to either side of his head, shoulder high, gazing into the camera with adamant, earnest eyes. The caption reads, "Father-Mother-Holy God, we come before you as anointed soldiers of Christ, to enslave Lucifer's rampant demons."

Here is another photo, Sorenson cupping his large head with his palms, eyes closed, face tilted upward, a beatific smile on his face. "Aum, holy name of names. Learn the secret path into your cosmic Eye, turn on the power of your cerebellum with one million watts of Bliss!"

My intellect boggles as I scan the mutilated, run-on text, a part of me wants to flee but I cannot, at least not yet. My fate has led me here to help this country-bumpkin yogi-shaman, I must give it my best shot. I must try to help him at whatever he's trying to do here in this bizarre hut on the outskirts of Nowhereville scattered along 101 like an after-thought. It's hard to imagine that anyone else is going to assist him with this project. And if by chance he does have the metaphysical key, okay then, I want to go through that door.

Assimilating these impressions, I stare at the last photo with an open mouth, trying to squelch the mirth cavorting inside me. Another portrait of the imposing reverend against a blank wall or a pale sheet. Torgie's leaning forward at the waist, his white-shirted belly paunched out, as though he's about to split his seams. He has a stern expression on his face, his forefinger points right at the camera, the caption shouts, "it's time to get down to business and develop your brain power! And no more jacking off!"

Evan snorts in my ear trying to control himself. I am all but panting in my effort not to erupt in a howl of delirious laughter, for without doubt this is like an insane metaphysical cartoon. Swallowing hard, I say, "Reverend Sorenson, who took these unusual photos of you?"

"Nobody," he says with obvious satisfaction. "I practiced for weeks in front of a full-length mirror, then set up the camera with a timer and took them myself. Pretty damn powerful, wouldn't you say?"

Chapter 11

S ORENSON PULLS US into his eccentric scheme despite our innate reluctance. My intense curiosity to see the arcane items stored in his iron safe is my vulnerability. The hand-made amulets and strange diagrams, the ancient Chaldean rituals and what he claims are secret unpublished writings of Yogananda himself. Then there's the bizarre stylized rants of his own unfinished pamphlets—"See it All, all in a Cosmic instant, with 360 degree Omnivision!" His looming face dominates the grainy photographs, the bulging eyes of a mad inspired sorcerer. Yes, I want a close look at the Kabbalist grimoires and other charred volumes of magikal conjuration behind those scorched curtains. The marathon meditation sessions with the oft-besotted reverend has sprung the padlock for us, the gate leans open.

The claustrophobic hitch is that now we must form a tight band. As I half-suspected, the meditations were just a prelude to the three of us hunkering together in the upper quarters of the Quonset hut. The cramped rooms above the country butcher shop becomes our new-age ashram. The reverend insists that it's necessary for the evolution of our esoteric work, the many moons of purification of our undisciplined and lustful imaginations. Only in this way can we prepare for the invocations of the supernatural and demonic entities. The occult net closes around me. No more will I be able to escape to my retreat on the vineyard farm across 101, away from the big monk's shepherding personality. But Evan and I both figure this strange experiment might be worth it, and I still believe in my luck like the thighbone of Jesus, so if we don't take the gamble how will we ever know?

The half-moon metal and concrete hut seems like an oven for souls to roast. We move into the Quonset in the oncoming swelter of Atascadero summer to pursue the promise of divine power. But Sorenson doesn't really try to fetter us to the place, he makes no attempt to restrict our comings and goings so long as it doesn't interfere with the ceremonial preparations, the core method that he refers to as "the purification".

The reverend preaches to us often about *the purification.* "You have to understand every detail of what's involved," he explains. "We have to make our own robes by hand, from consecrated linen, and each robe will be a different color. We need to make and hand-ink holy talismans of lambskin to ward off the evil counter-spells. We must find and sanctify antique swords made of steel, real swords, not toys, swords with which we will humble and command the infernal ones. All this must be accomplished according to the lunar signs and in the strictest secrecy."

The reverend brandishes his powerful arm in the air, eyes flared open. Then, nodding at the books on his shelves, he says, "yes, there's a lot of study involved and mastery of old rituals, that's how we'll make ourselves ready. There are no shortcuts unless you want to get fried like one of the sons of perdition. King David wrote in his psalm, "make me pure as new fallen snow, Oh Lord, make my heart and hands pure. Memorize that."

Listening to him ramble, considering my own recurrent lusts, I squirm a little. "All right, I can dig it, reverend. But when can we go into the sacred circle? To do some actual conjuring of the devils, to see how it works?"

"Oh, we're not even close to that yet," Torgie shakes his head.

"You have to learn to control the temptations of your imagination and of course there's no beating the meat. The confessions and coming clean takes some time, the river has to be dredged to the depths. Otherwise, if we go into the circle before we're ready, the arch-fiend can devour your wits. We'll be living over the hill in the state loony-bin."

Annoyed by such evasive answers, detesting superstitious blather and not wanting to spend years in this backwater metal attic, I persist, "okay, right on. But mas o menos, how long until we face them?"

"Oh, we're at least six months away from being able to enter the pentagram," Sorenson replies, swiveling away from me with a nonchalant air. "Otherwise, like I said, you go in too early you can short-circuit your noodle."

Short-circuiting my brain is not on my agenda, but neither is sitting on my hands. I want to find out whether and how this deal works. And exacerbating my sense of impatience is the worst case of hay-fever I've ever suffered in my life. Snot drools from my nose like a faucet. There's something in the air, some weird tree pollen, the profusion of drying grasses stirred by the withering heat that devastates my sinuses. I sneeze in wild, hiccuping spasms, often totally congested. I've gotten nose bleeds from hay fever in the past but I've never had it this bad. Not wanting to resort to drugstore medicines that leave you shaking like a leaf and unable to piss, I am driven to natural remedies. One must breathe, a yogi must conquer the ogre of mucus. Mrs Mallet lends me her metal kitchen grinder and I chop and mash up a half-pound of organic horseradish mixed with the juice of lemons and doused with cayenne pepper. Making myself swallow a couple tablespoons of this concoction has the instantaneous effect of clearing my plugged-up sinuses, but brings with it a laxative urgency. Aiyee, I am on the toilet gulping the copious release of snot and shitting like a goose at the same time, and miserably the relief is not permanent, only a respite. Consuming the entire half-pound if horseradish does not cure me as I had hoped. On my rural laundry route through the sere hills and ranch meadows my nasal affliction is intense. I am forced to resort to the hideous over-the-counter pills in order to communicate and not be openly pitied. As the summer deepens, living in the Quonset ashram with other beings takes on the lurid aspects of a homespun purgatory.

Relief comes to the afflicted in unexpected ways, almost when you're not looking. I try to figure out if I'm allergic to certain foods, is it the wine, is it this, is it that? On weekend nights, Torgie and I get into fierce metaphysical-political discussions fueled by the shoe-leather Rotta burgundy. Oddly, at these moments, I forget all about my hay-fever. It's there, it persists, but it doesn't matter. Our raucous debates range over the philosophical map, Evan sometimes joining in, sometimes off to the side reading. We evaluate Yogananda to Jesus to Moses to St. Germane, Hermes Trig to Milerepa, Gurdjieff to Leary to the Vedas and Upanishads, yes, we light up the mystical domain. One of the things I like about the reverend is his openness, he's not afraid to explore and ask new questions. Everything is sacred in its own right, yet nothing is immune to skeptical inquiry. I use as my yardstick the radical Fourth Way teachings of Gurdjieff, Sorenson draws from his Yogananda training mixed with arcane Solomonic magic. Following these spirited drunken bouts of ideas, I feel closer to him. We are breaking through to each other, gaining a sense of trust. He is steeped in occult lore, knowing the rare ceremonial grimoires almost by heart. It resonates with me how he is often in agreement with my mentor Gurdjieff on essential points, and outright dismisses self-deluded impostors like Aleister Crowley, the vain English meta-physician.

Rubbing the dome of his head, Sorenson takes another swig of the shoe-leather vino. "Gurdjieff was right," he laughs. "Crowley and that crowd were little more than metaphysical dabblers, they got sex and decadence all mixed up with the true teachings and tried to parade themselves around as gods. In fact, the whole Order of The Golden Dawn was pretty much bogus."

"Far out," Evan muses, listening in, "yeah, all you have to do is look at that Crowley dude's picture to see how twisted he was. The only one he loved was himself."

"That's astute, and yes, it's the old pitfall of the self-enamored ego," Torgie says, in a rare instance of articulate brilliance. "They all waste away in their own pretentious make-believe. But some of the early Theosophists like Blavatsky and her friends were on the right track. They were tapping into the Great White Brotherhood and that goes clear back to ancient Lemuria."

We ramble on deep into the night like drunken wise men, illuminating dusty rooms of concealed and forgotten artifacts in the attic of consciousness. How is one to know what is real and what is bullshit, and does it even matter? To be honest, I don't know much about those Victorian occultists, quack magicians, and Ouija Board dabblers. I do know that that iconoclastic teacher of self-awareness – Krishnamurti – dismissed their teachings as so much preposterous rubbish and turned away. The Theosophists claim to be dealing with a line of ascended masters, although disembodied ones. One of their early Utopian communities is right here in San Luis Obispo county, at Halcyon, in the foggy eucalyptus groves south of Arroyo Grande. I suspect that most seekers are as blind as moles in a maze of illusions, anxious to latch on to anything that promises something that transcends their bewilderment. And Torgen Sorenson, his rubescent face shining, pours the old-leather burgundy into our pickle jars and we rant and and rave deep into the mystical night, killing the ancient ghosts of loneliness.

HALCYON, IN THE eucalyptus groves of the south county, a dream-like place. In my laundry van ramblings the roads through the fog-shrouded terrain I've come across the village with its white theosophical temple back in the trees. Inquiring at the crossroads store, the bright-eyed lady tells me that only "true theosophists" and their families are allowed to live in Halcyon and that the fifty or so houses must be passed onto their descendants, never sold to outsiders. However, she confides in a sorrowful tone, most of the younger ones are drifting away to the fleshpots of Hollywood and San Francisco and joining the lascivious hippies and beatniks.

Disguising my amusement, I wonder, "is there any way my brother and I could see inside the white temple? We're involved in the teachings of Paramahansa Yogananda, we would come with a sense of reverence, not just curiosity."

"Oh my yes, you would be most welcome," the blue-haired lady assures me. "Yogananda was one of the great, great swamis. Yes, please bring your brother here for a visit. The Temple of The People stays open. The temple guardian is usually around and even if he's not, you may go right in. There are life-sized paintings of the ascended masters on the seven walls. Tell him that Emma from the shop sent you over. I'm sure you'll find it truly uplifting."

Driving off, I take another glance at the white triangular temple back in the misty trees. The idea of a utopia community seems good to me. I resolve to bring Evan down here on the weekend and take a peek inside that sanctuary. Who knows what we will find?

The raging hay-fever torments me, confusing my identity with my physical suffering. Only in those damp eucalyptus groves or along the breezy coast of Los Osos, Morro Bay and Cambria Pines do I gain a smidgen of relief. The yellow drugstore tablets decongestant and dries my nose, but the stuff is laced with Ephedrine to counteract the drowsiness. Those bitter pills jack me up; with the strong coffee that I love my pulse throbs like a drum. Where do these inexplicable afflictions come from? What is the root of such lousy karma? Even if some psychic tells you that you were a master herbalist in a medieval life that poisoned people for a fee, and that the wretched hay-fever is your payback, what good is that information? Such speculation is all but useless, it leads nowhere. I'm beginning to see that thought itself is a cunning trap, the insatiable torrent of compulsive thinking, aiyee, should we not just pluck our brains out and be free?

One sun-drenched afternoon on the coast south of Big Sur, I drive into the hamlet of San Simeon, parking my truck across from the general store in the shade of the tall Eucalyptus. The fabled Hearst Castle gleams on a distant bluff overlooking the sea, a power-obsessed rich man's fairy tale. I have almost no interest in it, I burn with a poetic transforming fire. My spiral notebook is on the seat beside me, I am always pulling over to scribble a few glorious insights. I have recently discovered the Bengali poet Rabindranath Tagore and the Sufi poet Jalaluddin Rumi, and a brilliant translucence has opened inside my mind.

And who is that lone bird
flying right out of the heart of the sun,
in the final blaze of sunset, straight
as an arrow in ecstasy homeward?

Mysteries abound in earth and sky
no human language can pretend
to know, revealed in a living script
as ancient and as present
as the fountains of the world.

San Simeon is quiet as a natural-born church. The air tastes of the surf washing the sand and shore rocks. Nobody stops here, I am by myself in my solitude. There's a hawk on the wing above the wind-bent cypress, a red-tail high in the blue air. Something draws my attention from beneath my eyelashes that I almost take for a hallucination. Beside my white van, the thick trunk and angular limbs of an old Eucalyptus seem to ripple with an iridescence in the sunlight. When I blink the image persists, a nascent tapestry of orange and yellow flickering on the tree, its branches and leaves. I get out of the truck in a sense of wonder and look up. The tall eucalyptus is covered from top to bottom in a fluttering cape of Monarch butterflies. The entire grove is covered in millions of wing-flickering, beautiful butterflies. Rooted to the spot, I am swept up in the miracle. I have happened upon pure creation itself, every cell of my being suffused in awe. I am the child of Eden once again.

DURING ANOTHER WINE-BESOTTED Friday confab, I fall into the ambush of the irrepressible Sorenson. From the moment I arrive at the Center of Light we start drinking ourselves into sheer metaphysical speculation. The Rotta burgundy tastes like the dregs of a godly elixir, the talk is punctuated by the reverend's burlesque farts. He takes off again about *the power inherent in*

shunned foods, power gained by devouring victuals scorned by ordinary folk. He includes in this repulsive menu moldering fruits and vegetables and, to my utter disgust, slimy meats, sausages, cheeses, baloney, rounds of Salami that are staring to rot and show mold.

"Don't cut that mold away, eat it," the big-bellied reverend advises. "The spirit endows these thrown-away foods with a potent force. Animals eat it with gusto but we humans are blind to it."

Evan, peeling a ripe banana, snorts in derision and turns away. Listening to such nonsense with raw fascination, I am half-convinced that this character is indeed deranged. After all, such ludicrous statements are embedded in his Center of Light discourses and although I myself have gone to extremes seeking revelation, there are limits. Does any intelligent man sit and devour rotting animal flesh in order to gain occult power? How insane! Only recently I've found out that old Mallet maintains a freezer locker out back among his inconceivable junk horde. He keeps this rusting unit plugged in with extension cords and humming 24 hours a day, the odious interior stocked with moldering cheeses and decaying meats. This is the hushed secret between the taciturn farmer and the obsessed monk, which they mutter about in private, the reverend's *"occult power food"* stash. Mallet goes around to the local markets and collects the garbage lunch meats, sausages and cheeses that are getting thrown out under the subterfuge that he feeds the stuff to his pigs. He brings it all home and stores it in the hidden refrigeration unit. Sorenson has confided all this to me, much to my revulsion. I have seen the cooler with my own eyes and been sworn to mute secrecy. Torgie's eyes gleam as he refills our pint jars with the red-dirt wine, gauging my visceral reactions. A massive brass padlock secures the rusting door to the refrigeration trailer, only he and Mallet have the key. The cool inner space reeks of odious, deliquescing baloney.

The reverend is testing me, testing us, I realize that. Glimpse by glimpse he reveals his bizarre, loathsome habits. Eyeballing me, he gnaws on a hunk of moldering dry salami. Slurping my wine, feeling his protuberant eyes on me, the kind regard of a saint, the beguiling stare of a madman, I say, "Get real, man. I mean, the idea of eating such garbage is beyond disgusting. It can make you deathly ill, you are aware of that? How do you even disguise such awful, putrid tastes?"

"Who said anything about disguising tastes? You wash it down with strong vino, just like this. Remember, you are not your physical body. There's a special initiation going on that people don't understand. In olden times they'd eat pieces of dried mummies in order to absorb the power."

"Mummies? Desiccated cadavers? Jesus Christ, Sorenson. Those were demented Catholic ascetics who lived out in the desert caves, mortifying their flesh. Count me out."

Laughing, enjoying himself immensely, Torgie guzzles more red wine. "Tell me," he says, "didn't your mentor Gurdjieff say that man in his natural state ought to be able to eat anything? That we've become weak and puny because we no loner eat like wild animals and birds?"

I acknowledge, with a crooked grin, that Gurdjieff had been openly contemptuous of modern man's dietary sensitivities. "Yeah, something along those lines. He said that people in true health should be able to digest anything, meat, roots, even grasses, even whole bones."

"And you agree with that?" the reverend prods. "With all due respect to Master's advice on fruitarianism, I'd like to know what you honestly think."

Glancing over at Yogananda's glowing lithograph above the alter, I say, "I think we should stop slaughtering animals by the millions for our food, it's totally barbaric We are the victims of our own delusions, is what I think. No, don't expect me to eat that rotten garbage in the trailer, I won't."

Torgie shrugs, unperturbed. Evan has checked out of this conversation, he's done with drinking. He's good for one pint and then he's off into his private world of books. The reverend and I are burning through the remnants of the Rotta rot-gut burgundy by ourselves. He lunges up and pushes through the bead curtain, crying, "gimme a minute, gimme a minute!"

My brother and I share an amused expression. What now? From the kitchen comes the intense aroma of frying meat, revolting and unusual, because Sorenson doesn't cook much. He eats at mom and pop cafes like the Rainbow Hut in Santa Margarita or in a pinch opens a can of chili and beans. I get up to check it out, the narrow kitchen is filled with spicy and amoral smoke. The fat monk forks a thick, bloody steak over in a sizzling cast iron skillet. I am flashed out on the strong wine, stomach growling, my mouth starts to salivate. Good holy God, two years of righteous pure eating and now I stand teetering on the unholy wildly brink!?

"A juicy tee-bone fresh from downstairs," the reverend says, "got one for us both, we both need the strength. And I know what I'm doing, I used to be a fry cook in the merchant marine."

I grimace. "No fucking way. I haven't eaten a bite of meat in over two years. Not about to start again. I'll go get a salad somewhere."

"Unbelievably gross," Evan says, looking on with disdain. "Did you space getting apples and bananas like I asked? Fuck, both you dudes are totally smashed." He backs out of the kitchen, muttering to himself. But I suspect he has a peanut candy bar stashed away, he always does.

"You're brother's right," Torgie points out, "you're too sloshed to be driving. Here, eat some rare steak, prove Gurdjieff's words for yourself. Take your power back, don't worship false notions! Remember what Jesus said, ye are gods, ye are gods!"

He slides the fragrant steak over in front of me, with a knife and fork, dripping with bloody juices. I hover over the platter like a famished wolf, all but drooling, my yogin senses in chaos. He flops another prime steak into the hot skillet, dosing it with salt and chili spices, refills our jars from the bottomless jug, clinks his glass to mine, his jovial face aglow with camaraderie. "Dig in, brother, dig in! I'm right behind you!"

My primitive instincts take over, aiyee, why the fuck not? I slice off a warm dripping chunk of meat and bite into it. It's indescribably delicious, my taste buds flood with pleasure. I chew and swallow chunk after carnal chunk with a ravenous appetite, aware that I am doing so without a twinge of guilt. I have always loved smashing the rules, I am the primordial man. I am an insouciant and unbounded and shameless apostate. I devour the juicy steak with a sublime and savage pleasure, my forehead breaking out in the rare meat sweats. Contemplating my action, I declare myself free of restraint. I am free to do as I wish and to eat every bite, even the succulent fat, and wash it down with this red country wine that tastes like sunshine and leather and clay.

Chapter 12

I COME ACROSS the ceremonial swords almost by accident, hanging in the window of a shabby pawn shop in North Hollywood. I am on my way back to my yellow Studebaker after a delicious lunch of machaca beef burrito spiced with jalapenos when they catch my eye, two antique swords, dangling from hooks in the dust-streaked window. There, a lean lethal rapier with a cross hilt and a strong naval cutlass with a cup hand-guard transfix my attention. Sorenson has instructed me to locate two antique steel swords to be restored and sanctified, that we'll use in the conjurations. Although a tad worn, I see at once this pair of swords will serve the purpose, maybe even with old blood on their blades. Torgie already has his own magician's wand, an enormous broad sword he keeps wrapped in a deer hide.

Now I have in my possession the quintessential, metaphysical weapons. Back in Atascadero, the occult preparations intensify out of sight of the others. Consulting medieval grimoires, Abramelin the Mage and Clavicula Salomonis Regis, the Legemeton, we fashion talismans by hand on patches of lambskin stretched to small frames and drawn in black indelible ink. These amulets are inscribed in Kabbahlist spells to protect us against the fiendish demons, meant to be worn around our necks on silken cords. The infernal powers to be summoned and bound are not trifling, they are described in grotesque and livid detail in the old scorched tomes of Ancient Ceremonial Magik.

There are 72 such major spirits that can be conjured within the pentagram of the sanctified circle, held in check with the sacred incantations and the double-seal of Solomon. They can appear in all manner of forms, beautiful creatures or as slavering beasties. We inscribe the symbol of the chief kings of these spirits into copper plates with metal hand tools, worn as a belt that cinch our robes. This is intricate and pain-staking work. While Evan and I go about it it, wondering as to our own motives, Sorenson slurps his barn-barrel wine and reads aloud passages that describe the fearsome visages of the demons we intend to evoke, interrupting their lewd feasts on the pitiable souls who have fallen under their sway. Aiyee, this is a twisted and somber and repugnant business, no frivolous entertainment.

"They won't be happy to be summoned," the reverend confides, ogling us, "to have their obscene pleasures rudely interfered with. They are apt to be quite wroth with us. That's why it's imperative that we are pure-hear ted and shame-free when we make our commands."

This is lunatic talk, almost sans doubt, but I've made an agreement with myself to suspend all judgment until I have evidence one way or the other. So I just nod and go on with my monastic handwork, listening intently.

Torgie goes back to his reading, almost muttering to himself, "For example, here's one of them that we'll have to face. He is one of Lucifer's great captains and holds authority over many of the lesser ones. His name is Amaymon, King of the East. The old texts all agree that he bears great vengeance and vehemence and that his face can be so terrible that the mere sight of him can cause mortals to shit their britches and fall into gibbering madness. They say he has horrible and putrid breath, and that one whiff of it makes men lose their wits and become his groveling slaves."

"Whoa, wait a minute Mr Sorenson, man," my brother exclaims. "Then why are we even messing with this dude – I mean, if he's even real? What the fuck?"

"Yeah, reverend," I say, only half-jesting, "that sounds like a really bad motherfucker or a bad, bad acid trip. I don't want one of those."

Listening to Torgie's soliloquy, Evan and I are fine-sanding the old swords down to the bare, shiny metal, removing every speck of rust and debris. But what good are antique swords against such a demonic monster?

Pushing his spectacles up on his nose, Sorenson nods. "Yes, those are good points. We have to take all the essential precautions. But number one, we're not ordinary men in this here sense. We are yoga-disciplined celibate sorcerers who can master our fears. And when we summon Amaymon, and we will, we'll command him to appear in a fair and comely form, no funny stuff."

"If you say so," I say with skepticism, "but it sounds like we're walking a precarious tight rope. I mean, dig, do these creatures actually exist, outside of the deranged imaginations of madmen?"

Huffing, imbibing his leathery wine, Torgie replies "Oh they exist all right and their behind all the wars and pestilence and horrors that plague humankind. The old Kabbalistic magicians and the Tibetan sorcerers were adepts at bending them to their will."

"But to what real purpose? Look around us, these wars, these horrible disturbances still go on. Why would such devils even want to help us?"

"Well, that's just it, and a damned good point. Most often these rituals were used for selfish purposes, for one entity to smash another. But when we summon them and bind them with the holy names of God, of Adonai and El Tetragamonon, they're compelled to serve us, they'll have no choice. Oh, at first they'll try to test and intimidate you, but once they see your purity of intent, they must submit. See, that's the key, our spiritual purity. All the sacred books stress this. We have to purge ourselves of any greed and lust or ambition for power's sake alone. What we do is for the good of mankind and all glory be to God, before whom the likes of these ones must cower."

Letting his words sink in, Torgie takes another wine-slurping pause. For a moment we lock eyes, he and I. Then he says in a dramatic undertone, "they will grovel and scrape before us, because remember, we are the highly exalted. We are the true ministers of the Lord Most High and they are compelled to do our bidding. Shoot man, I'm telling you, we can totally reverse how things are going in this fucked-up world."

I take a deep breath and with a sigh, just nod. As always, this Luciferian doctrine sounds lunatic to me, the flapping of wings in the reverend monk's overheated brain.

"I don't know," Even says, "can that even be real? Sounds like some thousand and one nights pipe-dream. If evil can be compelled to not do evil, then why haven't people done it already?"

"Yes, compelled," Sorenson insists, "compelled by the holy names and symbols and sacred formulas written in the Book of Life. And what's really nifty is that each of these powerful spirits has unique abilities and gifts they can confer on us, once we bind them, to do with as we please."

Laughing, my fascination for siddhic powers aroused, I ask, "really, you're quite sure about that? Alright then reverend, what kind of special abilities?"

"Okay, for instance, consider this here one." Torgie reads

from his scorched book, "Amaymon, who serves the great demon queen Astaroth, can confer on you the distinct power to appear and disappear at will, anytime, anywhere, even in more than one place at the same time. Is that far out enough? But he must be invoked under the holy guardian archangel ritual, otherwise his emanation is so vile that he can poison the soul."

"Dude," Evan scoffs, "are we supposed to believe these outrageous stories are for real?"

"Yes, quite real," Torgie retorts, "as real as the nose on your face, don't even doubt it. Some of them I've seen with my own eyes."

"You've seen them," I say, "you've seen these freaks? Then dig, like Evan is saying, should we even be messing around with these creatures? They sound like really wigged-out aliens to me. Maybe we should just leave them alone there in in Hell. Because if we fuck up and do the wrong thing, man, what then?"

"No, don't worry about that," Torgelananda reassures us, "you'll be covered from head to toe in the radiant mantle of the Cosmic Christ. You won't be vulnerable. They won't be allowed to lay a finger on you boys or me either."

"So you say, but there's always a risk, right? We're taking a major risk interfering with these bastards, and if there's going to be a risk there's got to be a pay-off. So, what are these powers you keep talking about?"

"Well, as I just described, this Amaymon can give you the power to appear in the midst of your enemies completely invisible and to humble them to their knees with a single gesture. And there's another special demon named Amen, yes Amen or Amon, who has the gift to reveal all hidden and lost treasures and to make us rich beyond all reckoning. Real treasure, not fake."

"Hmm, all right, that would be pretty amazing."

"I know, tell me about it. We'd be able to build a Center of Light church that would rival the Temple of Solomon itself. But listen here. There is another one called Anael, a spirit of great power, who shows you all the mysteries of the past, present and future. He gives you a ring to wear that when people see it at the slightest glance they are unable to lie to you."

"Right on! Even, you picking up on these vibes? Imagine what we could do."

"I'm hearing but it's kinda hard to believe. Sounds like abra-cadabra stuff to me."

"Yeah, I relate, man, but what if it's for real? I'm saying, what if? Consider that."

Sorenson chortles in amusement. "Oh they are real, they are real as a wart on your ass, you'll see. These are all infernal spirits of great wrath and trickery, who can cause anyone who tries to oppose our work to waste away into a trembling leper. By binding these infernal ones to our sanctified purpose we'll wrest control over this world to ourselves. That's how we'll restore the earth to its original pristine glory."

This is the most fabulous story that I've ever heard and it bears checking out, although Sorenson might be stark raving mad. He could be just a crazy mystical drunk. At the same time, he does have certain irrefutable credentials. And in the end if it all turns out to be pure bunk what have we actually lost? Nothing, nothing but time, and I've got to pass my border-bust probation in some worthwhile way. The idea of supernatural power with which to remake the world appeals to me greatly, I admit. Why be only ordinary if you can be truly extraordinary? Because this world is terribly fucked-up by malicious and scheming old men It cries to the skies to be helped.

The long hours of tedious work weigh on us – the fabrication of the Sanskrit amulets and Kabbalistic talismans of wisdom and divine protection. The weekday nights and weekends of meditation all bleed together in a hypnotic ritual of constant study, purification and preparation, tied together by Kriya mantras so that our dreams are not haunted by the foul spirits we intend to subdue. Outside of our self-intrigued enclave there is no one we can talk to about this endeavor. Our minds shine with a burning and secretive knowledge.

Reverend Torgie measures us from head to toe in fine linen material of diverse hues, our consecrated robes. At first he tries to sew the strips of cloth together on an old peddle-driven machine that he hauls upstairs and that we bless with candlelight prayers and solemn pipe organ music. But when the robes don't come together using this optimistic procedure, he concedes and takes them to a professional tailor. Evan and I go on with our mind-bending practices, the memorization of ritual conjurations, the identities and idiosyncrasies of the demon princes, blurred hours of contemplation and prayer. We make thick three-foot high candles out of blocks of paraffin, melted in handmade molds, and blessed with recitations of the 91st psalm. I fear I am going to blow my cool if we don't do some actual conjuration soon. Sometimes I dream of escape. In my restless sleep I flee on a Triumph motorcycle down into Mexico, into jungle Michoacan, into trackless country overlooking the sea where I am forever unknown.

MY BROTHER AND I work diligently over the old swords, sanding, polishing them into instruments of beauty. I paint the cup guard and handle of my navel cutlass a rich purple and gleaming gold;

Evan colors the hilt and handle of his rapier a royal blue and silver. The cutlass feels righteous in my hand, I feel ready take on the leering devils. Evan whisks his rapier in the air, grinning, "check it out, man." The blades are dull but Sorenson says that is no matter, we won't be contending with creatures of flesh and blood. Imagination aflame, I am eager to get into the ceremonies and force the suave and conning demons to do my will.

During the last stages of preparation, Torgen Sorenson begins shutting himself into the large empty locker out in the corridor. He locks himself behind the heavy hinged door armed with paint brushes and cans, hammer, nails, hand saw and boards, a Catholic bible of exorcism rituals tucked in his denim overalls. He does not allow anyone else into the locker during these days of solitary work, not even a peek, giving old man Mallet stern instructions to stay out. He only says to us brothers that this will be our holy ceremonial chamber, where we will sequester ourselves and summon the awful powers of Hell for the sake of peace on Earth.

Weirdly, in the midst of all this convoluted and esoteric activity, my probation office Camilo shows up on an impromptu visit from Los Angeles. It's a Saturday, he's almost on a holiday from his normal routine. Mr Camilo has never met the eccentric reverend and I've avoided going into much detail about the Center of Light. But I'm relieved to see Torgie handle this unexpected arrival with a aplomb, treating Camilo almost like an old, casual friend. He jokes about the surreal changes in Los Angeles, then compliments my attitude about life in a congenial way. There's no hint of the strange insanity afoot and no tell-tale jugs of the doctor's burgundy in sight.

Camilo hangs around for a few hours, he and I chat in private about where my head is at. Standing on the edge of Mallet's sprawling watermelon patch, looking at the dusty green oaks and dry hills, he says, "well my young friend, good work. You have a good, balanced life here and that helps my reports. One of these days I'll be cutting you loose of all this official nonsense."

Upon leaving, Camilo says with a touch of humor noir, "time for me to be heading back to the smog zone, Jake. That preacher Sorenson seems to have a positive influence on you and I'm glad to see it. But try not to sacrifice any pigeons or goats to the moon."

I watch him drive off with a smile on my face, wondering what lies beyond tomorrow.

Chapter 13

THE SUMMER HEAT wanes and we are in the throes of our occult catharsis when Torgie announces that he has arranged a face-to-face meeting for us with Sri Daya Mata, down at the Mt. Washington SRF headquarters. This blows our minds. First of all, it's almost impossible for outsiders to get a private interview with Daya Mata. She is reclusive and utterly devoted to of Yogananda's work. She does not seek the limelight and only makes a few public appearances each year. Second, this shows us that Sorenson still has clout with the inner circle of the Self-Realization Fellowship, despite being apart for the past fifteen years. In fact, my brother is profoundly impressed.

"I wrote her a letter and told her about you brothers in detail, about how Mokshananda sent you to me and your sincerity in following Master's teachings. I laid it on pretty good, let me tell you. I told her I was going to telephone her office and asked her to please answer when I called, if possible."

"Whoa Mr Sorenson," Evan exclaims, "and she did, she answered?" Privately I'm wondering what all this means for us. At heart I am leery of set-up situations, I much prefer things to just spontaneously happen.

"She surely did," the portly reverend affirms, his unshaven jowls bristling gray, "and she was as cordial as you can be. She was nice enough to give me a half-hour of her time. We reminisced about the days with Master, then I got down to business about what we're doing here at the Center of Light, our work for world peace. She listened carefully, she's a good listener. I emphasized how important I it is for you boys to meet with her and receive her personal blessing."

"That's really something, reverend," I say, "and she said okay? You told her about the ceremonial magic we're going to be doing here?"

"Yep," Sorenson beams, "we have an appointment two weeks from now on that Saturday. But no, I didn't go into the details about how we're doing what we're doing. That wasn't necessary, just the general idea. I stressed the peaceful purpose of our long meditations, and getting her green light is important for us. She's a spiritual power house. We want her prayers for our work."

"But won't she need a detailed picture of what we're trying to accomplish?"

"No, no, we're all on the same page, working for the same purpose. Don't sweat that stuff."

Holy Moses, this is a big deal. This coup brings every thing into high relief and dispels some of the my doubts about the worthiness of our efforts. Daya Mata is the living goddess of the SRF, Master's personally-trained disciple. If she grants us a private audience based on Torgie's request, obviously we're plugged into an esoteric network and this is real evidence. My brother and I surge with renewed inspiration about the whole, convoluted scene.

When the auspicious day comes we leave early in the morning, right after daybreak. Our appointment with Daya Mata is at high noon and the trip down to Mt Washington will take at least five hours. The reverend insists on taking his Ford painter's van, which has only two seats in the front. On the sides of the van are bright red letters – *Lucky Guy House Painting and Home Repair s.*

He rigs up a legless chair behind the center engine hump where Evan and I take turns sitting cross-legged, facing the highway in this awkward contraption. On the long way down Torgie drives like a tortoise, not more than 50 miles an hour, drawing angry honks and fleeting glimpses of scornful faces. Quite oblivious, he regales us with vivid Yogananda stories.

"I was rebellious and disobedient and always getting into trouble," Torgie confesses, slurping coffee, "Master saved my ass more than once. One time, down at the Encinitas seaside retreat – that's another chapel I helped to build – one day I wanted to go swimming but the sea was pretty rough. I'd seen some pretty rough seas in the merchant marine, so I figured no big deal. But Master sees me walking across the grounds with my swim suit on and he says, "Torgie, go get dressed. Those waves are much too dangerous today, it's no time to take a dip."

"Yogananda told you that?"

"Yeah, Yogananda's telling me, *don't go. Don't go out there,*"

"Okay, I got the picture."

"So, I oblige him and went and put my clothes back on, but rolled my trunks up in a towel and snuck behind the buildings and climbed down the bluff to the beach." Torgie bushes like a rueful boy, adding, "because I was determined to go swimming that day and I was in no mood to be told what to do."

"Hmm, bad muchacho. So what happened?"

"Like a young fool I dove in the surf and swam out a ways and got caught in the most ferocious riptide you can ever imagine. I was a good strong swimmer but I was almost helpless in the grip of that tide. No matter how I fought to get back in it kept carrying me out, and it wasn't long before I was tuckered out and feeling desperate."

"Whoa dude, how far from the shore were you? Could you see

the SRF on the bluff?"

"Oh, that tide pushed me at least a mile out, and yeah, I could still see the retreat. But I was so exhausted I figured I was a goner. I flopped over on my back so I could keep my face above water, I started praying. I prayed to Yogananda and to Jesus Christ, I said, "please, I'm sorry I'm such an arrogant asshole, I'm sorry but please my strength is almost gone, so if there's anything you want me to do please help." And in that very next instant it was like a powerful hand shot down out of the sky and smacked me plumb in the chest. It smacked me so hard that it drove me clear to the bottom, I hit the sea floor with a thud."

"Reverend Sorenson, you serious, for fucking real?"

"I'm telling you God's honest truth, no exaggeration" Torgie implores, swiveling his face back and forth. "I hit the ocean bottom so hard I saw stars, and then it was like being dragged by the collar by a tremendous force. I could feel my back and shoulders scrapping and when I was about to pass out, I got flung up onto the beach like a drowning seal. I just lay there panting, I'm telling you, man, I was at the end."

Evan and I are beside ourselves with mirth, despite the gravity with which Sorenson relates the episode. After a moment he starts laughing too, tears filling his clear blue eyes. "Yeah, that's right, it's awful funny looking back, it is, it is."

"Did Master ever find out? Did he know?"

"Oh hell yes, he knew," Torgie replies. "When I got enough strength back I climbed up the cliff dragging my stuff. I was dripping blood from where my back and legs scraped on the seabed. I'm going across the grounds and he comes walking past me in his saffron robes going the other way."

"Man oh man, what a scene! Hah ha ha!"

"Master, I says, wanting to apologize, Master – and he says,

Shut up, Torgie. Next time I tell you not to go swimming, you listen to me. We're not involved in kindergarden here. Now, go have someone dress those wounds and don't pester me for anymore miracles."

"Wow, reverend," Evan murmurs, "he said that? Those were his words?"

"Yes, yes, those were his exact words, I'll never forget them. And believe you me I was humbled to the marrow of my bones."

UPSTAIRS IN THE grand old hotel of the Mt Washington headquarters, Evan and I sit quietly in a hallway beside tall windows that look out on the graceful palms of the SRF grounds. The Los Angeles skies are smog-smudged a metallic blue and a deep hum arises from the city as always. The Mt Washington ashram is a beautiful, flowering place. As we sit waiting for Sorenson to conclude his private talk with Daya Mata, I'm cogitating on how great it would be to have such an estate for our own work, and why not? If we can throw Satan into chains and make him do our bidding, then the bread to buy such a place should be no problem. We might be able to buy a string of the elegant old resorts and turn them into esoteric centers, across the country, across the whole world.

Torgie sticks his head out of a nearby doorway and says, "come on, she's ready to meet you guys come on."

He's beaming and happy, garbed in his tight black minister's suit. We follow him through the door and into a window-lit solarium, more than a little nervous. She is there, the matriarch of the SRF, peaceful and radiant, sitting on a blue couch taking us in as Sorenson makes the introductions. Another saffron-robed woman is with Daya Mata, introduced as her sister and secretary. The reverend finishes with his little spiel and Daya Mata deftly takes charge.

"Well, I certainly see what you were telling me, Torgie," she observes in a gentle voice. "These young men have the most striking auras. It's quite clear to me that you two brothers are involved in Master's teachings." We are seated across from her, Evan and I, in cushioned wicker chairs and Sorenson is seated in a large plush chair to our right.

"That is true, mamm," I say, playing it by the book, not sure what Torgie has said to her. "We've been deeply following his discourses and meditations for the past couple years, and lately with Mr Sorenson's guidance. It's a real honor to be here with you."

"Thank you, Jake Acree," Daya Mata smiles. "Let me just say that the devotion and dedication really shows in your faces. And you in particular have an extraordinary intensity. I think that you can accomplish just about whatever you set your mind to in this life."

Taken aback by this frank statement, I mumble my thanks. Did I hear her right?

Then, to Evan, she says, "and you, young man, have a heart that naturally overflows with kindness and devotion. In fact, I think that devotion could be your middle name. If you hold to that your progress into the God-consciousness will be swift. I'm tempted to steal you away from Mr Sorenson right on the spot and fit you into an orange robe."

Blushing, my brother stammers, "wow, thanks, that's quite an invitation. I might just take you up on that one of these days."

"Well, be sure to let me know when you're ready," Daya Mata laughs, putting all of us at ease.

"Okay now, wow," Sorenson joins in, lifting his hands from his knees, "we're all one family. And I've been telling Sri Daya Ma and sister Ananda here about our meditation ceremonies for world peace, about how that's our main focus at the Center of Light."

"Absolutely, and yes, we're serious about that," I affirm, looking directly at Daya Mata. "We're intent on bringing this awful war and all wars on this earth to a final end."

Daya Mata regards me with grave thoughtfulness, then says, "Master taught that world peace was entirely possible and that it is within our human ability. It depends on enough people waking up to their birthright of loving God awareness so that misunderstanding stops."

"And do you believe that can actually happen in our lifetime?"

"I think that it's possible, yes. And I believe we must try our utmost to make it so."

"And in my view," Sorenson says, "in order to influence people in the right way and get them to cooperate, we need to reimpose upon society the elaborate religious ceremonies that inspire mass worship, like the Roman Catholic and Byzantine church once had. We need to bring the glory of the old church back."

Hearing this, I wince, my body twitches. To me this is a loathsome idea, orthodox brainwashing, ritualistic nonsense designed to induce a fearful and witless compliance. Sorenson and I hotly argue this point. During our wine sessions it's our most volatile disagreement, his wish to resurrect the delusional bombast of the medieval church and my wish to see all such parasitic coercion wiped from the earth. To my surprise, a subtle disapproval passes across Daya Mata's face as if she'd just heard something ridiculous.

"Oh now wait," Daya Mata responds with feeling, "I'm afraid I cannot agree with that. Bringing back the old rituals of the Catholic Roman Church is the last thing this confused world requires. That all belonged to a certain time and place, but no more. What people are reaching out for now is to be liberated from all those ancient patterns of religious ignorance."

Her rebuke seem to fluster Torgie, but he takes it in good grace. In fact, he is literally beaming in the benign energy of this meeting. Nothing's going to spoil it for him. Daya Mata meets my subtle nod with an open gaze, then turns her affectionate smile on my brother, who is gazing at her as if he's fallen in love.

"Now, if I may with your permission, I'd like to ask these two young men one or two questions."

My brother and I murmur our agreement, Torgie saying, "By all means, Daya Mata, please do. Ask away."

"All right, then tell me, each of you," she says, looking at Evan, then at me, "what is your main aspiration in delving so deeply into Yogananda's teachings? Because it's obvious that you're doing this, it shows. And I'm interested to know why, in you own words, what motivates you?"

Considering this unexpected question, I nod at Evan, saying, "go ahead, man."

My brother hesitates just for a second, blinking, then says, "I want to know my oneness with God. I believe in what Master teaches about and I want to realize that, for myself. I want to be able to live in that transcendental state."

"How wonderful," Daya Mata murmurs. Here sister Ananda, smiling, leans toward my brother and gently admonishes him, "then you must be very careful of your imagination wandering into areas of lust. Watch out for that."

"Okay, I will, I understand that," my brother blushes. "Yes, thank you, I'll remember."

This exchange strikes me as rather peculiar and I almost have to conceal a smirk. Turning her candid eyes on me, Daya Mata asks, "and you, Jake? What drives you in this quest?"

"Well, what my brother just said, I'm in agreement with that. I want to know who I am in total God-awareness, I want to realize my eternal self. And in realizing that, I want to bring peace to humanity and to this beautiful earth – an end to war. That's my purpose."

Daya Mata nods, considering me without blinking, and says, "if there is a more noble work than that, I cannot think of it."

Her approval sends a surge of enthusiasm through my whole body. She asks us a few more questions, where do our parents live, how do they feel about our spiritual aspirations, how do you deal with loneliness? We answer honestly, without embarrassment. There is no need to shy away or embellish anything, we feel like we're being bathed in a gentle, cleansing peace.

"I'd like to commend you both," she tells us, hands folded in her orange-robed lap: "It's been refreshing talking with you. And now I have a request. I'd like us all to a few minutes in silent meditation together. Would that be all right with everyone?"

We agree that hell yes it would be, Torgie expressing his appreciation, in the dappled light of this serene solarium where Yogananda himself passed many quite hours, we go into meditation. My heart feels humbled, suffused with the pure radiance and presence of this transparent space.

After awhile, Daya Mata gently brings us out of it. "That was very nice," she says, "thanks to us all. It would make me glad if you two young men would stay in touch, write us a letter every so often, and let us know how you're doing."

"We will do that, yes mamm, we will, for sure we will."

Daya Mata looks out the tall windows at the elegant palms, the blue patches of sky, as if deciding something. Then says, "and one more thing, Reverend Sorenson. What you asked me about earlier, I can give you that green light now, I received the go-ahead while we meditated. These young men have earned it. You have permission to initiate them into the higher Kriya mantras that Master taught those of us living in the ashram. And occasionally, to special devotees who are living out in the world."

Her statement catches us toff-guard. Torgie, whose round boyish face opens, blue eyes wide, stammers, "oh my God, that's fantastic, sister. Yes, I felt his presence too, I felt it, but didn't expect such a blessing."

Evan and I are momentarily speechless, stunned by this good luck. So disoriented that I can't remember exactly what she said in words, only her calm and radiant kindness, as if washed in light my photogenic mind temporarily switched off.

ONCE ON THE way back home, rattling up 101 in the paint truck, I press reverend Sorenson for details. "She mentioned that you discussed the higher initiations with her, before we even came in. That was for us?"

"Yes, we talked about it as a possibility. I asked her if there was some way you fellows could get the Kriya initiations, just like Master used to give one on one. Those are the sacred initiations, they don't go out in the discourses anymore and almost never to anyone living outside the ashram."

"Man, I'm blown away, thank you, thank you, Mr Sorenson!" Evan laughs, fixing me with a jubilant gaze, for he was the one who first brought home "Autobiography Of A Yogi" for us to read.

Smiling at mt brother, I say, "yeah, incredibly cool, reverend, such a gift! But you seemed surprised yourself?"

"Oh I was, I was," he replies, puttering along the freeway at 45 mile per hour and getting honked at, his huge belly propped on the steering wheel. "I know what they are, those Sanskrit tones, and I still have Master's initiation booklets locked in my safe, the sacred names of God. But I don't have the authority on my own to bestow them. I needed Daya Mata's okay to give them to you, so I asked her. Shoot, you never know until you ask. I asked her if it was possible for you to receive those initiations, and she said maybe, maybe some day, but not to expect it anytime soon. But then, after meeting you boys, lo and behold she gave the go-ahead."

"Wow, man, fantastic," I say almost to myself, the sun-glinting off the turquoise ocean on the shoreline above Santa Barbara. "Things sure are happening fast."

"Yes, you can say that again," Torgie affirms, kicking up his highway speed a notch. "But it just goes to prove what I've been saying all along. Master sent you two brothers and you are being richly blessed. It just underscores the magnificent work we've got ahead of us."

"When? When do we start?"

"I'd say almost any day now. Especially after what just went down."

Chapter 14

THE MAD REVEREND monk brings home the beautiful, hand-fashioned linen robes, one for me, one for Evan. He intends to stick with the SRF saffron robes that Yogananda gave him years ago. Mine is a royal purple fringed with red and green silk thread, my brothers is pure white linen interwoven with golden thread. We cinch these robes around the waist with the hand-wrought copper amulets strung on a tasseled rope. Around our necks we wear a silk cord that drapes the lambskin talisman on our chest. On these talismans, front and back, are inscribed the minute words – "I conjure thee by the ineffable name Tetragrammaton Jehovia Adonai, to now appear before me in fair and friendly shape and do my commands."

Solemn and austerely sober, Reverend Sorenson takes us through a dress rehearsal. After dark, we march out along the dim corridor and into the renovated meat locker. We go in our sock feet, clean white socks, so as not to defile the holy chamber. We carry our swords in one hand and a sacred book in the other. Handing me his heavy implements for a moment, Torgie unlocks the brass padlock on the heavy door and swings it open, we go inside. Then he locks the door again from the inside, leaving the key in the lock.

"That's in case we have to leave this place in a hurry," he says tersely.

The burly reverend clearly has done a lot of work in here. He has rigged up some recessed lighting that dimly illuminates the deep, hollow space, and removed the metal hooks in the overhead conveyor belt. He's painted the ceiling of the room a sky blue, all the walls and floor are painted immaculate white. A large alter has been built against the back wall, draped in yards of white linen. There are incense burners and seven heavy brass candelabras on the alter, holding tall handmade candles about three inches in diameter. Pictures of Yogananda and the SRF depiction of Jesus Christ stand sentinel at each end of the alter, angled inward. In the center of this edifice a striking gold cross stands, its arms inscribed with arcane symbols.

"That is to put the fear of God into the haughty and arrogant ones," Sorenson mutters.

On the white floor of the chamber there is a large circle painted in Tibetan red, yellow and blue. Our straight-backed chairs are positioned in this circle, facing the alter. Torgie has rigged a shelf-like table in front of the chairs, to accommodate our swords and sacred books of conjuration. In front of the circle, between us and the alter, he has painted a large pentagram in brilliant gold. This five-pointed star is where we will cause the infernal demons to manifest and yield to our will. I check these elements out with keen interest, while my brother mumbles to himself.

"This is how we enter," the reverend instructs, "in silence, with our minds focused on God, no distracting thoughts. We'll come in, light the candles, burn some frankincense and myrrh, then take our seats. Me here, Jake you in the middle, Evan you there. We'll invoke the Heavenly Father, the Divine Mother, the Holy Spirit and Jesus the Christ, along with the SRF ascended masters. After a few minutes of silent meditation and of visualizing the Light of Perfect Protection, we'll begin. No frivolous chit-chat or fooling around. We'll get right down to the serious business."

"Far out, Mr Sorenson," I murmur in appreciation. "And how long should we expect to stay in this chamber?"

"It all depends," Torgie says, lofting his bushy eyebrows. "Depends on what kind of results we get. But this is showtime, so I'd say be prepared to spend several hours in here at a stretch. That means no breaks by the way, we can't leave the circle once the ritual begins. So take a pee or a dump first."

Evan sighs, none too enthused. "Uh, that sounds pretty heavy. Are we gonna fast too?"

"Yes, thanks for reminding me," Sorenson replies, "We are going to do our first invocation in nine days, on a Friday night, with the new moon in Virgo. That will give us all weekend to work in here, and right, fasting is mandatory. We have to fast for three days of purification leading up, then eat a meal of cheese and fruit before getting started. That has to last us for at least 24 hours."

Contemplating those days of sipping the canned grapefruit juice that Torgie favors, I shudder. But at least he isn't insisting on some ritualistic consumption of rancid salami, and at last we're finally going into action.

"We have to honor our discipline," the reverend emphasizes. "As long as we're going in and out of the circle and conjuring the infernal powers, we can indulge in only one light meal a day. And only a few sips of consecrated wine, no other liquor of any kind. We have to be able to resist any and all sensual temptations, just like Jesus did."

"Sensual temptations?" my brother speculates "but what if they materialize as some irresistible sexy goddess and offer us the world for a blowjob, what then? I mean, you talk about doing as Jesus did but we're not Jesus, were just yogi hippies trying to sublimate our desires."

"Yeah," I say in a wicked tone, "what happens if that happens? Are we doomed?"

"That could happen," Sorenson allows, "and we have to resist it. We have to stand firm against their lascivious wiles. We have to demand and claim power on our own terms, not theirs. So spend some extra time in prayer and meditation to strengthen your will. Don't even imagine that you will falter. Spend at least three hours each night in meditation and prayer in the days leading up, pray to Master, build your light. No telling what we're gonna run into once we get started, we need to put on the whole armor of the Lord."

After our robed ceremonial rehearsal we eat some of Mrs Mallet's homegrown peach pie and drink strong Mexican coffee, each of us absorbed in our thoughts. These are strange days, things are getting weird. Weirdness has never bothered me much but this is radically different. I'm wondering what I've gotten myself into and what it's going to be coming out the other side of this trip, and I'm pretty sure my brother is thinking much the same thing. Finally, it's demon showtime.

DURING THE NINE day interlude, Torgelananda gets into his orange swami robes and turns us on to the higher Kriya initiations. The sacred Sanskrit tones are more complex than the basic meditation techniques that Yogananda imparts in his home discourse booklets. These esoteric mantras consist of ancient names of God that must be chanted in a certain, silent order. At first, you listen to the words spoken aloud, then you repeat and memorize them. After that initiation, you're not permitted to utter them aloud again, only silently, nor are you supposed to write them down. The exact sequence of the inner chant is important and deep practice is intended to awaken you again to the Cosmic Source Divine.

Fantastic, but for me these strange words are hard to remember, I already have an overload of ritual formulas in my head. I keep getting the sequence jumbled up. For days I keep going back to Torgie for confirmation and finally he lets me write them down to memorize them. I pen these Sanskrit tones inside the flyleaf of the leather bible that my mother sent me as a birthday gift, hoping I'd come to my senses, surely a blasphemous act. My blue-eyed southern mother fears that Evan and I have become wayward-soul, pagan mystics. Ah well, nothing is ever quite as it seems.

During the ink-blot nights of ardent meditation leading up to the magical ceremonies our dreams are twisted, populated with nameless anxieties. I have no idea from where such frightful images arise, from what repressed currents of consciousness. I follow Yogananda's simple advice to turn over on your opposite side if you're caught in a nightmare. If you remember to do that, the freaky stuff quickly dissipate. The long nights in the Quonset hut feel like a surreal womb. Evan wanders into the outer corridor groggy and half asleep, to take a piss, but passes by the bathroom. He shuffles into the pitch blackness and runs face-first into something hideous. His awful shrieks bring Sorenson and I awake in wild-eyed alertness.

"Agggh, fucking monster, agggh, fuck, fucckk!" Evan screams from the hollow darkness, flailing like a rabbit in a trap, "get it off me, get it off, aggghh!"

Even as the reverend and I bat our way through the beaded curtain, flicking on the light, Evan blunders his way into the kitchen, his yogi skin pale and waxen, his handsome face a taut canvas of shock. A yellow stain spreads in his white shorts where he peed himself.

"Fucking Jesus God," Evan babbles, his eyes like lamp sockets, "something horrible out there, something hairy and disgusting hanging from the roof, rubbing all over me—"

"Whoa man, calm down bro," I say, taking him by his arms, fighting my own superstitious dread. "What is it, what are you saying? No, no, you're all right now, it's cool, you're safe, man, you're safe!"

My kid brother, hangs on to my forearms, gasping, "no dude, dig, dig, I'm telling ya, something hideous out there in the darkness, I ran right into it, something huge clutching at me and it stank, maybe those things are already sneaking around—"

"Well for Christ's sake," Sorenson mutters, rummaging around in one of the drawers, finding a flashlight. "Let's go see what's what. . ."

He comes up with a red pipe wrench and pads his way out the door in his fat man's undies. The bulb has burned out in the corridor, it's inky black. The cacophonous machinery comes on with a shriek of old fan belts. I follow him with my brother, our senses on total alert.

"Awfully dark, I'll grant you that," Torgie calls back, then a moment later starts laughing. "Well, I'll be damned, I see what you stumbled into. Damned big bastard, too."

"Well, what the hell is it?" I demand, not moving. Torgie shines his light my way, he's over by the meat locker but all I can see is his beam.

"Come see, come over here, but watch your step. It's almost unbelievable, got to be old man Mallet's doing."

We make our way across the plywood flooring of the corridor, more blinded than helped by his flashlight. When we get in close he points his beam at a black hirsute carcass hanging from the conveyor belt with a meat hook in its slit throat. It's some kind of monstrous hog with glassy red eyes, slung up tat face level, ah for true, a hideous diabolical creature. I begin to snicker under my breath, my poor brother shuffled out here and ran smack dab into that thing.

"Holy shit," Evan mumbles in revulsion, "what the hell is that?"

"It's one of those big feral pigs that hang out in the Salinas river bottom," Sorenson says. "Somebody must have shot it and hauled it into the butcher shop late. So they hoisted it up here to let the ticks fall off. That's all it is, just a dead scary hog."

We all convulse into spasms of laughter, there in the flashlight and faint kitchen glow, realizing our foolishness, breathing in our psychological relief.

"I'm gonna have a talk with Mallet in the morning," Sorenson vows. "I don't think it was malicious but I'm gonna put a stop to any random activity. From now on, this whole upstairs is off-limits to anybody but us. Come on, let's go get some shut-eye."

Chapter 15

ONCE THE FINAL days of fasting are under our belts, we don our elegant robes, unsheathe our swords, look each other in the eye, then stride into the cavernous meat locker transformed into a ceremonial chamber. Evan in his pure white robes carries a King Jame's Version of the Bible; Torgelananda in his saffron robes holds the leather clad Holy Roman Catholic Ritual of Exorcism; me in my purple robes clutching a medieval grimoire of demonic conjuration that can be traced back to King Solomon himself. We light the candles in the windowless room, we ignite the frankincense and myrrh. We take our seats in the consecrated circle, Evan on my left, Torgelananda on my right. We lay our swords on the narrow table and open the sacred books. The reverend lifts his palms to the sides of his head, we all do, and invokes the Holy Spirit, the Christ Consciousness, all the SRF saints and masters for their presence and protection. Evan takes his Bible and in a stern, fortified voice recites the 91st psalm. Then we go inward for about fifteen minutes of silent meditation.

"Let us begin," Torgie says in my right ear, "the time is auspicious. We'll go until around midnight or until the infernal ones appear."

And thus, after months of study and preparation, we at last begin a real-life conjuration. Aiyee, we summon the leering Arch-Devil himself and most of the grunt work falls to me. When Sorenson told me that I was to take the lead in the invocations, I was flattered. But once we get down to the arduous work at hand, I soon realize that I'm in for it—

"I invoke and conjure thee, O Spirit N., and, fortified with the power of the Supreme Majesty, I strongly command thee by BARALAMENSIS, BALDACHIENSIS, PAUMACHIE, APOLORESEDES *and the most potent princes* GENIO, LIACHIDE, *Ministers of the Tartarean Seat, chief princes of the seat of* APOLOGIA *in the ninth region; I exorcise and command thee, O Spirit N., by Him Who spake and it was done, by the Most Holy and glorious Names* ADONAI, EL, ELOHIM, ELOHE, ZEBAOTH, ELION, ESCHERCE, JAH, TETRAGRAMMATON, SADAI: *do thou forthwith appear and shew thyself unto me, here before this circle, in a fair and human shape, without any deformity or horror; do thou come forthwith, from whatever part of the world, and make rational answers to my questions; come presently, come visibly, come affably, manifest that which I desire, being conjured by the Name of the Eternal, Living and True God,* HELIOREM; *I conjure thee also by the particular and true Name of thy God to whom thou owest thine obedience; by the name of the King who rules over thee, do thou come without tarrying; come, fulfill my desires; persist unto the end, according, to mine intentions."*

These incantations have to be repeated with commanding force, over and again. Since I am working with nothing visible, all I can do is do my imaginary best. It seems that visualization plays a key part in the rituals, in the early stages, until some phenomena starts to manifest. But it's hard to know exactly what to visualize—a fearsome man-beast or a suave beguiling devil? And it's crucial to conjure them within the confines of the pentagram so they can do no mischief or wreak harm our bodies and minds, so the old texts warn.

This proves to be exhausting work and time drags along. At

first things go all right, we will ourselves into the ceremonial routine, I orate my ethereal commands, I brandish my sword in the incense-rich air above the radiant circle and make known our demands. Reverend Sorenson and my good brother, flanking me in fellowship, chime in at regular intervals with chants of protection from the Psalms of David. But if we have been hoping for quick results we are soon disabused of that notion. No gleaming devil or leering demon pops into the space, not even a ripple of supernatural light or unusual noise, just the droning of my own voice trying to conjure something out of nothing.

To my annoyance things begin to break down before the first hour has passed. Evan starts to check out on me, whether from sheer monotony or disinterest, who knows? He nods off with spasmodic jerks, drooling on his white-linen chest, then swoons into an oblivious coma. I nudge him awake with my elbow, growling, "come on, buba, I need your help in this. Stay with it!"

Evan grunts, jerks upright, mumbles, "oh, sorry, okay, I'm gonna concentrate." He picks up his rapier and waves it in the candle lit air next to my cutlass. But these swords are not paper mache, they're heavy steel, our shoulders and arms soon ache. I take a sip of water from the jar, wetting my mouth, and move aggressively into the ritual of demonic conjuration. The demons are surely gathering, I must make it happen. There are twelve such rituals, each with its own invocation of the Infernal Hierarchy. Sorenson and I have memorized most of them in the months of tedious study, my occult text is bookmarked at the relevant pages. We figure that one of these forbidden spells is bound to do the trick.

The wax candles flicker in a sudden wandering draft, instilling a little hope, because how can there be any draft in this hollow sealed chamber? Drawing on my courage, I command the invisible ones to materialize before me, manifest you diabolical miscreants, I do command you in the name and power of all that's Holy! The biblical incense smudges the atmosphere, time drags, speech slurs, the body begins to revolt in this mighty contest of will. Time itself ceases to have much meaning for me – I rasp out my incantations, fighting my own mad and desperate urge to escape, my back muscles ache, my sword arm trembles. This is worse than the marathon meditations, far worse. Captive to this performance, there is no inner refuge to be gained. I must keep my bloodshot eyes focused on the sacred pentagram for any sign of fiendish disturbance, the slightest ripple in the air. We are trying to force something into manifestation that might not even be real, and even if it is real why should it cooperate with us? I mean, if I were a powerful and cunning devil would I knowingly cooperate with my own materialization and bondage? Of course not.

My brother has more or less conked out on me. Although he remains more or less upright, his chin has collapsed, his face droops downward The lazy bastard doesn't respond to my soto voce entreaties or to my elbow. On my other side, reverend Sorenson's condition is not much better. The fat monk has settled his orange-robed bulk into a slumbering lump, his whiskery jowls bob on his chest, his breath sonorous. Neither one of them have stayed awake with me during this grueling ceremony, both have nodded away, leaving me to go it alone. A slow-burning knot of anger congeals in my chest.

"Keep going, keep going," Torgie mumbles in a whiskey-dream voice, not even opening his peepers, making me wonder if he's nipping the vodka again. "They're congregating, they're coming in."

All right, so be it; smothering my doubt and resentment, I

press ahead. It's taken me months of intense preparation to reach this stage of hardcore performance, I don't want to be counted as a stupendous fool. I recharge myself, I plunge into the strident orations.

Show yourselves, O ye fiends of Hell, in fair and comely form, with compliant demeanor, appear and do my holy bidding!

Verily, I push deep into this psychotic no-man's zone, this brow-beating occult fog, voicing these mantras and brandishing my sword in the aura of the golden pentagram painted on the Chinese red floor. I give it all my strength, I orate and rant, but it is not enough. The stubborn devils outlast me and at last I am worn out. The candles have burned down but still gutter and flicker, made to last for days. One thing about this converted carcass locker is its muffled silence due to the heavy insulation. You almost feel entombed. We sense the shudder of the old cooling equipment going on and off, but can barely hear the racket. It's doubtful that anyone standing outside could even hear our voices.

"I can't go on, I'm totally bushed," I confess to Sorenson. "I've got to lie down for awhile."

The reverend, as if reading my thoughts, opens one eye and says, "it's very interesting. We're getting quite a lot of resistance from the other side. But that's to be expected, we have to keep pushing through the membrane."

"The membrane?"

"The curtain of unknowing, we have to rend it open. But yes, let's get some rest now, it's been a good start. We've definitely got their attention, just know that our determination is being tested. You are doing a fantastic job."

My brother rouses from his stupor, we bring ourselves together and close with prayers of thanksgiving to the most high and holy God, although I'm beginning to wonder why God needs so many high and holy names? Did man in his desperate and deranged longing invent these names and exotic notions, trying to invent a solution to his chaotic stupidity and blundering? But I am too tired to investigate this intriguing thought, I need to piss and a bite to ear and then crash. Our metaphysical manipulations will begin again at daybreak, even as old man Mallet's rooster crows.

AND AS THE sun rises in a rose patina over the Indian summer hills, we march back into the holy chamber and chase the phantoms of ceremonial magic for many more demented hours, me, commanding the protean ether, stabbing the air with my iron cutlass, doing my utmost to conjure from the film of thought some satanic being, suave or obscene, for what we need is real evidence that we are involved in an intelligent action, not just a madman's agonizing obsession. Sorenson mutters and snores beside me, urging me onward, don't slack off, he mutters, we're getting close, the benign spirits are gathering in protection, encircling the room in light, the wicked ones are being dragged forth. Problem he is the only person who beholds this astral vision is the reverend himself, the interpreter, one must continue this arduous battle in imagination alone. I find myself struggling with this presumed authority, with what cannot be verified by anyone other than Sorenson, the sense of blind imbalance. Because my brother and don't see shit. The muted echoes of the chamber ferment the conflicting thoughts in my brain, setting up a grim current of revolt in my mind that feels like a whip.

My kid brother labors beside me, making an erstwhile effort to stay awake. He senses my inner struggle and wants to help. But our bodies are in torment and I can tell that Evan has no real interest in what we're doing. He has no passion for this demon business and in fact is repulsed by the whole scene. He'd rather be wandering around somewhere picking figs out of trees.

Only last night as we sat around recovering, eating cheese and apples and imbibing a smidgen of Rotta-gutta, Evan said, "listen, I've been thinking, maybe you need some psychedelics to make this trip happen. I mean, to open up the psyche. Maybe those old Hebrew magicians were tripping on some kind of mushroom and then flashed into their supernatural visions."

"Hah ha, yeah," I offer, finishing a muscle-relaxing half-pint of wine, "I had the same thought while I was slugging through that last ceremony. Because this is no magic carpet ride, it's a real grind. Those old sorcerers might've been chewing some powerful herbs in order to see such bizarre creatures."

Torgie, sitting in his sweat-stained underwear, breaks into uproarious laughter. "Aha, psychedelics," he shouts, "hah ha ha, you want psychedelics to see a vision? All right then, I'll give you some potent psychedelics! My dingleberries are psychedelic, here, let me pick some out of the hairs of my ass."

"What," Evan sputters, "say what, your dingleberries? What the fuck you talking about?"

"My acid-infused dingleberries," Sorenson huffs, beet-faced and blinking, digging around in the seat of his underwear with blunt fingers.

"Hee, hee hee, here," he says, offering us a hard little ball of shit with a hair stuck in it. "Here, chew on it and you'll have the wildest visions imaginable, I guarantee it."

"Are you crazy? That's nothing but a dried up turd. You are fucking crazy, yes you are."

"Psychedelic dingleberries, 100 percent organic," Sorenson

cries in lunatic delight. "Don't disparage what you haven't yet tried."

Evan and I double over in insane laughter, wheezing for air, scarcely believing what we're seeing. The reverend is laughing so hard tears are streaming down his cheeks. Waving him off, we go to our sleeping pallets, murmuring our incredulity, and fall into the deep and dreamless sleep.

Yes, unbounded madness, and now, half-way through the Saturday conjugations, the war within my head oscillates between fantastic expectations and the bitter facts. Nothing unusual is happening at our whipping post. No ethereal spirits are showing their faces in this ceremonial asylum, neither angelic nor diabolic. Acute rebellion mounts within me. Evan has plunged into a mindless stupor, mumbling to himself. Torgelananda is dead to the world, his gray-whiskered chin slumped on his barrel chest, snoring. My tired voice is cracking, almost giving out. I forge ahead, though the invocations no longer make any sense to me. I seem to be garbling out meaningless sounds, nonsensical noises. My right arm aches so that I can barely lift my painted sword. I've drained the water jar, I need to piss ferociously. Somehow a fly has gotten into this sealed room, one of those obnoxious blue-bottle flies, the hideous creature keeps buzzing round my face.

Worst yet, I cannot escape the terrible conviction that we have been conned, even flat-out tricked. Tricked into believing that all this occult gibberish is anything more than a fantastic joke played on gullible fools searching for magical words. Aiyee, such a ludicrous scam!

"Abracadabra, you demon fuckers, fuck off," I croak, dissolving into hysterical laughter even as the loathsome fly dive-bombs me again. Teeming with righteous fury, I bring this lunatic ritual to a sudden halt. Elbowing my brother awake, pushing the leaning orange-robed Sorenson upright with my shoulder, I tell them, "come on, that's it, I'm wasted, I'm done. This has been a total no-show, man, I need to get out of here for some fresh air."

Bowing our heads, we pray together, then vacate the stifling incense and fart-suffused chamber, shuffling off to the kitchen. I've been chewing on my disillusionment, I need to express it, but I don't want to sound petty. This ordeal has been incredibly frustrating, not at all like we imagined. And if this occult theosophy is nothing more than hocus-pocus, what does that say about the fanciful nonsense floating around all the other new-age sects, making their hallowed claims of authenticity? If nothing can be really verified, what then can be called real?

We sit around and eat red apples and cream cheese, sipping spring water and wine, comparing notes. Reverend Sorenson presses us, wanting to know what we saw, what we thought we saw, even a hallucinatory flicker to justify all our hermetic work and effort.

Evan shakes his head, long-faced, despondent. "No, nothing, sorry Mr Sorenson. I didn't see anything. Okay, maybe some jumbled fragments but I can't remember what. Nothing made much sense to me, it was just total weirdness."

Sorenson turns to me, imploring me, "what about you, maestro, think. In all those hours of conjuration, didn't you see anything unusual?"

"Nope, not really, sorry" I reply, exhausted and dissatisfied. "And believe me, after all those high-octane acid and trips that I took, I was alert for any kind of unusual phenomena. Nada, reverend, nothing happened."

"Nothing, you saw nothing?" Torgie retorts in frustration. "Not even the slightest glimpse?"

"No sir, I'm telling you straight. It was like knocking my head against a wall You two were both zonked out, how could you know? Toward the end I was in agony. And there was this goddamned fat black fly trapped in there, buzzing around, buzzing my face, it was repulsive."

Sorenson peers at me, blinking his luminous eyes, considering my words. "A fly, you say? You saw a black fly in there?"

"Yeah, there was a fly. A really nasty bastard, too. It kept dive-bombing me."

"Jesus Christ," Sorenson blurts, tilting his head back and gulping his wine. Wiping his mouth with his fingers, he leans in close to me, his sweating face, he says, "I wish the hell you woulda told me that before we quit. That fly was what we've been waiting for. That damned fly was the lord of demons himself."

"What, say what? Come again?" I say, eyeballing the deranged fanatical monk. For I have no doubt that Torgen Sorenson is quite mad, the only question is to what extent.

"I'm telling ya," he insists, staring at me, "that angry fat fly had to be Beelzebub, that was Beelzebub manifesting for us. We've got to go back in the circle. We gave up too soon."

Part Two

"I searched for God and found only myself,
I searched for myself and found only God."

—Rumi

Chapter 16

T HAT TURNS OUT to be the fly in the ointment of tolerance, for me. Fanatical I may be too, fool I am not. Torgen Sorenson's insistence that we return to the circle of delusion in order to conjure the Lord of Darkness, that the trapped bluebottle fly was Beelzebub taunting us, snaps my patience. After almost one year of being sequestered in the austere Quonset hut, chasing phantasmagoria, I make the decision to break away. But at first I keep this surge of rebellion to myself, not even confiding in my brother. Never show your hand until you're ready to play it.

I spend a Saturday morning driving around the wooded Atascadero neighborhoods and on a hillside street not far from the stoplight downtown, I hit pay-dirt. There's a wooden duplex sitting back under some oak trees, with off-street parking. A mailbox sign reads, "one bedroom, partially furnished, $75.00 per month, utilities included. No weirdos."

Parking my yellow Studebaker along side an old '54 Ford turquoise station wagon, I check out the scene. There are a few toys scattered in the yard and up on one porch, not a good sign for a sanctuary-seeking yogi, but neither sight nor sound of any kids. Brushing my longish hair back with both hands, I call out, "hello, anybody here, anybody around? Hello?"

For a minute there's no response, only a TV murmuring in the background. Then, the screen door cracks open and a feminine voice says, "ahh, were you looking for someone?"

"Well no, not actually. I mean, it's about the place for rent."

A lucid moment passes, she says, "oh, right, just a sec," then after a muffled comment to someone inside, she appears on the porch. A young woman in her early twenties, a shy and friendly smile, in blue jeans and a simple draw-string blouse. She's slender and curvaceous, with gray-green eyes and honey-blonde hair across her shoulders. "Maybe I can help you with that," she says in a lilting voice, "if you want to take a look I have the key."

"Yeah, that'd be cool," I say, swallowing. "I'd like to see it."

"Okay," she flashes me another smile, saying, "be right back."

I stand there for a moment, my thoughts beating like wings. This chick is devastatingly pretty. I say to myself, "shut the fuck up."

She takes me around to the other side, making friendly small talk. The wooden-floored duplex is nothing special, standard one bedroom, one bath with an original tub and shower, an old kitchen, stove and fridge, a screened back porch that seems to conjoin the other porch through a service door. "My name's Shandy," she tells me, giving me a look-around, pointing out how the whole house is shaded by trees. It doesn't get too hot and there are birds in the morning and this street is a quiet one, almost no traffic. But I'm only half-listening, because the most delicious sensuality is humming between us. Her olive skin and fresh girl scent has me almost panting, like a caress impossible to ignore. And it seems to me the feeling is mutual, she seems delighted.

"Oh my gosh, well, what do you think?" she says with a self-conscious laugh. "It sure would be nice to have a good neighbor. The last guy who lived here was a drunken slob, so bad the landlord made him move."

"Hmm, I can dig that," I sympathize, my winning smile, devil that I am, with syrup in my throat, hot sap rising in my celibate balls. "And so Shandy, you would be my neighbor? And who lives with you . . .?"

"Oh, it's just me and my two little kids, Randall and Shelly, but they're good kids." She gives her lovely hair a little toss, adding, "And their no-good father is long gone, he ditched us. He went and shacked up with some Mexican chick over in Bakersfield, such an asshole, and good riddance, too.

"Sounds a little complicated," I say, absorbing this news with conflicting emotions.

"No, not complicated anymore. It's simple now. It's just me and the kids and the little dog, but he doesn't even hardly bark. Plus right now my girlfriend's staying with me for a few days until she moves into her own place. So it might be just right. Would you like to try living here?"

I tell this disarming chick that I like the place just fine, that my only concern is that it's quiet. I'm a writer and a poet and I meditate early in the morning for at least one hour. This facile nonsense comes out of my mouth without any hesitation. Shandy takes it in with a blink of her jade green eyes, her lips slightly open.

"Really, a writer," she says, "that's impressive. And you know meditation too? I've been wanting someone to explain that to me. I think I worry too much, you know? It would be neat to be able to switch my mind off."

"I could probably help you with that, it's not so hard. There's a method to it."

"Gosh, maybe this is our lucky day," she smiles. "And just so you know, my kids and I don't make a fuss. I'd be the best neighbor in the world. I'll even help you fix the place up, some curtains and things like that, if you want."

My thoughts are like wild flowers in a humid breeze as I leave, telling her that I'm going to call the landlord and talk it over. I have been voluntarily celibate for the past two years. Me moving out of the Center of Light has nothing to do with renouncing my Kriya yoga practices. If anything, it's meant to recover my own pure approach to spiritual awareness without the occult embellishment. I don't consider myself as one of the lost tribes of Israel, as Sorenson speculates, nor are those Old Testament characters my heroes. I just need to make it all more real. And after spending twenty minutes with this adorable, friendly girl, my loins are like a biblical furnace.

I drive around aimlessly for awhile, trying to sort out the swarming beehive of new feelings. What am I doing, what is my intention? I am day-dreaming like a thief, my mouth suffused with the scent of her. I stop at a phone booth and call the easy-going landlord, going over some details. I rent the place that same afternoon.

Torgie takes my moving out in an almost nonchalant way. In his mind, I am only moving around the corner, not far away. He shrugs in the claustrophobic air of the Quonset hut, oblivious to the air compressors screeching in the corridor. "I know how it is," he says. "it gets pretty intense at times. A little break in the routine won't hurt anyone."

My brother is more perturbed by my abrupt decision. A born dreamer, he still doesn't have a paying job, other than the few bucks Mallet gives him to help out in the watermelon patch. Now, he's stuck in the Quonset hut by himself with reverend Sorenson's monkish obsessions. He shoots me a wounded look. But I reassure them both that I'll be around, I'm not abandoning the exalted path, I'll be doing my solitary meditations and coming over for the regular meditation services. Not much will change, I hear myself say, yet knowing something already has.

What my sudden departure signifies, in a non-verbal way, is that I am done with Sorenson's authority. Not that he has lorded it over us, no, he has treated us as self-determining individuals. But I am finished with the convoluted ceremonial work and all of its fanciful expectations. The occult project has exhausted and disillusioned me. I'd rather sip bitter Datura trumpet flower tea on a mountain than spend anymore time in those rituals. Let's get get back to natural mysticism, no more of this psychic hocus-pocus.

The day I move into my new digs, Shandy and her unseen kids are nowhere around. Only the other woman Marge is there rounding up the toys flung around the yard. She greets me, mentioning with a smile how happy Shandy seems that I'm going to be their new neighbor. This tidbit of news has an exhilarating effect, as though some clandestine part of me is hungry for feminine attention. And without it, perhaps, that is how the self-emasculated monks go mad.

It's no big chore, I make the move in two carloads of my gear and books. I drag over a double mattress roped to the roof of my yellow Lark, then I drive out to the Rotta Winery in Templeton. The old woman leads me into the shadowed barn, telling me in her Italian-accented English that she has a new batch of the famous Doctor's Burgundy, especially rich and strong. From a large wooden cask she fills three loop-handled glass jugs for me, smiling and mumbling to herself, three gallons for only six bucks, such an amorous and treacherous elixir. Although in my head I am not imagining anything, nor discounting any possibility. In fact, I refuse to think ahead. For months I've been planning and performing every aspect of my life like a master-controller. Let's just go with the flow and see what the spontaneous moment brings forth on its own.

This new sense of freedom is revitalizing. I throw the mattress with sheets and pillows on the wood floor, hang a few towels in the plain bathroom and hook-up my portable dual speaker hi-fi. Taking a stock of 33 rpm records out of their dusty box, I realize I need to visit the hip record shop in San Luis Obispo my next trip down the hill. It's high time for some new sounds. The landlord has left a comfortable old couch in the front room, around which I create a beatnik ensemble, oriental-style rug, scarred coffee table, and a couple of stick chairs. There's a chest of drawers in the bedroom for my socks, underwear, buck knives and personal stuff. A peeling dinette set compliments the old gas stove and rattling fridge in the kitchen. I stash the beautiful jugs of red wine on the tree-shaded, screened back porch, in full view. I am ready to roll, for whatever.

Whatever shows up just as twilight falls. Chiquita Cornsilk comes tapping at my back door. Chiquita Cornsilk is the pet name I've given Shandy because of her long, silken, sun-kissed hair. Greeting me with a playful smile, and a mason jar of blue and yellow wildflowers in her hands, Shandy says, "I hope you like flowers. I went out in a field and picked them, some for your place and or mine. Welcome to the private house."

Delighted, I say, "yeah, they're beautiful, wow." Opening the door, I bring her inside. It's just the slightest touch of our hands but she feels quite delicious.

"Ohh," she says, "all that wine sure looks tempting. You planning a party?"

"Only if it's spontaneous and now that you mention it, a little house-warming might be just the thing. You like wine yourself?" For someone who has lived like a Tibetan cave monk I feel quite at ease with her. Her svelte nearness and flirtatious touch on my forearm turns my balls into molten wax. I give her a poetic spiel about how rich the wine is, the picturesque place it comes from, wine made for laughing happiness.

"Hey," she blushes, "that sounds awfully inviting. I have to admit I don't know much about wine, but I'd like to drink some with you. How would it be if I come back over around eight, after I get the kids to bed? Marge can baby-sit. That is, if you're not doing anything?"

Ah, she just took a vulnerable leap and I adore her for that. I almost stammer letting her know, yes, oh yes, eight would be fine, taking her hands and lightly kissing her fingers. Where that little move comes from I don't really know, I astonish myself. But she seems enthralled and flutters away aglow. There's nothing ever quite like now.

I hop in my Studebaker and go down to the Atascadero market, where I buy some red apples, green grapes, and Tilamook yellow cheese. Feeling light and insouciant, I banish all conflicting thoughts. Just go with the flow, man, don't get hung-up, just see what happens. When I get back the fireflies are in the air outside. I put her little jar of yellow and blue flowers on the coffee table, starting to wilt. I arrange the sliced cheese, apples and seedless grapes on a clear glass plate, plunk a jug of shoe-leather wine down beside them with a couple of white mugs, twisting off the cap, letting it breathe. When the clock in the bedroom ticks to 7:30, I pour myself a liberal portion to calm my nerves. It's been awhile since I've been in an intimate scene with a come-hither girl, way too long. It's easy to forget that life can be more than just an ascetic pursuit.

When she taps on my porch screen door, Shandy is anything but disappointing. She gives me a girlish smile, her lips touched with coral lipstick, her gray-green eyes optimistic, her lustrous hair falling over her bare rounded shoulders. She's got on tight faded jeans and a white pull-over blouse with a low neckline, showing me her kissable flesh. She isn't using any perfume but smells utterly delicious.

A little self-conscious, Shandy says, "Margie said she'd be glad to babysit, so we're in luck. I have some free time tonight."

Sucking the drool off my lips, murmuring some inviting words, I lead her into my spare abode, not a painting or poster on the wall yet, sit her on the couch and put Marvin Gaye on the turntable. Then I pour us mouth-watering portions of Rotta's finest, super-strong, hippy vino.

"To the sweet serendipity of this place and meeting you," I say, clacking her mug with mine, a smile on my lips, wishing, to get her naked and in my bed with my tongue between her luscious thighs as soon as possible, oh yes, my darling.

"Down the hatch," Shandy giggles, bravely taking three good swallows in a row. Pausing for air, she says, "wow, this stuff really puckers your lips, doesn't it?"

"Yeah, it does," I laugh, "and it's strong too, it'll sneak right up on you."

"Well good," she teases, "I want it strong. I'm tired of drinking milkshakes with the kids and I need to change my luck."

I'm charmed by how unscripted she is and the barnyard burgundy has us flying in no time. She begins to confide her secrets to me, saying, "Jake, this is so much fun for me. It almost feels like I'm on a date. I haven't been on a date in over three years."

"That long? But why, you're so pretty, tell me why."

"Believe me," she says, "there's been nobody around and I haven't been missing anybody."

Our sudden rapport feels magical, I refill out mugs from the copious jug. In the attitude of hoping it won't bother me, Shandy clues me in on the details of her life. Turns out she has sole responsibility for her wild youngsters, the father split on her and has not reappeared. She's mentions him with a wariness, whoever that dude is he has an ominous vibe.

"I kind of hate to say it, he's their father, but he's nothing but scooter trash."

Well, definitely stuff to ponder only not now. I put Surrealistic Pillow on the turntable and take us higher, she comes my way, sliding closer, yearning to be kissed. It's good to know that the ex-boyfriend or ex-husband or whoever-the-fuck is nowhere around. Her lips glisten, her hand rests on my thigh, her soft eyes are wells of desire We want it and our first kiss is pure dynamite. A kiss that starts out a little shy, then goes deep and hot and wild, leaving us breathless. My burgeoning cock seems about ready to split open my button-fly jeans. "Hmm," she murmurs, caressing my leg, "you suppose we could try that again?"

Our yearning tongues seek, she whimpers with desire, our young bodies blaze and tremble. Ayiee fuck, there's not the vaguest doubt where this is going and the ruby red wine cannot be blamed, the match that lit the wick. The taste of her mouth is intoxicating, I want to eat this girl alive. Her blouse comes off like a flimsy afterthought, surrendering her luscious breasts to my lips, our bodies on fire, incinerating any censoring thoughts. Shandy removes any lingering question by taking hold of my hot, hard prick and saying, "oh my god yes Jake, yes, let's do it, yes!"

No one can say this explosion was expected, for there was no plan. Only the bold flirtation and willingness to let something new happen. We are quickly consumed with pleasure so intense and ravishing that it leaves us naked on the bed, stunned, a trail of clothes on the pine floor, cannibals on mescaline, panting for words. My still tumescent cock oozes its few last drops of rich yogic sperm and this precious girl nuzzles me like a Kama Sutra dakini.

"Boy oh boy," she exclaims softly, "I never even imagined. That was beyond wild."

"Honey-child," I say, thoughts spinning, "that was beyond words. You are beyond words."

"Well you too, my beautiful man. But listen, I need to go check on the kids. But I'd really like to come over tomorrow, so we can talk? Would that be okay?"

"Sure, that'd be fine, uh huh," I murmur, caressing her smooth back and fragrant tresses, already aroused again. "Around dark, the perfect time for us, when the fireflies come out."

"Okay, beautiful," she whispers, kissing me. She slips into her coral panties, smooths her hair with a pleased expression, another kiss, then leaves me with an ardent little wave.

O me oh my, fuck me girl, fuck me all night and every night if you like, although in that passionate twinkling two and a half years of celibacy are burned to a cinder, my balls drained in a shuddering orgasm and churning again with hot sap. What an incredibly delicious female, now what? A niggling sense of guilt tries to creep in but I swat it away. Guilt is nothing but a trap, a social-control mechanism. Guilt rules those who live in fear, fuck that. There is no moral authority over your other than yourself, that one must know.

Nonetheless, the suddenness of this voluptuous explosion leaves me slack-jawed with wonder. There's no way that she and I are not going to dive into this river again together, and soon, oh soon! And now I am a reckless and wayward yogi, aiyee. Her passionate nubile body has turned into an insatiable lion, and she's already gone on me, I see it in her wistful eyes. Obviously I'm going to have to start practicing some Tantric sexual techniques, I've read some of the books, I understand the theory. Otherwise this adorable chick might avidly drain me of so much vital spurt ting cum that I'm left but a quivering husk of myself, one of the doomed fallen ones.

Naturally I don't tell reverend Sorenson or my curious brother about what's happening, no contrite confessions. This is between me, God, and Chiquita Cornsilk, nobody else. There is the matter of trust, but if you can't trust yourself you are always behind the cosmic eight ball.

No, on the surface of things I keep up my appearances. I attend the regular Center of Light meditations, maintaining a placid saintly face. I do my dawn Kriya meditation regardless of last night's escapades. I continue to drop by the Quonset hut every so often to visit with Evan and Torgie, always excusing myself around twilight to go home and do some metaphysical research. The implication is that I'm involved in the investigation of the clairvoyant use of Tarot cards, and this isn't untrue. I am studying the classic Tarot deck, trying to see if I can reliably use them to predict the outcome of things. It's an ambiguous business, one as to sort through layers of false thinking. Behind it all my clandestine and torrid investigation of sexual pleasure with my wild-child, country girl is what's really going down and I worry if that can even be hidden?

Ah, the flagrant truth is she comes to my porch door every night just past eight, starlight in her eyes, dew on her lovely lips, and fireflies in her hair. We sit on the couch together, our bodies like amorous torches, sharing a few loose fragments about out day, sipping the heady wine, tasting the nectar of feverish desire. It's as though a lascivious and rejuvenating wildfire consumes us, burning past taboos. But this is a dangerous game, I cannot lose myself like she does. The yoga adept trying to control his volcanic eruptions into her honeycomb orifices is a tricky business. Shandy herself, dazed with sensual pleasure and released from all bondage, can't quite get why I want to restrain my orgasms. I try to convey the esoteric principles, the precious subliminal seed, its transmutation up the spinal chakras, but with my artful fingers deep inside her delicious cunt, she seeks my dripping organ with crazed abandon. Yes, it's a dangerous game and never for a moment does this insatiable beauty slack off. She usually wins. She comes up for air glowing and infused with erotic energy, in shy triumph saying, "wow, I swallowed every bit of that. Did that feel good, baby? Do you like the way I suck you?"

Oh wicked yogi bad, bad, lustful and hedonistic yogi, I am! I take her adorable face in my hands and kiss her pliant, sperm-moist lips and tell her that she is wonderful, fucking wonderful, and wonder what in the name of all that's sacred am I doing, what have I done?

Chapter 17

T ORGELANANDA IS SOON up to his tricks, pulling another wild card out of his hat, determined on keeping us all together. Reconciled for the time being to my refusal to go back into the occult chamber and chase Beelzebub with him, he announces with a magnanimous air that we have reached important milestones in our spiritual development.

"You boys have distinguished yourselves," he tells us, "that is beyond question."

Gathering in his office above the country butcher shop, he in his oak rocker and us on the padded milkcans, the reverend takes from his iron safe a folder with a red ribbon around it Adjusting his spectacles, he unties the ribbon and opens the folder, saying to us, "you have earned these degrees and it's time to formally honor your achievements."

"Degrees?" I say, perplexed. "I don't follow. Degrees for what?"

"Jake Acree," he says with aplomb, "hereby, by the legal authority invested in me and the Church of the Center of Light, you are hereby deemed a Doctor of Divinity. And Evan Acree, so are you."

Torgie hands us each a parchment document imprinted with black and gold embossed letters, the import of his words – our full names, Doctor of Divinity, Center of Light Church and Seminary, a non-profit religious organization authorized by the state of

California, dated and notarized. Evan and I stare at this declaration, our mouths slightly agape, not knowing whether to guffaw or applaud. It is like a gift completely unasked for, not in the least desired, and never even discussed.

"Ah, reverend Sorenson," Evan says, face tinging red, "is this on the level?"

"Damn straight it's on the level," the reverend asserts, "you are now bonafide minsters in the work of God, with certain legal rights in the eyes of California. And here's the next one. This second degree appoints you two as the first ordained ministers of this Center of Light, other than me myself. You can now preach and teach and spread the holy message."

He slips the second document into my hands, which I regard in disbelief—

Jake Acree, Minister of Religious Science, Church of the Center Of Light, etc.

"That one's especially valuable," Torgie points out, "it gives you the legal privilege to conduct services anywhere and anytime just like Jesus' apostles, to counsel and marry people, and even to conduct services at their funerals. It's for serious business."

Shaking my head, I mutter to myself, "Good Lord."

Evan throws me a what-the-fuck look. I think he wants to hoot, but senses how important this is to our avuncular, beaming mentor. This presentation is out of nowhere, and had I known, I would have requested that he not formalize things in such a way. Although noble distinctions, these fancy titles are an attempt to bind us to the COL for the nebulous future, and I will not be bound.

Shifting on my stool, cogitating, I consider outright rejecting these honors. But Mr Sorenson proudly states, "and here's the icing on the cake! These credentials make your status clear to anyone who wonders by what authority you do your ceremonial acts, and don't worry, we're going to get formal frames under glass for all five designations."

"Come again? You're giving us five of these declarations? But why?"

Torgie, festooned in his tight black minister's outfit, hands us three more embossed parchments with notarized seal over his scrawled signature. Plain as day, these documents ballyhoo that we are master adepts to be reckoned with – Doctor of Metaphysical Science, Master of Occult Ceremonial Arts, and Advanced Practitioner of Ancient Yoga Knowledge. If words made reality, we've got it clinched. But if I have been looking for side-door to slide through, the wily reverend just made it complicated. There's a weird craziness about all this and it keeps getting deeper.

The big-bellied monk doesn't allow us to bask in the cockeyed light of these degrees, not that we know what to make of them. The next day, unlocking again his antique safe, wheezing in his spattered overalls and painter's cap, Torgie takes out a large manila envelope lumpy with paper-clipped contents and drops it on the desk beneath the scorched book shelves.

Fixing his luminous eyes on us, he confides, "this here is a secret project of the utmost importance. It's going to save tens of thousands of innocent lives."

From the envelope he slides out several more of the black and white photos of himself in religious garb, posing in stances before the camera's lens, punctuated by arrows of mind-bending captions:

"Supercharge your brain power and illuminate your dormant pineal gland! Learn to see in all directions simul-

taneously! 365 degree Omni-Vision!"

"Develop total global vision with ancient foolproof yoga techniques! Turn off the inferior cockpit radar, you will no longer need it!"

"It's tie to get down to business and develop your cosmic brain power! No more wasting your life-force in jacking off or other in-flight shenanigans!"

Aiyee, there, before my eyes, these deranged assertions and madcap photos! I am speechless. The barrel-shaped reverend accosts the reader with his stern stare, thrusting his blunt finger. These eye-poppers highlight thirty or so pages of rambling text, another bizarre pamphlet to be whipped into shape. "We have the opportunity here to bring these terrible airline crashes to an end," Torgie states as I scan the typed manifesto with an incredulous eye. "All we need to do is polish this up and see that it goes right to the top of the Federal Aviation Administration."

Nodding, half-mumbling to myself, I hand the pages over to my brother. Trying to smother his garbled snorts, Evan gapes at the ink drawings of airplanes falling out of the sky and blurts, "dude, wait, for real? This is for real? It seems like a twisted cartoon."

"No, not a cartoon," the reverend scoffs, "although I agree it's rough, it needs some finishing touches. That's why we're moving it to the front burner, the timing is critical."

Sorenson elaborates the details of this ambitious proposal to the FAA – a plan to train all of its passenger airline pilots in the metaphysical art of "360 Degree Omni-Vision," an advanced psychic technique that will enable their cockpit crews to envision the total airspace around their plane and for many miles out. According to the manifesto, this supernatural ability that can be activated by thought-power alone once one learns the esoteric secret. It will render current radar completely obsolete and make pilot error a thing of the past.

The pamphlet contains several drawings, done by a skilled hand, showing how pilot omni-vision works, emanating from the navigator's brain and radiating out around the aircraft in flight. While in fact, science fiction aside, is so preposterous that it renders me almost voiceless.

"Uhh, dig, reverend, how long does this special pilot training take to work? I mean, to reach the supernatural omni-vision state?"

"Not that long," he tells me confidently, holding up specific pages. "It takes about six months of intensive training, eight hours each day and in small classes. Everyone has to get full one-on-one teaching, we have to train all the licensed jet pilots. The FAA is in desperate need of this, we just have to make them aware of it. Once they sign off on this project and we get rolling, we're going to be fantastically busy."

"Riot on, if you say so," I mutter, perusing the pages. The manifesto goes on to explain that there will be three stages, Basic, Advanced, and Master Aviator's Grade, and for this work the US government will pay the Center of Light the cool, clean sum of $750,000 in cash.

"Reverend, three quarters of a million, are you serious? This training is all in the realm of speculation, there's no proof!"

"Speculation? No, bullshit, we will demonstrate the validity one hundred percent. And damned right, three quarters of a million and no paper money, only US Mint gold coins. Hell, man, that's chicken feed to them but that'll bankroll our operations world-wide!"

I squint at my brother, who looks somberly back at me, once

again on the lip of the rabbit hole. We have been involved with this bizarre monk and his crazy schemes for the past year and a half. This wiggy notion that the FAA is going to leap all over his crackpot scheme to train their pilots in cosmic clairvoyance and finance us to the tune of 750 grand in gold double eagles is too much. It's all I can do to keep the skeptical leer off my face.

"Mr Sorenson," I say in a wry voice, "what makes you think the FAA is going to entrust us with this kind of work? What are our actual qualifications? You say validate, but where's the evidence? I don't know about you, but I don't posses anything like 360 Degree Omni-Vision."

"Yeah," Evan puts in, "they'll just take us for a bunch of new-age weirdos. Who's gonna teach the pilots? Not me."

"Naw, you'll pick right up on the knack as you teach it, you'll see," Torgie counters, fishing a booger out of his nose. "Bear in mind, they're under tremendous pressure to solve their air crash problem. More passenger planes are in the air all the time and they could start dropping like flies. The existing radar technology is too flawed. When I was out of the body awhile back they showed me the whole dire situation."

"Showed you? Who showed you?"

"The Spirit. The spirit-guides showed me in a real-life vision. It was very clear-cut that the people in charge of the FAA would be open to a far-ranging solution of this kind."

Evan pushes his nose thoughtfully, shifting his eyes at me. Haven't we heard this stuff before? Yet there is no arguing with the reverend's skewered logic, always in favor of someone who can see something that others can't. But interpreted according to what criteria?

Out of respect, we agree to dig into the arduous line-by-line rewrite of the 360 Degree Omni-Vision project, so at least we won't feel embarrassed by the brochure. Reverend Sorenson is going to show this metaphysical proposal to anybody who will listen. But my intuition is already willing to bet on the outcome even if the FAA bothers to respond.

Meanwhile, my Tantric double life with Chiquita Cornsilk burns up the sheets at night in orgasmic lust. We scarcely need more than a swallow of wine and the scent and taste of each other. These wild indulgences are addicting, her beauteous wanton lips, her desirable ass bent over the plush arm of the couch. Shandy confesses her lurid secrets. It seems that the sullen father of her two brats was a swaggering member of Satan's Disciples who dealt methedrine on the side and spent his bread on chroming out his panhead chopper. He used to brag how he was gonna blow the heads off of hippie queers with a sawed-off 16 gauge. When she dared to complain, he used to whip her with his studded belt. The last time she saw this pendejo he told her to get her ass on welfare and warned her that he might show up at any time. If he ever found out that she was putting out for another dude there would be freaking hell to pay. None of this sounds too groovy to my refined ears, and I don't even ask her how she got involved with such a character. What is, is, people fuck up, personal karma has some weird twists. You've got to be ready to deal with whatever because whatever is hanging around. It won't be the first time I've kept a hickory baseball bat behind my front door.

The reality of being a fallen yogi, juggling volatile sexual energies, keeps me focused. It won't hurt to call in some extra metaphysical protection on this tricky scene. Shandy keeps asking how can she meditate and if I think she'll benefit from the practice. This usually happens after we've had wild, disheveling sex and she sobers up and starts to worry about her life. But I'm not selling her short, she might take to meditation, who knows?

Since I'm the one who's turned her on and flicked her switch, I need to lead her to the river.

I mention Shandy to the reverend Sorenson, describing her as my pleasant neighbor who has shown an interest in learning how to meditate. I broach the subject a bit nervously.

"By all means," Torgie says in a benign tone, "new faces are always welcome here. New people bring fresh energy and we need some new recruits for the work ahead."

"Hold on," Evan says. "You're bringing some chick you met to meditation?" He looks up from his book of the lives of Catholic saints, scrutinizing me. He knows me from way back.

"Yeah, no big deal," I reply nonchalantly. "She's a young mother with two little kids who's trying to improve her life. It might help her."

My brother grunts, wondering what kind of a secret life I might be living. He remembers my notorious pre-yoga history with chicks. I frown at him, then I ignore him.

"And the FAA proposal, Mr Sorenson? Anything happening?"

"I sent it off a few days ago by certified mail, soon as I got it back from the printer. You did a beautiful job on the remake, that's all it took to get the project off the ground."

"Well," I say with a poker face, "I guess we'll see sooner or later."

"You can bet your bottom dollar we'll be hearing from them," Torgie says confidently. "And if your lady friend can't find a baby-sitter tell her to bring her little ones with her. The younger you start learning meditation, the better."

The notion of bringing Shandy's irascible kids to our meditation meetings strikes me as absurd. Both kids are insanely rambunctious, the little girl actually the worst. They bicker violently, chasing each other with garden hoes around the yard, ignoring pleas to play nice. But I tell Sorenson that I'll bring Shandy over to the Center of Light, inwardly questioning my common sense. Am I trying to appease my muffled conscience or what?

Chiquita Cornsilk comes with me to the mid-week meditation, curious, self-conscious, and quite alluring to my consternation. She wants it to be known that she and I have something special going on, and she's put off by my aloofness. I don't prep her, I'm completely winging this deal. She's bewildered by the religious atmosphere and the Paramahansa readings and fidgets through the t meditation like she's got ants in her tight white pants. But she keeps up a pleasant demeanor and responds in enthusiastic ways to everyone.

"Is your family from the Atascadero area, dear?" Mrs Mallet slurs in her kindly tones.

"Oh no, it's just me and the kids up here," Shandy say, glancing at me for clues. "Mom lives down in south LA with a black jazz musician."

This spontaneous tidbit goes over like a lead balloon in the horseshoe chapel, even I'm surprised, even though she mentioned this to me before while we were drunk and naked.

"Well, you are welcome here," says reverend Torgie, glossing over the redneck shock. "Master's ashram was open to all four winds of culture and I hope you start coming and study with us."

"Oh yes, we surely do," Mrs Mallet chimes in, "we need new blood."

"I guess I could," Shandy says uncertainly, flicking her eyes at me, wondering how much the congenial reverend knows about out nocturnal secrets. I'm wondering that myself, just what kind of impressions is the aura-reading Torgelananda picking up on? Chewing my inner lip, I cast my glance at my brother.

Evan is ogling Shandy with a furtive but intense interest. He knows there's something between us, there's no doubt in his mind. But I can count on him to keep his brooding to himself, although it's clear she doesn't want to be here. She is here because of me, to tie us closer together. What ties us together is her honey-dripping vagina and wanton desire for my hard cock, why pretend otherwise? And I want to keep all of this separate, I don't want to mix it up it. What was I thinking in bringing her to the group meditation? Was I looking for some sort of absolution for fucking over my celibate vows? This scene is not for her – the saintly pictures, the ritual ceremony, the exotic chants, dejection is painted all over her pretty face.

"I didn't realized it would be so religious," Shandy murmurs s on the way home, her hand on my thigh, pressing her breast to my arm, giving me a feverish hardon.

"It doesn't have to be," I say, tasting my avid desire to fuck her. "Meditation can be about pure awareness, essence, it doesn't to be religious at all. That's the Zen approach."

"Then why do they make it that way, do you believe in all that stuff? And why did you act like we hardly know each other?"

That remark hits me right in the chest, I glance at her in com- plete candor. "To be honest, Shandy, I neither believe nor disbelieve it. I'm after the truth. I'm trying to find out what's real. And I'm sorry, I didn't mean to come across that way."

And indeed, why have we made it so elaborate? What is it about indescribable reality that frightens us? Why steep it in such religious trappings, which if anything obscures what we are seeking – true freedom. Freedom from the ego persona, for the domination of the incessant mind, from the illusion of "me, individual me, mine." All these verbal blessings and formulas and ritual prayers do not Reality make. Only pure awareness opens that door.

Shandy snuggles closer in the front seat of my yellow Lark, her cool shameless hand finding my hot and shameless cock. In a wistful voice, she says, "I guess I just need a little reassurance now and then, about what we're doing, you know?"

All right yes baby, oh yes praise Jesus, your shrill little kids are going to have to hang in with Marge in this marvelous moonlight, because I'm gonna reassure you. Shandy whispers in my ear, with a throaty murmur, unzips my pants and goes down on me with unabashed urgency to make her point. Aiyee, oh doctor, oh darling, my doctora, Doctor of Divinity where art thou?

On the weekend, Shandy follows me to Sunday meditation in her turquoise Ford, bringing her youngsters with her. Mrs Mallet, Sorenson, and my brother we are the only ones present at the service, the others apparently taking a break. Shandy sits there on her milk stool, looking at me with a sad expression, showing me she is willing if she must. But I don't insist, not at all, it's all too ridiculous. Her little urchins fidget and squirm and glare at me, identifying me as the target of their resentment. Am I not the bastard who has seduced their momma, into whose house she disappears bathed and excited for those secretive night hours? No, these children do not appreciate me and why should they? I can barely remember their names and outside of the occasional proffered chocolate bar, I show them little interest. They in fact hate me, it is quite clear, just as their violent and surly father would hate me. It's in their blood.

Behold, the two squirming brats make a wreck of the meditation service, taking a perverse delight in their antics. But no one wants to be where they don't want to be. Whispering embarrassed apologies, Shandy shoos them out and takes them home, casting me a forlorn glance. "See you later," I mouth to her silently.

What more can I do? I am cognizant of my rueful mistake in trying to bring her in and as Torgie has quipped in his jovial, wine-infused moods, "A stiff prick has no conscience." Ah, well. After we patch the meeting up with the reverend's benevolent prayers, Mrs Mallet comes over and pats me on the hand. "Be patient," she tells me, "I'm sure you and your lady friend are going to be fine. Kids like that need a firm and patient hand, spank them hard if you must and don't worry about what anyone else thinks – just do your own thing."

Egad, her words leave me in a state of shocked self-perception. My own thing? If I wanted a family to raise I would probably be with Dawn and blond-headed Tia, yes, blond, like my mother, but that once-fond notion has also gone off the tracks. Dawn doesn't write much these days, she's grown distant and hints of other plans. And I am good at ignoring what I don't want to hear.

Torgelananda pours me a pint jar of wine has something perceptive to say. "She's an interesting young woman. She aspires to be more than her karmic limitations have so far allowed. And she has her hands full with those two young ones, both of them are extremely jealous."

"Tell me something I don't know," I say with a wan smile. "But they're not mine."

"They'd probably get over that in time. But I have a suggestion, if you'll hear me out."

"Please, Mr Sorenson, I have no intention of getting married. But sure, lay it on me."

"Well, like we've talked, we need to expand our core ceremonial group with new people, fresh energy. And this new friend of yours is a perfect candidate, her aura is compatible and she's quite attached to you. So you should encourage her to meditate and bring her over here, get her involved in our work. I don't think that celibacy would bother her out much, maybe at first but then no, she'll follow your lead. And those wild kids, we can always arrange for a babysitter. We can form our new, secret power group, comprised this time of both men and women. Each of us needs his devoted female counterpart. That's how Jesus did it, like Levi describes in the Aquarian Gospel. Then in about six months we can all go back in the ceremonial circle and accomplish our real aims."

In amazement I squint at Sorenson, peering into the bald madness of his obsession. He believes, he believes in the crazed metaphysics of his plan for world control. He believes he can convert sex-crazed chicks like Chiquita Cornsilk into obedient yogini nuns, and with their reverent help throw Beelzebub and Lucifer into shackles. For sanity's sake it is all too ludicrous, but Torgie resolutely believes. There in nothing I can say, no coherent words come to mind. I just blink and nod once or twice, a twisted half-smile on my lips, and look away. One might just as well mix gasoline and water and throw a match.

Chapter 18

S EVERAL ODD INCIDENTS converge on the heels of one another like psychedelic cartwheels. Sometimes life is laughable, sometimes it is plainly cruel, sometimes it's a trick bag. We can get lucky on occasion and other times seem quite helpless. And one never knows, never really knows, never knows more than an intuitive flash of what's coming down next.

On my way home from work in San Luis Obispo I pass by the Center Of Light. The brooding Sorenson shows me, without much comment, an official-looking letter that he has received from the Federal Aviation Administration by certified mail. On US Government letterhead, we read:

Dear Rev. Sorenson, Center Of Light, Atascadero, California,

The FAA wants to thank you for your organization's interesting and thoughtful proposal to train American pilots in extrasensory perception "365° OmniVision" in order to eliminate airline disasters. We appreciate the time and effort that your team put into this ingenious training program.

However, after careful consideration, we must decline your offer to establish this course of training at the FAA headquarters in Washington, DC. Unfortunately, it's proposed cost is not in our congressional mandated budget and we are currently exploring other flight safety measures. The agency will keep your booklet and proposal letter on file for possible future review.

Sincerely, Robert Parker, Deputy Director, Federal Aviation Administration

"So," I quip in an undertone, "the bureaucratic dullards. There goes 750 grand out the window."

"Afraid that's about right," the reverend grunts "but at least we got their attention. We'll make another run at them after a few more plane crashes. Sooner or later these superior brain methods will force their hand."

"Right on, reverend, right on. We'll see what comes down the lost highway."

ON A COOL Autumn evening I take Shandy to visit my chiropractor friend in Arroyo Grande. This eccentric doctor of spinal-adjustment science, Delgado Sanchez, is one of my few friends on the remote central coast. We met by chance when he called into the dry cleaners to have someone pickup his old-fashioned suits, so I swung by in my van. He scrutinized me with keen interest, a man with a disciplined mind. When I delivered his clean serge suits a few days later, he invited me into his rear office for a cup of coffee. The coffee was strong and black, Mexican style, and in our convivial chat we hit on number of mutual philosophical interests. Sanchez had made a study of the Hindu Upanishads and Vedas as well as Rosicrucian metaphysics, and had rejected the Catholic version of reality as childish. He professed a strong interest in learning how to read auras in order to heal people, because healing was his chosen life's purpose.

A peculiar and witty character, Delgado and I shared a sardonic laugh about the meddling of government in every important area of human affairs from health treatment to food production, not forgetting the horrors of their eager war in Vietnam. Why do intelligent people even need such an insane government? People know what to do at heart and always act accordingly, they have no need of blustering overlords. I liked Doc Sanchez at once, a revolutionary Mexican-American who had deep respect of Jeffersonian principles and an instinctive loathing of authority. I told him about our esoteric work at the Center of Light and he seemed quite curious. But he was outright in his dismissal of celibacy as a means of accruing special personal power.

"No, my young friend," he says to me, peering through his brass-rim spectacles, "and I hope you will forgive my bluntness. But all that is nonsense, a total waste of your time. You might as well go chew hallucinatory plants like Carlos Castaneda did. And trying to give voluntary celibacy some special health or psychological benefits has no scientific credibility at all. In fact, just the opposite is true. Both men and women should have plenty of sex, it's healthy for the human body. That's a lot of hooey invented by deranged, lustful monks."

We hit it off together, Delgado and I, he was not not locked into rigid ideology. Sanchez allowed that the metaphysical practices might lead to an extraordinary outcome, and we had to intelligently experiment. Our early conversations took place before I fell off my yogic high horse and got swept up in the turbulence of tantra sex.

On another visit to his Arroyo Grande office, Sanchez takes me into a dim side room, switches on the light, and pulls a blue drape off a solid piece of equipment that stood about five feet high, similar an old movie projector with a side tray of various-hued glass lenses. The machine operates on electric current and the lenses slide in front of a light projector that generates rays of bright colors. This Light-Therapy Instrument, Sanchez murmurs in my ear, gained intense notoriety in the 1930's and 40's. It kills cancer and malignant diseases in the human body and was so successful in treatments that it drew the denunciation of the American medical establishment. You didn't have to be a licensed doctor to own or operate one, so a smear campaign was launched against these advanced machines, accusations of "quack and bogus" were hurled at the inventor. The federal government seized and destroyed hundreds of them so they would not fall into the hands of unscrupulous scam-artists. This particular machine, Delgado whispers, covering it back up, happens to be one of the last ones in existence. He swears me to absolute confidence.

To be honest, another intriguing thing about Sanchez is his young, flirtatious Mexican wife. Lupita is in her mid twenties, vivaciously pretty, about half his age, and speaks very little English. Delgado met her on one of his forays into old Mexico for native herbs, became enamored, romanced her, then married her in a traditional family ceremony and brought her home. But Lupita doesn't act traditional, she loves to flirt in provocative ways and can't seem to help herself. She is the reason the intellectual chiropractor takes such a dim view of any philosophy advocating sexual abstinence.

One foggy evening over dark run daiquiris, Nicaraguan cigars, and spirited conversation, Delgado and I become real comrades, feasting on Lupita's marinated goat tacos. She joins us in the fun in her short, flouncy skirt, made up like a ravishing teenager, and quickly downs a few glasses from the jug of burgundy I brought as a gift. She turns giddy, flushed, and starts to outrageously flirt with me in front of her husband. At first Delgado takes this with an indulgent shrug, he winks, then begins to glower. Ah me, no bueno, no bueno.

Half-drunk myself and all but licking my lips, I make light of her shameless behavior. "Ah what the hell," I say to Sanchez, "she is just enjoying herself. It's this home-made Rotta vino, it sneaks up on you in a hurry."

Knowing that I'm talking about her, this naughty mail-order bride flashes her dark eyes at me. Burying her giggling face in her hands, she rocks back on the couch in such a way that I am given a delicious glimpse of her sleek thighs and pink panties. Seething with displeasure, Delgado barks at his young wife. His voice carries such a charge of anger that Lupita jumps from the sofa and flees from the room, overcome with embarrassment.

"You act like that right in front of me," Sanchez shouts, "your husband? Like a shameless little puta, in the face of my new friend!"

Our cozy little party crashes and burns in a moment, the exuberant mood and high-flying talk shot to hell. Showing me glumly to the door, Delgado mutters, "I might have to take her back to Guadalajara if she doesn't shape up. She's a goddess in bed, but after only one or two drinks she becomes a social calamity."

"Don't be too hard on her," I say. "I bet she's under a lot of stress being so far from her family. That wine just hit her too fast, that's all it was."

"Ah, my friend, you are too kind. She flirts like a little whore, I have eyes. She all but threw her panties at you. Although I suspect that you have that affect on women – and isn't that strange, you being a celibate and all? If you would drop that pretentious nonsense you would be a prince in their world, yes, listen to me. Your moody aloofness drives them crazy."

"What, no, Delgado, come on, it's all just a momentary thing. In the morning it will be forgotten, it means nothing—"

"To me it does," Sanchez cuts me off. "I won't tolerate that in my wife, I am going to punish her. But I appreciate our unusual conversations, you have a brilliant mind. We have talk talk again but Lupita will be banished to the back room."

Feeling a drunken and lustful remorse, I say, "Ah comprendo, things between men and women get so complicated. It seems fucking impossible at times. But you'll still come up to Atascadero this Sunday for the meditation service?"

"Yes, I'll be there for the group meditation, you've piqued my curiosity. I want to meet this Yogananda disciple of yours, this mystical reverend Sorenson."

GOOD FOR HIS word, Delgado shows up at the Quonset hut on Sunday morning but alone, for which I feel a twinge of sensual loss. He pays total attention to everything, being an ardent student of Gnosticism. He is cordial with everyone, particularly with Mrs Mallet who asks him several questions about his holistic health practice. She complains of needling pains in her shins and ankles that wake her at night. Sanchez tells her to lie on her back and elevate her feet about 10 inches above her head for at least fifteen minutes per session.

"Put them up on firm rolled blankets," he advises in a kindly tone. "If you'll do this at least once a day you'll feel some relief. Do it before going to sleep, it should help. But if the pain still bothers you, come and see me and I'll treat the nerves involved."

After meditation, in Torgie's study, I mention to Delgado how similar his advice is to the Hatha yoga benefits of the inverted postures, reversing the gravity effects to induce a therapeutic blood flow.

Listening with a quizzical expression, Delgado says, "yes, I think you are right on that point. Using gravity to alleviate the pressure on the extremities, the replenishment of oxygen to the feet and ankles, that can make a big difference in how one feels. And what are we without a feeling-good body?"

"Without a feeling-good body we are usually in a bad mood," I laugh.

The four of us, my brother and I, Sorenson and Sanchez, are gathered together sipping the reverend's ceremonial wine. For Sanchez, a rather small wiry man, it's almost like a sparring session with the burly reverend. He's not a stranger to metaphysics and in the end Delgado bluntly tells Sorenson, "with due respect to your devotion, sir, and to your noble teacher Yogananda, I'm afraid we will always disagree on the value of celibacy. As I've said to Jake, I consider that little more than religious hogwash. The voluntary practice of sexual abstinence is a mistake based on brainwashed superstitions It can cause serious disruption of a person's psychological health and even lead to moral insanity. There have been many insane monks who have done untold harm to others, especially children. No, reverend Sorenson, celibacy is a sham invented by psychopathic priests to make people feel guilty about their natural urges and bilk them out of money. That's all."

I break into an involuntary snort of laughter at this bold and astonishing statement, it seems that Sanchez is taunting the reverend with these barbed words. Torgie seems taken aback, one of the few times I've ever seen him at a loss. "Well, doc Sanchez," he manage to say, "I hope you'll stay open-minded to give me a chance to expand your point-of-view."

"No," Delgado leers, having scored his coup, "on that muddled point you shouldn't get your hopes up. But I do agree that an hour or so a day of meditation is beneficial for out mental health, just as orgasms are vital for our physiological happiness. May I suggest that you try it sometime? A good roll in the hay won't hurt anyone at all and the sky won't fall in."

Torgie goes beet-faced and turns away. Sanchez says to me, "I would like to come here and meditate with you on occasion, I appreciate the peaceful vibrations, Jake. And I confess to being interested in this mentor of yours – what's his name, Gurdjieff? His ideas on human development are intriguing to say the least. I'm going to do some library research on his teachings."

"Gurdjieff," I say, swallowing my amusement. "Yeah, he and Ouspensky put out some some amazing books, The All And Everything, In Search Of The Miraculous, incredible stuff. And Delgado, feel free to come here and meditate with us anytime. Bring Lupita too, she might benefit."

"Oh no," Sanchez laughs softly, "she has no interest at all in mystical subjects. I tried to teach her some visualization exercises but it was a no-go. She just falls asleep. She'd much rather look at soap operas and snack on pastries, I'm afraid she's going to get fat and lazy like her mother."

I walk my friend down to his car, a blue Nash Rambler, and mention that I now have a pretty new girlfriend. At once he's intensely interested, his carnal antenna goes right up. He insists that I bring Shandy down for an evening of wine and fun with he and his wife at their south county pad.

"So, you're coming around?" he needles me. "Well, I'm dying to meet this sultry wench who's tempted you away from that apple cart of pretentious nonsense."

Laughing nervously, saying that I will, I see him off with a wave, noting the Luciferian gleam off his forehead. Back upstairs, Torgie, still in his formal minister's outfit, says to me, "He's an unusual individual, quite magnetic. Unfortunately he's got his facts all twisted up. If he'd ever stop dribbling his power out the end of his pecker he'd become a great leader. As it is though, he's a metaphysical wiseacre. But keep bringing him back here for group meditations, we've got to entice him onto the higher path."

"I'm not so sure he's at all that interested," I reply in my apostate voice, shrugging. I suspect that the reverend is addressing me as much as Sanchez. Assuming my best poker face, I say, "he's into his own thing and he's got a young and sexy Latina wife."

"Don't give up on it," Torgie says, not looking at me, looking at one of his scribbled notebooks, "there's too much at stake. Always remember what's at stake."

ACTING ON DELGADO'S invitation, I take Shandy and a jug of red shoe-leather wine down to Arroyo Grande, on one of those evenings when fog hangs in the ghostly Eucalyptus trees. Doc Sanchez sees at once that this come-hither young woman would fail miserably as my Platonic companion, he all but smirks in my face And to be honest, I have never understood how one can just be friends with an alluring woman and not want to fuck her. That seems like such idealized nonsense, or what?

The evening gets off to a beautiful start. We are all soon feeling exuberant, quaffing the d north county burgundy and snacking on carne asada fajitas drowned in Serrano sauce. Lupita is a fabulous Mexican cook, that is beyond petite. Delgado boosts our mood by bringing forth a bottle of aged Spanish brandy, pouring shots into little green glasses. Lupita puts on some hot

Latin dance music and begins to shimmy around in her short flimsy skirt, one hot little number. At first Delgado seems pleased by this sensual display, smiling ear to ear, but then sensing that her performance is not really for his benefit, he begins to glower With an air of abandonment, Lupita pulls me into a thigh-joined salsa, her parted lips making her interest much too obvious. My head is swimming, it's only a game, I laugh and go with the flow. To refuse her would be rude, to stop and ask permission seems ridiculous. Sanchez himself has gotten us all so wildly drunk, go with it, don't throw shadows on the celebration.

But all at once Delgado and his hot-blooded wife are in a furious argument. Malicious words singe the air, Mexicano slang, denunciations. He shouts at her to stop acting like a barroom slut, she retorts in broken English that if he would pay attention in their bedroom maybe she wouldn't, he is always lost in his books! Tossing her glossy black hair, flashing her eyes, mumbling apologies to us, she snaps off the hi-fi and rushes from the room in a haughty pout, slamming a door!

"That damned little mujer is driving me crazy," Sanchez fumes, "she is tormenting me, she knows what she's doing! I'm afraid I must ask you both to leave, please take your things, that wine too. I apologize for all this chaos."

Muttering confused, self-conscious words, as Shandy tries to sooth him, Delgado shows us to the door. "Take care and drive safely," he counsels, his morose face hanging in the lamplight, "we are all quite devilishly drunk."

Back in my Studebaker, as I fumble with the key and push-button ignition, giggling, Shandy fishes a joint out of her purse and fires it up. She puts it to my lips, ah yes, the night is young, porque no, let's not wag that finger. "Hmm," she says in my ear, "I think I'm feeling kind of jealous. That little Mexican tart has the hots for you. No wonder he's pissed."

Laughing together, we roll onto 101 and head north, there's fog all the way, my headlights dance in the ghostly haze, thirty five miles to make it home, not many cars on the road. We turn on the radio and groove, slap in a 8-track, Creadence Clearwater, flamboyant rock and roll. It's marvelous to be alive in this moment with this beautiful girl in this glittering mystery of night.

We lumber up the long Cuesta Grade in my little Lark, I have blown the engine of a Ford Falcon on this steep hill, I laugh, I pray that we make it. We veer off 101 at the lonely Santa Margarita exit and take the old road into Atascadero, mindlessly high and happy, meandering through the fields and trees of the sleepy countryside.

And I am so witty tonight, oh I am a clever dude, I have Shandy giggling in stitches. But there seems to be something amiss with my headlights, I can't quite tell if they're on or not. Flicking my light switch, I try to see if this anomaly is in the car's electrical circuits or in my brain. Coming over the wooded rise near the mental hospital shrouded in darkness off to our right, swept away in admiration, my darling girlfriend slides into my lap and starts giving me a knock-out blowjob and it's all I can do to stay on the pavement.

Stroking her adorable head, murmuring my appreciation, I glance in the rearview. There seems to be something back there, shadowing us. There are no street lamps on this lonesome stretch of road, and I am the only car. Are my eyes playing tricks on me? Then to my sudden horror the red piercing lights flash behind me – Aiyee oh fuck, oh fuck, fuck me, the heat, the cops, a cop cruiser tweaks its siren!

"Shandy, baby, stop, no more," I gasp, "there's a cop right on our bumper, ayy fuck, this could be bad!"

"Huh, what," she mumbles, lifting her pleasure-dazed face as I tug on her hair. Her eyes are like jade, her lipstick smeared, glistening, her blouse unbuttoned, her luscious round breasts, she is so fucking desirable.

"Cops," I croak, swallowing my drool, "must be highway patrol, right behind us."

"Oh no, oh please god no," she whimpers, scrunching up in the seat, trying to button back up. She leaves me unzipped and exposed with a huge, oozing hardon.

Since I'm the only other vehicle on this gloaming road, I can't feign ignorance. I steer onto the shoulder with my left hand, trying to tuck away my cock with my right hand, but about halfway the zipper gets stuck.

"Okay sweetheart," I mutter, stuffing my tumescent tool into my pants, "I'm getting out and talk to them. Be cool, be hip, if they ask you anything just say you were taking a nap."

As usual, my mind in a crisis is moving at light speed although I'm winging it. I step out of the car with my hands in a neutral position, squinting back into the harsh cruiser spotlight.

"Stand where you are please," a voice says, and two cops come silhouetted into view, one on either side of my car. They move warily, but with guns holstered. One carries a large flashlight that he shines into the backseat, then into the front seat, illuminating Chiquita's worried face. She looks illicitly sexy and disheveled.

"You can stand at ease, sir," the trooper says, "we can see that you and your lady here are peaceful. But we need to ask you a few questions."

"Yes sir, I am a man of peace. In fact, I'm a minister of the Center of Light right down the road a ways. You really surprised me because I don't think I was speeding, was I?" The words come out on the slurry edge, but articulate. In my mind's eye flashes the guilty roach in the ashtray, ayy no, Jesus help me, my probation officer's face leers in my back-brain.

"Well no, you weren't speeding," the other cop replies. "But a few miles back there we observed you flashing your headlights on and off, so we followed you. We couldn't help but notice that you folks were having a little party and you were weaving a bit."

"Yeah, that's true," I admit with a sheepish grin. "We were getting carried a way, see, we just got engaged. The good thing is that it's only about a mile and we'll be home."

"Uh huh, all right then. You mind showing us some I.D?"

"No sir, not at all," I say, pinned in the flashlight's beam. I reach into my hip pocket and pull out my wallet, but something goes wrong. As I'm bringing it up into the light the wallet flips out of my hand, somersaulting into the air, its two halves flaring open like blunt wings. It reaches an apex at head level, then falls with a thunk onto the hood of the car. We stare at this inexplicable phenomena, the wallet laying there as though opened and placed by my own fingers. Shandy breaks into giggle, burying her face in her hands on the other side of the windshield. The two troopers slide there eyes at each other, then back at the wallet, the one probing it with his inquiring flashlight.

"Damn, whatever that was," I grimace, "it was one in a million. But anyway, look, it's open right at my driver's license and here's my minister's card too."

Extracting these two items, I hand them over to the officer who's been asking the questions, they scrutinize the cards under the flashlight. "Oh Lord please," I beg under my breath, "I could really use a little slack here. This would look real bad on my probation report."

After a few plaintive heartbeats, the boss cop says, "all right, Mr Acree, this is all in order and we've noted that both your headlights and your taillights are working fine."

"Well that's good, good to to know," I say, staring at him with my mouth agape. "It's always good to be on the safe side."

Almost smiling, he says, "we're going to ask that you drive directly on home now. I'm sure you'll agree that would be in the best interests of everybody."

He hands me my license and minister card back with a wry squint. "Well hallelujah man," I almost blurt, but instead say, "yeah you're right, yes sir, that's what we're going to do. We're heading right on home, it's just a hop and a skip down the road and thanks, thanks a ton."

Both of them wish us a good night, then walk away in their tall boots to their cruiser. I slide into the front seat, muttering, "holy fuck, they're giving me a pass, can you believe it, they're letting us go, incredible, incredible."

"Oh you are so lucky," Shandy says, scooting in close to me. "You're eyes are so red, in that flashlight you looked really bizarre. I thought we were busted for sure."

Pulling off the gravel shoulder and back onto the road, I keep my eyes glued to the rearview. I'm still spooked, leery that it might be a trap, that the amused cops might change their mind and swoop in for the kill, slamming me with a DWI. I've never met such nice cops before. But no, as I drive away, they turn off their flashers and make a U-turn, heading back down the road to their hidey-hole. Their fender spotlight is still on, making a crazy swath across the dark fields.

We drive on home, Chiquita and me, insanely happy in our wild good luck, her hand caressing me, my hand squeezing her lush mini-skirted thigh. Route 101 is off to our left in the night, the noise of semis booming along. We cruise past the darkened Center of Light at a modest speed, thrilled with our apparent immortality, hang a right at the lone town stoplight and a few more blocks to our duplex in the oaks. We sneak into my side, put on Janis and her marvelous voice, guzzle a glass of shoe-leather burgundy, then peel off our clothes and make ravenous, insatiable love. Things are not what they seem as far as I know, nor have they ever been. I don't know why this chick affects me the way she does, but she does, oh she does, yes she does.

And in the morning I awake with a euphoric hangover and a splitting ache in my lower left jaw. I am 23 years old and have never had a toothache in my life, not so much as a cavity. As a young boy I used to blithely crunch ice cubes to bits, my teeth are indestructible. It's been at least seven years since I've even visited a dentist, loathing their metallic probings and bright obnoxious lights, But this is different. This pain is more than enough to cross my eyes and drive me to the phone booth.

Chapter 19

THE PAIN IN my jaw does not slacken or go away like I first hoped. The pain is so intense that it's impossible to think. I distrust dentists just as much as I do regular doctors – through their national political clout they promote all kinds of horrible shit detrimental to our natural health. Fluoride in drinking water rots the brain, lethal mercury fillings leaking in your teeth, insidious Nazi toot canals, no way man. When I learned of the dangers of fluoride a few years back while smoking a fat joint, I threw away the toothpaste and began using baking soda and hydrogen peroxide. I've never had teeth problems of any kind but now I'm spurred to an unknown dentist by this monstrous agony.

The local dentist gives me an examination, probing my ravaged jaw, x-rays my mouth, then writes me a prescription for penicillin and codeine. "I'm sending you to an oral surgeon in San Luis Obispo," he says. "What you've got in there causing the problem is an impacted wisdom tooth. Soon as the swelling subsides and the pain goes down go see him, and don't put it off that molar is only going to get much worse."

Egad, an oral surgeon? What hellish karma is this? I who chewed ice cubes and gnawed on rib bones with nary a chip. But I realize I have to cooperate and a few days later I drive down the long hill into SLO, dreading to know I know not what.

"Ah indeed, my, my," says the mordant white-smocked doctor with his German accent, studying his own x-rays of my jaw with peculiar satisfaction. "That's a real doozy, I have no choice but to cut it out. We need to operate soon or it's going to infect your entire jaw."

Aghast, I listen as he describes the grisly procedure, although he blithely assures me not too worry. The operation isn't that big of a deal.

"Why do you say that, doctor? It sounds fucking awful."

"No, hah, well maybe a little, it can get a bit bloody," he admits. "I have to cut away the gum in order to grind the roots of that bad molar out of the jawbone itself."

"Good God, man," I plead, "is there no other way?"

"No, not really, I'm afraid not," he muses, eyeballing me with clinical interest. "But you won't feel a thing, not even a speck of pain."

"Nothing at all? Are you sure?"

"Quite sure, yes. I'm going to give you a sedative first that will completely block all pain. This procedure will take about an hour unless we have complications, but you will sleep like a baby."

"Doctor, I prefer not to lose consciousness. Is there a way to do it without knocking me out?"

"Ah, actually, in that case, I give you a special solution that will allow you to remain alert through the operation but you'll feel absolutely nothing. How would that be?"

"Perfect, yes, perfect, that's the ticket," I reply, experiencing a morbid curiosity as to what it will be like. I have never had any kind of operation in my life, never suffered even a broken bone through my rambunctious childhood and passion for motorcycles. How weird will it be?

When the dreaded appointment comes Chiquita Cornsilk drives me down 101 into SLO in her '54 Ford wagon. She's in a bright and cheerful mood. She tells me that after the operation, when I'm feeling better, she has a surprise for me. She wants to show me a little ranch that's for rent in the country, an old tree-shaded house with a corral and barn, even a friendly horse.

"A horse," I say, distracted, "how do you know it's friendly? I've been thrown off horses, they can be dangerous, believe me."

"No, not this one, you can tell right away this one likes people," Shandy says, "and I think this place would be perfect for us. The house is old-fashioned but it's got a nice kitchen where I can bake. And there are enough rooms so everybody gets some privacy, plus an upstairs bedroom for us with a window that opens right into the oak limbs. There's a least ten acres out there, trees and fields, it's really super-neat."

Pretty much doped up from the painkillers I've been taking, I mumble my no-hassle assent. "Okay babe, sounds cool. Only let's see how I feel after this ordeal, okay? But yeah, we'll go out there and look around, I want to see it."

In the reclining dentist's chair, a nurse in a green smock prepares me. I haven't seen the brusque oral surgeon yet, he's presumably off in another sound-proof room torturing somebody. This stoic nurse is busy securing my arms and legs with straps to the chair.

"Is that necessary?" I protest. "I mean, it's not like I'm going to leap up and run away."

"Oh of course not I know," she placates. "This is just to prevent any random unconscious movements during surgery. It's a fairly complicated procedure."

"Well, dig, it's not like I won't be aware of what's going on, and I realize this sore tooth has to come out."

"I hardly think that will be the case," she says blandly. "But we're going to make sure you don't feel a thing."

Before I can ask her what she means by that, or even blink, she inserts a needle device into the crook of my elbow and begins infusing a vial of clear fluid into my bloodstream. "What's that stuff?" I mutter in revulsion.

"Sodium Pentathol, back in world war two it was called 'truth serum' because people being interrogated would always tell the truth under its influence. But it's also one of the greatest pain-killers going. You won't feel anything."

"But I thought the doctor said he was going to give me some kind of oral solution? I detest needles, ever since one bent off in my arm when I was getting vaccinated. Damn."

"Not too worry, not today, tisk tisk. This IV will go right to your brain like a light switch."

"Huh? I don't get it, like a light switch? Is it hallucinogenic? Maybe you should know, I've had thousands of mikes of pure acid flood through my cerebellum, not recently, but before."

"How very peculiar," she murmurs, not really paying attention to me, instead peering at the now emptied vial inserted in my arm. "Don't you feel any unusual sensations?"

"No, nothing at all," I tell her confidently. "As I was saying, I'm fairly experienced in psychoactive chemicals."

"How unusual," she says, studying my eyes. "Don't you feel more relaxed?"

"Yeah, I do feel pretty relaxed, but lucid. . . just like he prom-ised."

"Okay, well, just a moment. I'm going to go consult the doc-tor. Be right back."

There's an odd metallic ringing in my eardrums, but no visual effects at all. I can hear the dentist's accented voice out in the corridor. She returns almost immediately, with plump, pale cheeks and curious brown squirrel eyes.

"He says to give you a tad more," she says, "apparently you

have a strong resistance."

"Yeah, that's usually been the case with me, stronger dose, no problem," I murmur, watching her install another creepy transfusion into my arm. I watch as she watches, the transparent fluid being pushed by her thumb into my vein. Hollow seconds tick by, it's at the halfway mark.

"Still feel nothing?" the nurse asks warily, peering at my eyes.

"Umm no, not really, what am I supposed to feel?"

And at that instant all the light in my head winks out. Heavy black shutters drop behind my eyes, thought flickers out, extinguished, utterly soundless, bottomless oblivion ensues.

There is no sensation of time, although at some vague pint I become aware that something is urging me toward the surface. I hear anxious women's voices and I recognize Shandy's sweet voice, speaking down a long tunnel to me.

"Jake, Jake honey," she says, flustered and worried, "can you hear me? Please talk to me."

"Sure I hear you," I smile, or I think I smile, opening my peepers, her face flickers into view, her jade-green eyes looking down into mine. "What's happening?"

"Oh, he's back, he's back," she cries in sudden relief. "Oh wow, I was so worried."

"Of course I'm back," I say, sitting up in the chair, no longer strapped down or hooked up. "What the hell happened? How long was I out?"

"Oh a long time, sweetheart, way too long."

The weird nurse nudges Shandy aside, coming in close, checking my pulse and my eyes. "Oh my, Mr Acree, you gave us quite a fright. You've been under for two hours, we couldn't bring you around. We were on the verge of calling an ambulance. How do you feel?"

"Hmm, like there's bright open spaces up in my head, but a least I'm awake." Gingerly touching the tender lump in my lower jaw, I say, "where is that doctor? I want to talk to him."

The nurse glances at another nurse in the doorway, whose face is knit with concern. Shaking her head, she says, "I'm afraid he's not in the building right now, he went to lunch."

"That lying bastard," I grimace, getting to my feet, a trifle woozy, "he lied to me about the sedative. Why didn't he just tell me the real deal?"

"Oh, Mr Acree, now please, take it easy," the nurse soothes. "The operation was a complete success, the bad tooth is gone for good."

Waving them off, with Shandy's help, I walk out to the Turquoise Ford brooding with satisfaction. The Machiavellian dentist must be made to pay for his outrageous deception. As my eyes focus, I stare at the brochure the nurse gave me, detailing the side-effects of the "medication" they pumped into my bloodstream.

"Oh my god," Chiquita tells me, "I was scared too, Jake. You were totally out of it, you wouldn't wake up. They we're ready to freak out. That head nurse was about to dial an ambulance and send you to the ER."

"Funny, but not funny," I muse, trying to make sense of the pamphlet. "That doctor lied to me about this sodium pentathol. He said I would be completely lucid through the whole procedure. Then she had to give me an extra dose, due to my tolerance levels. Did he actually leave before I came around or was that just another story?"

"No, he left the building, I was kind of shocked. He just up and split, saying you were a difficult patient but that you'd come out of it sooner or later. To be honest, he gives me the creeps. He sounds a little like that awful man Henry Kissinger."

"What an asshole," I say, feeling thirsty. "I think I'll screw him on the balance of the bill, fuck him. Why does someone like that lie to his clients? Why not just say what is?"

My eyes focus in on the blurry brochure. It cautions me about the ungroovy withdrawal symptoms from the codeine I've been taking, and warns me about the weird side-effects of sodium pentathol. In certain doses it makes people babble freely about things they would normally censor. Hence the reputation of a "truth serum" which the droll nurse had mentioned. In stronger doses it's a heavy-duty knock-out potion, eclipsing consciousness and all sensory input to the brain. But it's also known as an "amnesic cocktail" because for several days after transfusion the patient tends to forget what he has been doing or saying for many hours at a time. Some truly bizarre CIA shit.

"Listen, Shandy, honey," I say, "this drug they shot me up with? It can make me act really strange for awhile. So please, if I seem off-kilter, try not to take it the wrong way."

"Oh don't you worry, sweetheart," she says, driving, throwing me a smile. "I'm taking care of you now. We're gonna be super-good together."

"Super-good? You honestly believe that?"

"Yep, like bees and honey, you'll see. And like you say, don't sweat the small stuff."

We stop and have a late lunch in Santa Margarita, a chicken salad sandwich and iced tea, at the Rainbow Hut. My thoughts are clearing, Shandy persuades me into let her take me to see the pretty farm house she has found. She's excited, my adorable girl, she's glowing with anticipation. "Okay, sounds good," I smile, going with the flow. "I'm not ready to go home yet anyway."

The place is on the far westside of Atascadero, well past the mirage of 101, set back in clustered oaks and a peach orchard. The plain wooden house is rustic, but has its charm. There's some pasture out back, a small barn, and even a corral. Shandy leads me around, she prattles on about how happy we will be here as my heart contracts into a mute cloud of foreboding.

There is a horse, a large sorrel horse in the corral. The horse comes right over to us, quite curious, ears perked, maybe hoping for an apple. Its long nose slopes toward my austere face.

"He's so friendly," Shandy laughs, "the owner says he can stay and live in the barn if we don't mind. It might be cool. I'd love for the kids to learn to ride. Do you know how to ride?"

"Yes. I learned up in Montana when I was thirteen. A horse almost killed me one day running down the mountain and slamming me into the side of a barn. But I've always loved horses."

"Are you all right, Jake? You sound kind of funny."

A ominous sense of being trapped engulfs me, congealing in my chest. A deep inward stare, what am I doing? The horse stares at me, flicking one ear, look into the horse's soulful brown eyes.

"Have you lost your mind?" the horse says to me. "It will never ever work out."

"I honestly don't know," I murmur, "maybe I have lost it, it's confusing. It wasn't my intention to get so entangled."

"What?" Shandy wants to know, pressing against me. "What did you say, I don't get it?"

She usually gives me a monumental hardon, the feel of her, but I don't have one now. I feel like a seashell with energy wafting through me. I feel rather like daylight itself. I look at her with a gentle half-smile, words forming but still unspoken on my lips.

"You need to tell her like it is," the horse nudges me, bobbing its noble head. "She dreams of you being her husband. Better to set it straight."

"That's complicated," I say, looking into the horse's intelligent face. The animal snorts brusquely and swishes its tail.

"Don't be afraid," the horse says to me.

"Yeah, time to get real," I say, nodding, "and you know what's weird? I wasn't clear about this until this very moment."

"Clear on what?" Shandy demands, pulling away from me, giving me a perplexed look. "Are you trying to make a joke or what?"

"Shandy, no, I'm not... But listen, I need to tell you something."

"Well, you're starting to really freak me out."

"No, I don't mean to. But I just realized I can't do this with you, this family farm scene. I'm not ready."

"What's the matter?" she demands, her beautiful eyes tearing up. "Oh my god, what are you saying? How can you do this to us, Jake, after all this?"

The horse drops its head, snorts, turns and walks away, swishing it's long tail. "Shandy, honey, I'm sorry. I don't mean to hurt you but I'm just not ready. I thought maybe I was, but I'm not."

"Oh please, please tell me you're just trying to be funny. It's that crazy drug they gave you, this isn't you!"

"I would never joke about this. I'm telling you the way it is."

She gives me an accusing look, a stricken look, a look I've never wanted to see on her face. Breaking away, she sobs "oh you bastard," and runs to her turquoise car, jumps in, slams it into reverse and throws dirt and gravel turning around. She disappears down the road like a woman with her life on fire, my darling, my Chiquita Cornsilk. I stand there blinking in the dust, tasting ashes, as something like a rock sinks in my chest.

After a moment, I take a ragged breath. The horse swivels its head and looks at me. "There you have it, man," I say, noting the dull thud of my heart, "I guess it's my day to walk."

THE TRUTH IS what it is, no promises had been given. No, I'm not ready or willing to shoehorn myself into a mundane domestic scene. If I were ready and willing, I'd first try it with Dawn and baby Tia. But those wistful ideas have fallen on stony ground. Over the past months of other-worldly existence at the Center of Light our letters became less frequent, our cross-country phone calls put on hiatus. The whole emotional vibe changed when Shandy entered the picture. Dawn wrote, saying she had met a man that she appreciated and who seemed to really appreciate her and the children. This guy wanted them all to live together in his house. Naturally, I read this news with a wince. The other shoe had finally hit the floor.

Dawn asked me what I thought about this idea, saying that sh needed to make some decisions about her future. To me, there is nothing more nebulous than *the future,* but I knew where she was coming from. I thought it over, feeling strangely liberated. We were a long ways from our wild psychedelic romance. I wrote back, encouraging that she should do what she felt best, and thanking her for being who she is. My own life was still so unusual in many ways – yes, unusual, abnormal – and no matter how you slice it facts are the facts. I was not ready to play husband or father. I promised that I'd keep sending some money back for her and Tia as I was able. It's been almost three years since I've laid eyes on Dawn, and I have never even met Tia. Time flies and one thing is certain, it takes you to some pretty strange places.

After the incident with the prescient horse, Shandy vanishes from my view like a mirage of eroticism. In the subsequent days of amnesiac shadows caused by the insidious truth serum, she moves out of the next door duplex without so much a murmured good-bye. She was gone before I even knew it.

And as my head clears, that becomes the lop-eyed mystery.— Gone where? No one knows. Her friend Marge, who regards me now like an odious pariah, will only say that she left town and doesn't know to where. Frustrated, I ask around of people who seemed to know her, the butcher, the local market, the gas-pump operator, but nobody has seen Chiquita Cornsilk anywhere around. It's as if she has slipped off the face of the earth.

Over at reverend Sorenson's Quonset hut I own up to my bewilderment, as he listens with an thoughtful air. After a minute, Torgie says, "that is odd, her to have disappeared like that. She was over here for the meditation service just last Wednesday evening."

"Shandy? Shandy came here to meditate?"

"Sure did, she just showed up out of the blue. I think she was hoping to find you here. She told your brother that you two had had a falling out, she seemed pretty distraught by it. Afterwards, Evan took her down to the diner for some blueberry pie."

"Yeah, that's what happened," I mutter dejectedly. "I had to come clean with her, Mr Sorenson. I told her that I couldn't set up house with her and those kids, that I have other priorities. I guess it blew her away, although I tried to be gentle."

"Uh huh, I see, that makes sense. She was definitely blaming you for something. But that's what happens when the blood runs hot, those situations blow up just as quickly as they start."

"Huh, I suppose so, reverend, But I would really like to know that she's all right."

"Well, while you're investigating," Torgie replies, "see if you can solve a puzzle for me. I haven't seen your brother in over three days. Last time we spoke he was going down to LA with you to visit friends, but that obviously was a story. Do you have any idea where he might be?"

"Hell, I don't have a clue. Man, that is weird. I haven't seen him since before my tooth operation, But I'll check around, I'll ask our cousin down in SLO if he's been around."

"All right, I appreciate that. I have to admit I'm a bit mystified. It's really unlike him to fib. And please come back over and meditate with us, we've been missing you."

"All right, reverend, I'll do that," I say, "and I'll keep you in the loop, don't worry."

I RETURN TO my laundry service job, the bizarre absent-mindedness clearing from my head. I run my truck routes up and down the coastal communities and in the evenings I search for some sign of her, and now Evan, too. I consider the possibility of them disappearing together but dismiss it. Although Evan had the mournful eyes of a lustful celibate for Shandy, there's no way he could stand her scatter-brained ways and feral kids, nor had she shown the slightest interest in him other than to say he seemed like a sweet guy. No, to be real, my brother finally flipped out over the restrictions of living with the mad imposing monk and flew the coop. My own bold defection had brought things to a breaking point. Evan probably hopped on a Greyhound bus to Los Angeles, where he's holed up with some of our bohemian friends. He might even be sucking on a Moroccan hooka right now, quien sabe?

No, the real question for me is how this girl has vanished into thin air? I feel a little miserable about the way I broke with her, but I only spoke the plain truth. The last thing I wanted to do was hurt her, she had already been hurt enough. But how strange things turn out, that by being honest you bring pain to another. Is this always the fruit of pure, magical, spontaneous sex?

My restless search for Shandy leads me back out to the romantic farmhouse, the scene of the crime. The horse is gone, my long-nosed friend, but to my alarm someone else is there. Three motorcycles are in the dirt yard, two bad-ass Harley choppers and an older BMW. A scruffy dude in mechanic's overalls is working on the Beamer, kneeling in the dirt. I park my yellow Studebaker, then saunter over and put a question to him.

"I wouldn't know about that," he says, without looking at me. "I think the guy you want to talk to is inside. Hey, you know anything about the timing on these goddamned kraut bikes? I can't keep this fucker running."

"No, not a thing, sorry," I say, "I always rode British."

The dude grunts, glances up at me, nods toward the house. I walk up onto the porch and knock, wondering who's inside and what he knows. Shandy told me more than once that her ex-husband was an outlaw and mean-tempered biker.

I knock again, an irate voice calls out, "it ain't locked!"

Going warily inside, I walk through the kitchen and into the front room. A fat hairy man in torn jeans is disappearing up the stairs. Another man, wiry and and shirtless, sporting a few prison tattoos, squints at me from the couch. A 30-30 lever-action carbine and a double-barreled shotgun lean against the wall next to him. The guns put me on edge at once. He's probably a speed and crank dealer living day and night on the fumes of raw paranoia, I've seen it all before.

"Huh, I thought you was someone else," the man says in an suspicious tone. "Do you have some reason for being here?"

"Yeah, actually I do. I'm looking for a girl who's turned up missing," I say evenly. "Chick by the name of Shandy. She drives an old turquoise Ford and has two young kids. She was interested in renting this place, that's why I'm here. Any chance you've seen her around?"

The skinny doper blinks, a quizzical sneer forming on one side of his face. "Well, who's asking? You her brother or old man or what?"

"No, man, I'm just a friend. She's got friends in town and were all a little concerned where she up and went."

"Okay, I got it," he sniffs, pursing his lips. He relights a joint with his Zippo, offering me a hit. "No, not right now," I shake my head, "thanks anyway."

"You some kind of cop?"

"No, fuck no, hah. Like I say, I'm just a friend trying to find her."

The tweaker hits the roach hard, turning it into a burning ember. Exhaling, he hacks out his distrust. "Yeah, alright," he mutters, sliding his glassy eyes at me. "Yeah, she was out here for awhile, her and those brats. A real honey, but sad, a sad-faced one, and never would sit still, you know? I thought she was gonna move in here with us. I told her she could stay for free, with free dope if she'd take care of the house and she was tempted. But then that religious freak showed up and started preaching to her, blah blah, talking his shit. It seemed like it was his mission to rescue her from herself."

"What religious freak?"

"The vegetarian-type dude. Bragged about living on carrots and whatnot, apple juice enemas for the soul, hah ha ha. Don't know his name, a young guy, with a super-serious face. But she knew him, Shandy did."

"When you say religious, how do you know? Religious in what

way?"

"Cause she fucking told me after her left the first time. Said he lived with that fat yogi preacher who lives in the Quonset hut on the southside of town. Some kind of mystical church."

"Well fuck me, my god, no, no way. I'll be goddamned."

"Why, man? Hey, you look like a crow shit on your head, hee hee hee. Who is that? You know who that dude was?"

"Yeah man, I know who that was," I say, grimacing into the bleak reality-check. "That was my ex-girlfriend and he's my younger brother."

The scrawny biker doubles over, snorting with laughter. "Whooee, shit can be a bitch, ain't it fucking true? Looks like your kid brother ran off with your sad-eyed old lady."

"Yep, sure as fuck does. You have any idea where they went?"

"Not a clue. All I know is he came back out here all righteous like, and I'm gonna kick his ass, but she says to leave him alone, so I did. Then they packed up that station wagon of hers and split with the kids, pillows and some suitcases. All she said was they were leaving and going a long ways from here."

Chapter 20

THERE ARE THESE shocks in life when you realize you can't psyche out everything in your favor. You imagine that you're in control, but you're not. When I got busted at Tecate in '66 for smuggling primo Mexican weed it shocked me to the core, and now this, my faithful brother running off with Chiquita Cornsilk really blows my mind. No doubt Evan felt he was rescuing her from some dark and undeserving fate, dreamer that he is, but for Shandy, ahh—it was pure revenge. Aiyee, I feel like roadkill on the center stripe of 101. They knowingly betrayed me, probably gleeful to boot. But after a few bitter days I begin to laugh off, taking stock of my radically new situation. Nothing is going to be the same again and that means you can remake things any way you want, dig it.

Life seems to happen with an inexplicable synchronicity. Right around this same time, halfway across the country in a roadside bar in Gonzales, Texas, my father had a boozer's epiphany. A small picturesque town overlooking a green river, Gonzales, where he and mom were resting in their eastward migration from Arizona. The aerospace gig in Phoenix had gone down the tubes. A maverick jet-plane designer of the 1950's, my old man walked off the job in a disagreement with a younger supervisor and out of the moon-shooting rocket industry for good.

My stoic father was struggling with his love of good whiskey and one can only wonder if he was drunk when he told Lockheed or Grumman or whoever it was to go fuck themselves. The fact is he was undergoing a deep philosophical change at this point, abandoning his agnostic stance toward anything religious. He had taken up the study of Vedanta as expounded by Swami Vivekananda, along with The Infinite Way ponderings of someone named Joel Goldsmith. I'd never heard of Goldsmith but I was quite familiar with Vivekananda from my LA days. One of my prized books is his commentary on the Patanjali Yoga Sutras that had been with me in Oaxaca, and I had spent some acid-infused meditations in the Hollywood Vedanta Center, my black 600cc Matchless cooling in the shade of the Jacaranda trees.

Now, sitting at the Center of Light, reading my mother's chatty letter that my darkly brilliant father has taken up Vedanta Yoga frankly blows my mind and inspires me. I recall one misty evening a few years ago when he and I stood in their Santa Monica backyard conversing before I took off for Mexico. He offered me a swing out of his pocket flask of his favorite Canadian blended whiskey, a pure Bogart gesture. I fished into my shirt pocket and came up with a double-ought gelatin cap of ultra-deluxe acid, saying, "dad, I'll drink that with you when you drop this with me."

"What is it?" he asked curiously.

"500 micro grams of pure Lsd."

My father smiled at me fondly, and said, "son, let me consider that."

Anyway, on a withering summer day in this year of 1968, a ruthless year of rice-paddy death and mayhem and political assassination, my old man walked into a bridge bar on the green banks of the Guadalupe River, a whiskey-itch parching his throat. He asked the bartender for a bottle of cold Schlitz and a shot of Four Roses, settling himself on a red bar stool in the air-conditioned draft. Mom was back at their motel room presumably taking a nap. Of course my father knew he ought not to imbibe, not with hundreds of miles of road still ahead of them. It would only cause grief with Margaret, his beloved and loyal wife of 35 years. He had already drank his way out of a high-paying aerospace career, they didn't want iconoclasts like him anymore. But there are times when you just say fuck it to all such rationalization and follow your private instincts, and whiskey was his true confidant. For as long as I've known my father he had always been a courageous loner and that's the way it was.

The long afternoon sun filtered in through the neon slatted windows. Martin Acree's red pack of Pall Mall kings lay at hand, with the book of matches. He always preferred matches to a Zippo, he liked to light that cardboard match wit his thumb and he liked his whiskey straight. He poured himself a perspiring glass of chilled beer, then lifted the shot of amber spirits to the window light, to admire it for a moment before throwing it down the hatch. But in that monumental pause something happened. That moment became a long minute and my old man became engrossed in a quiet voice inside his head, that said, "forget that, you you don't need it anymore. It's a worn-out story and in your way now. Move on, my friend."

My father blinked, then nodded and set the shot glass down on the bar untasted, next to the tall foamy glass of beer. He sat and mused on what he had heard in his inner ear, then he stood up, put a few dollars on the bar, and walked out into the dusty sunlight. He was 58 years old and didn't know if that was the last drink he would never have, but figured it just might be.

I learned of these salient details a month or so later, when my father's 29 page long-hand letter showed up at my Center Of Light postbox. He and mom had continued their eastward journey, crossing the Mississippi River at New Orleans, and were presently living in a motel cabin out on Airline Highway. He was sober as a sun-bleached bone and sounded determined to stay that way. His legal-pad epistle started out by thanking Evan and I for the honest curiosity we had caused in him by our dedication to the yoga philosophy and practice, inspiring his own research into Vedanta and the Upanishads. He confessed that this esoteric study had radically changed his life. Even though my mother had mentioned this change in him, yeegods, it still floors me. My intellectual father has given up his agnostic's whiskey for the mysticism of the Vedas?

In his hand-written letter, tinged by a certain lunacy, my old man speculates that he might have been Paul the Apostle of the New Testament, the author of many deranged speculations. He thinks that he has reincarnated this time to finish the unfinished work, glad-hearted that he has awoken from forty years of boozer's rebellion He sounds serenely confident and brimming with purpose, even feels that his faltering health will be restored. This optimism makes my brows furrow, since my mother has said that he is suffering from worsening emphysema. His forty year, two pack a day habit has caught up with him. It's with a deep sadness that that I learn that my father, my wilderness mentor and friend, is hooked up every evening to a portable oxygen tank.

Nonetheless, I have the deepest respect for his keen and in-quiring intelligence, still undaunted. I wing off a return letter asking his opinion on a handful of pertinent questions. Is it plausible to imagine that a band of super-conscious individuals could wrest control of the world through metaphysical means from the sold-my-soul swine now in charge? Or is that merely a ridiculous and egotistical pursuit? Can the dream of the world be made more real somehow, for the betterment of all?

My father answered these questions in a sagacious way, with a sardonic wink to their audacity. He thought that such an event is theoretically possible, maybe even doable, if certain conditions are met – one, the unswerving devotion to the cause of all people involved; two, validate that authentic methods are used by verifying results as you go along, not waiting for the elusive pie-in-the-sky, the bane and bullshit of all religious sects and political teachings. My droll father is a skeptical anarchist at heart and for that I have always loved him. Lastly, he reminds me that there have been various cults all through history, Christ-oriented and otherwise, who in the name of their God tried to gain control of the worldly powers that make for such irredeemable suffering, and all these movements had failed. They all failed, according to my old man, because of a basic and fatal flaw in human nature. Their pied-piper leaders and core disciples were invariably deluded, believing as all fanatics do that they alone had been elected by God to take charge and dictate new rules and lord it over all the others. They became lost in their own imaginary version of the world.

Reading my father's insightful words, I find myself laughing deep down inside. He holds up a mirror. He goes on to say that in such a situation one needed to ask who or what "God" they served and why, making damned sure it wasn't the Lord of their Vainglorious Ego. History is populated with mystical charlatans who had a persuasive story to tell linked to your salvation. We are all in stages of *trying to become* what we aspire to be, a practice rife with its own contradictions. Our obsession of thinking constantly about ourselves seems to be the sibilant root of our madness.

AIYEE, THE LEERING fact persists, they deserted me, my sensual

Chiquita Cornsilk and my once loyal brother, run off together to some hidden place. After moping around with my feverish and unrequited erections, I begin to lighten up and regain my natural buoyancy. In order to avoid the mocking images, I do some soul-searching. What is it now that I really want to do? My life does not depend on what anyone else does, only on what I do. What is lost must always be transmuted into something new, and what is the price, this new act of creation? You don't get something for nothing, unless more of nothing.

After pondering for awhile, I go over to see the inimitable Sorenson with a nascent plan. It's a Saturday afternoon, I bring with me a jug of red-dirt burgundy, along with a pad of scribbled notes and ideas. I've been avoiding Torgie of late, knowing that he has been despondent over the ruins of our supernatural plans. The Quonset hut glints in the sunlight like a giant metal toad. To my surprise, the gordito reverend greets me with enthusiasm, his blue eyes lit. "All right, I've been hoping you'd drop by, I've got some things I want to talk about. It's been lonely around here since you and Evan both went over the hill. Say, whatcha got there in that sack?"

"Well, me too, so looks like were on the same page," I say, hoisting the glass jug by its finger loop. "Thought I'd bring over some new testament reconciliation."

"Okay then," the reverend laughs, smacking his lips. "Pull up a chair, I'll get some glasses. You're timing couldn't be better. I haven't been doing much except feeling sorry for myself."

It's easy talking to Torgie, the big disheveled monk loves to hobnob, loves to tell his stories, likes making you laugh. He's in his stained white tee and denim overalls, his gnarly white feet sockless. His graying hair flares at the temples like bat's wings beneath his balding pate. We put away glass of the old woman's wine and pour another, sharing a few philosophical shrugs laced with twisted humor. When the wheels come off the celestial chariot they bounce in all directions.

"Tell me what's on your mind," he urges me, "I can see you've been thinking on something."

"Yeah, that I have. And I'd like to run some ideas by you, get your take. Maybe see if we can work together on a new endeavor."

"Well hell yes, man, I've been wondering the same thing myself. It'd be a crying shame to throw away all the work we've done without giving it a new try. There's more than one way to skin a cat. So lay it on me."

The reverend takes a long, thick cigar out of his desk drawer, nips the end with his teeth, lights it up with a wooden match. I've had no inkling that he liked cigars, and never seen him smoke one. It smells delicious at once. Impressed, I say, "hey, where did you get that?"

"Cameroon wrapper," Torgie says, blowing thick blue smoke rings, "mighty fucking tasty."

"Right on, Mr Sorenson, right on. Okay, dig, consider this and hear me out. Gurdjieff founded a special school over in France that he called 'The Institute For The Harmonious Development Of Man.' He set up branches of the school in England, Russia, and America. He had students from all over the world studying the art and science of spiritual awareness. You remember me talking about this?"

"Yes, yes I do," he acknowledges, in that rapt manner as if murmuring to himself. "He taught advanced movement training to awaken the chakras, dances set to sacred music."

"Yes, that's right, along with the I Am meditation, not that we'd be trying to copy what he was doing. His methods were Sufi-oriented and grounded in the yoga Vedic sciences, like us. But I love the way he organized his trip, the network of esoteric schools dedicated to self-awareness. Not ashrams per se, but centers of learning where people came and studied advanced meditation methods to awaken to their fullest potential. You see where I'm going with this?"

"I'm pretty sure I do," Sorenson enthuses, "and I love it. Here, have some more jugos de vino. That approach would put us in touch with literally hundreds of folks in short order, then we could pick the cream of the crop for the higher work. But how would you go about setting it up up? In what locations? And what kind of moolah are we talking about?"

"Moolah, money? I don' really know, I haven't gotten into all that yet. I'm still working on the conceptual aspects, on what to offer seekers."

"Fine and dandy, but you've got to recognize that that kind of teaching can generate a helluva revenue stream." The reverend takes a lusty gulp of the red wine, his eyes glistening, then puffs vigorously on his long, fragrant stogie.

"All right, I see your point, set a value. No pearls before swine and all that. Money coming in allows us to expand and do even more. So dig, I see these schools up and down the west coast, each center being self-sustaining, along the lines of new-age communes. There's an esoteric curriculum of study and core practice that gets deeper as one gets involved, and that's where you come in, reverend. You've got a very important role in this scenario."

"I'm all ears," Torgie says, leaning forward with beaming interest.

"Well, you, and *the Center of Light* here on the central coast, will be the secret mystery center behind the schools. Eventually all the students who qualify have to come here to receive the higher initiations, and you will be the grand yogi potentate who authorizes those initiations because of your direct lineage to Yoganan-daji. Of course I'll need to set this up in the right way."

"Ohh I love it, that is a great idea," Torgelananda laughs, his big face wreathed in cherubic energy. "And why the heck not? I can always wrap a kind of satin turban around my head."

"Hah ha ha, yeah, I can totally dig it, and you can wear your long saffron SRF robes for the ceremonies. In my opinion those robes are much more impressive than your minister's outfit. I can always wear my purple robes too, if it seems appropriate."

"Well, damned straight. We have to give you a title of some kind, an exalted title."

"No, reverend, no, I don't want a title. I don't to strut around showing off."

"You are going to need a title of distinction, trust me. President of operations, executive director, something impressive like that."

"Well, maybe, we'll see. Let me think about that."

"Okay then, and my god yes, we're on to something really good here!" Torgie refreshes our pint jars with the brujo wine. "When you bring them here, it'll be showtime for the new initiates, we have to put on a show. And what are you going to call these satellite schools,? Clue me in."

"Not the Center of Light, the Center of Light has to be the one of a kind kingpin. I'm thinking of a separate trip called the Kama-Kala Foundation, that gets legalized under California laws as a non-profit spiritual organization. Just like you did here."

"The Kama-Kala Foundation, that's got a good ring to it. But what does it mean?"

"It comes from the Sanskrit language and means, more or less, as I interpret it, the creative will manifested in time. I take it to mean the divine will manifesting in the illusion of time, and in the nick of time, to make a crucial difference in the world."

"Holy Moses, my friend, that's good, that's brilliant! I am beginning to envision this whole grand thing! How did you hit on that?"

"I don't know, these ideas come into my head when I meditate and I just jot them down. The first thing I'm gonna do is to go down to LA and spend a few days with my old friends. Some of them are interested in esoteric self-development and I need to find out what's happening there. They might come right into the group wit us and LA's definitely a prime location. What I'm envisioning is a multi-faceted approach to self-awakening – a method that uses the ancient yoga sciences combined with contemporary psychological techniques."

Sorenson exhales a cloud of smoke from his cigar, burnt about half-way down. "I gotcha," he says, "and that's smart. Make it more modern, but give me a for-example."

"I'm still sorting it out, but maybe something like this—We can streamline a practice that includes Gurdjieff self-remembering concepts, pranayama breathing exercises, some nada-bindu hatha combined with Yogananda's revitalization exercises, along with a basic initiation into the So-Hawng mantra. Throw in some of the unique angles of Castaneda and DeRopp to give it a hip vibe—see where I'm going? We can include some of Maslow's 'self-actualization' method and hook people up to these new bio-feedback machines to give them an valid, conscious experience. Really a montage of techniques that get you involved in your own self-realization, stage by stage, then the final trip, the crowning stage will be the royal kriya ceremony given by Sri Reverend Sorenson here at the mystical Center Of Light."

"Oh my God, that's absolutely fantastic, I love it!" Sorenson exclaims. "I always told old man Mallet you were a genius this just goes show it. He's always been a little jealous of you, in case you didn't know it, that one million watt brain of yours."

This oblique flattery catches me by surprise, for a moment I lose my train of thought. The rich cigar smells delicious, the dense wafting smoke makes my mouth water. But the reverend's enthusiasm for what I'm describing can't be denied. His luminous eyes are lit up like headlamps, the mad monk sees to be chomping at the bit. I pause, and clear my throat.

"Listen," I say, with a half-smile, "you don't happen to have another of those stogies around, do you? Smells fucking outrageous, man, la aroma divino."

"Nope, sorry," Torgie chuckles, "it's my last one. But I'm gonna pick up another box next time I'm in Pasadena. I've got a pal down there, an ex-SRF monk, who runs a barber shop and imports these from Spain. Sure beats the hell out of White Owl, don't it?"

"Oh man, no comparison. Yeah, okay, I'm cool. I'll take ten or twelve of those babies if you can swing it."

"Hell's bells, compadre, I'm gonna get you a whole box. My buddy says they're almost one hundred percent custom blend from Fidel Castro's own plantation."

"Whoa, right on, right on, wow. Anyway, listen, like I was saying, first we establish three or four schools up and down the coast. Los Angeles, Santa Monica, maybe in Santa Barbara, then I'm going to San Francisco to see if I can meet some new people up there. The bay area has become a new age oracle, and we need to tap into that. Maybe another one in Santa Cruz as we go along."

"Jake, you've never been short on guts or ambition, I've got to hand you that," Torgie says in admiration, polishing off his tumbler of shoe-leather Rotta. "I'll drink to that plan!"

"Well, if you say so," I laugh, "but for me it's intuitive. Something tells me this will all come together as we get it rolling. We should have stream of new-age aspirants coming in to help us build our network of schools. Hell, there's no reason we can't go coast to coast with this project."

"All right now, all right now," Torgie says happily, clinking my glass as we nod together like conspirators, by now pretty damn drunk. To my dismay he stubs his cigar out in a chipped plate, into a smoldering heap, smothering the rich blend so that now it will begin to stink.

"And I've got to say again," he toasts, "that plan of yours is brilliant, a real money-maker. When do you plan on kicking off this metaphysical shindig?"

"Pretty damn soon," I say, "there's not much holding us back, my probation officer indicated I'd be off probation soon. After that, there's no use in sitting around Atascadero."

Laughing, Sorenson upends the well depleted jug and guzzles directly from the spout, burps loudly, lips glistening, then holds it out to me. "What say ye?"

I welcome his friendly gesture and take a lusty swig. It seems to me that the reverend is getting fatter, he's slabbing on the fat, maybe pushing 400 pounds now. His fleshy jowls and bursting britches are in your face, a huge jovial crazy monk, but I don't say anything. It's his trip and we're about to become partners in this new-age brainstorm.

"So here's our grand new deal, Mr Sorenson," I point out, "beyond even what we imagined. Are you good with it?"

"I am in complete agreement," he says, "and your brother will be too. Oh, Evan will be back, don't worry about that. And I see the donations pouring into our treasure chest, we're back on track. This will finance our entire ceremonial endeavor and then some. You've come up with the golden solution, it's beautiful. But now listen, let me tell you what I'm designing to build right here on this spot. I'm going to show you something fantastic!"

"Designing to build? You mean here, in Atascadero? Some sort of church?"

"Yes, yesiree, only much grander than an everyday church. First of all, I see now, with my share of these new funds I'm gonna buy Mallet out lock, stock and barrel, the whole ball of wax, Quonset hut, the farm house, the whole forty acres and all his precious junk. I'll pay him top dollar, then make him a deacon in the holy new temple which will tickle him pink."

"What new temple? What are you rambling about?"

"Just hold your horses and let me explain. This is my secret so listen up, 'cause it dovetails perfectly with what you plan to do. One hand always washes the other, right?"

"Yeah, right on, my turn to listen, shoot."

"Well, not too long ago I had this fantastic vision as clear as day. It showed that you were gonna come back in with a powerful idea, and that idea was gonna put us on the map. It didn't show all the details, but now I see how all the pieces are falling together. These branch schools will supply us with dozens of evolved seekers who we can train into an elite corps of light masters to control the whole show. And some of these new-comers will have deep pockets, you can bet on it!"

"What the fuck, reverend, I'm not sure we're on the same wave-length here. I want to bring people into the art of self-realization, not some grandiose scheme to take over the world. And I'm not going back into that occult ceremonial circle, so forget that."

"Oh come on Jake, don't look at me like that. You know you want it just like I do, don't play naive. Just because you blew off some of your brain power with that hot little gal doesn't change your destiny. You're still the one who's gonna throw Satan into chains. And when your brother gets tired of goofing off and comes back, he'll follow your lead, you'll see."

"Man oh man, you are truly obsessed, Sorenson."

Torgie gleefully quaffs from his pint jar, the gallon jug going on empty. He wipes his lips with the back of his hand, and says, "and in the end, we'll win. With all the loot these newcomers will be dropping on us, I'll be able to build the magnificent new temple."

"What temple? You didn't explain. What magnificent new temple?"

"The one that I see in my visions, a huge triumphant temple that were going to erect on this property. It'll cover one whole square city block, man, you'll be able to see it from 101."

"Reverend, dude, you're really tripping," I retort, wanting to get back on our original track. I wonder again whether he and I have ever spoken the same language, or has the past two years been a harebrained assumption on everyone's part?

Torgelananda raises his callused hands, then launches into a description of his imagined temple. The monolithic structure shall be an immense rectangle covering at least ten acres of Mallet's farm, modeled after Solomon's own temple in the Bible. This imposing structure will be seven stories high and have hundreds of rooms to house the student-devotees, with several large kitchens to feed them, scores of bathrooms and spacious lecture halls for the edifying presentations by those who are the wise ones. At least twenty acres of land will be dedicated to growing enough organic crops to feed everyone, and there'll be a parking lost big enough for one hundred cars. Sorenson's febrile mind has worked out every detail. All I do is listen with a kind of twisted fascination.

"There's two crowning features," Torgie confides, slurping his vino dregs, fixing me with his bulging eyes. "There's gonna be a worship shrine right at the heart of the building, an exact replica of the Ark of The Covenant told about in the Book of Revelations, although big enough to seat one hundred and eleven worshipers. This will be the central initiation hall for all your new people. Some magnificent pictures will be hanging there, big tall pictures hanging from the domed ceiling, all illuminated, the SRF masters and our pictures too as the founders. Oh yes, your picture is gonna be hanging there along with mine."

"Wait a minute, Mr Sorenson," I say defensively, "you're going over the edge. The purpose of these schools isn't to parade ourselves around like demigods, it's to awaken people to their true self. We don't need all this fancy pomp and ceremony to that. We just have to turn them on to real methods of self-transformation and give them some guidance."

"No, it's important because we have to establish a hierarchy. Master's picture along with Jesus' will be at the pinnacle of the dome, giant life-like photos, and we need to be there too to show who's who. That will be the ultimate initiation, the ceremony that will totally blow their minds open. We're gonna install the world's largest pipe organ in the balcony, bigger than the one in the Mormon tabernacle. It'll be incredibly awe-inspiring."

"Aha ha ha, more like insanity, all this cult-circus madness. Why don't you just buy a glitzy hotel with a neon ballroom? All I want to do is help people flash into their own self-realization."

"Hah, we might do that too. But don't worry about that. All your wishes are coming true."

"All right, Sorenson, all right, and what's the other thing? You said there were two crowning things about this stupendous temple of yours."

"That's right, there is," the big monk grins, flaring his tufted eyebrows, "and that's the kicker. On top of this huge complex, way up on the roof of the seventh floor, we're going to build an oval skating rink, a really big one. This rink will be the main place for daily exercise and fun, along with the garden work. It'll be open 24 hours round the clock so the yogis and yoginis an blow off steam anytime they feel the need."

Incredulous, I'm not sure I've heard him right. A roller rink on top of a yoga tabernacle? The idea itself of one hundred spiritual aspirants tucked away into their nests in a giant metaphysical hatchery here in Atascadero strikes me as absurd. But to top it off with a roller derby? It's all I can do to not break out in derisive snorts and hoots.

Instead, after a moment, I say, "Mr Sorenson, you want a roller skating rink on top of your vast holy temple? Skating into cosmic-consciousness? Doesn't that seem to you a bit weird?"

"No, hell no, not roller skating," Torgie retorts. "This is gonna be a huge ice-skating rink to help folks cool down their sexual lusts and transmute that energy!"

"Come again? An ice-skating rink on the roof in 100 degree summer heat? Reverend, get real, that ice will never even freeze."

"Nonsense, you're not seeing it yet, yes, yes it will freeze. We're gonna clap a weather-proof fiberglass roof over the rink and freeze the ice from underneath. When I buy Mallet out I'm gonna take control of all these old freezer compressors, and we'll put them to better use. I've come to realize we've got to get rid of these meat lockers, it's a turn-off for most spiritual seekers. we'll reinstall all the refrigeration equipment under the temple roof in order to frost and maintain the ice. Those old machines are practically indestructible, they'll be humming around the clock. Man, it's gonna be one of the most phenomenal sights people have ever seen!"

"Good God, dude, forgive me, but that's madness. I mean, just imagine the electric bills to run that show, they'll drive you into the poor house."

"Hah, well, my ingenious friend, that's where you and your new-age foundation comes in. I have all the confidence in the world that before long we'll be rolling in loot."

"But the fucking noise, the racket from all that old machinery, it's maddening!"

"Naw, not a problem," Torgie enunciates, pushing his dentures out of his mouth, "oh, we'll rig up some kind of sound insulation for sure, good point, and make sure that there's always guest rooms available. Because people are gonna be coming from all over the world to ice skate there and study the sacred teachings."

I begin to laugh, a deep belly-shaking laugh, I can't help it, the flagrant assumption is just too much. Torgie starts laughing too, great ribald guffaws, tears streaming down his rubescent cheeks. I don't think he is laughing for the same reasons I am, is he in love with his own madness? After a moment or so, gasping for air in snickering hiccups, I pull myself together.

"All right then, reverend," I say in a serious tone, "you're into this idea of mine? Establishing these hybrid yoga schools and using you as the esoteric kingpin? I'll bring people together in a self-awareness training and then we'll connect to the mystical Center Of Light as the gateway to higher consciousness. Eventually all the students have to make the pilgrimage here to get the sacred initiations, and you are the grand initiator. You all in on this deal?"

"Damn right I am, I'm totally in. It's pure genius and it's just the shot in the arm we need And I have no doubt you have the charisma to pull it off. You do your part and I'll do mine and all that past stuff is forgiven. One step leads to the next and the bullshit falls by the wayside."

We lean forward and clasp hands, Torgelananda and me, with crazy, inebriated grins. "Right on, right on," I murmur with satisfaction, "I think the plan is good. I think we can do something special together."

Sorenson grunts in approval, a huge happy bear in his cups. "There you go then," he nods in aplomb, topping off out glasses with the dregs of the jug. "And remember what I told you. The mighty will bow and scrape at your feet, I've seen it all as plain as day. You don't have to believe it 'cause you're gonna see, you are gonna see."

I say nothing, I just rock back and forth with a smile. It's like having a lovable metaphysical uncle who's stark raving mad. One thing is certain, though. My whole sense of purpose is renewed, the doldrums are peeling away. Whatever qualms have been nagging me, I throw out the window. Now it's time to see if we can make an angel food cake or a mud pie.

Chapter 21

WHENEVER YOU'RE REALLY up on your horse of consciousness, the universe seems to conspire to bring about great good fortune. How that happens I don't know, but it happens. Right after Torgie and I strike our glittering deal, I get an official letter from my probation officer summoning me to Los Angeles. Mr Camilo has never made this request before. He has always made random visits up the picturesque coast to see how I was doing. I'm not sure what to make of it and Camilo gives me no hints. But I figure it's got to be good news because I've had no black marks against me.

I make the long drive down 101 to LA with several purposes in mind, but first I go see Mr Camilo. He greets me with his usual weary smile, a friendly warmth in his eyes, offers me a cardboard cup of burnt coffee and gets right down to the business between us.

"I had planned to drive up to Atascadero to give you the news," he says, "but I've been bombed by this damned circus. Too many of your former colleagues getting popped and booted onto probation, the lucky ones, I should say. But Jake, I'm glad to say your life is improving again."

"Does that mean what I think it might mean?" I ask tentatively.

"Yeah, probably it does. I'm cutting you loose early, Jake. Right here on the desk are the release papers for you to sign off on. You've fulfilled your end of the bargain, you've kept your act clean, and it's my privilege to take the legal restrictions off your back."

"Wow, Mr Camilo, that's incredible news. And this means I no longer report to you?"

"That's right," he says out of the side of his mouth, "you're a free man and I better not see your face again. Keep going forward in your life and don't backtrack into any old ways."

"Oh hah, I promise you, I won't be doing that. No need for me to revisit the past."

"Glad to hear that. Here, my friend, sign these three pages. Now, according to the terms of your court conviction, with your probation obligations satisfied, that court sentence is going to get expunged. Within a matter of six to eight weeks your record will be wiped clean. Not a bad deal, all things considered."

"Fantastic, yeah, I remember that provision! God, man, it's all been worth it. So now I'm free to travel?"

"Oh yeah, you're free to travel anywhere you want, including back into old Mexico. You know the score."

In a surge of jubilation I reach over and grasp Camilo's hand, this man who befriended me from the day I stepped into his supervision under court orders. I hasten to scrawl my name on the release documents.

"One other thing," Camilo says, lighting up one of his eternal Parliaments. "Technically I'm supposed to tell the Selective Service System that you are no longer under federal probation, so they can reclassify your ass."

"Those bastards," I mutter warily, "all they'll do is try to draft me into their fucking war."

"Yep, I think that's about right and you and I feel the same about that miserable war. And with Nixon and that insane

Kissinger in charge it's only going to get worse. So, what's going to happen is that I'm going to forget to file the notification to the draft board. I'm so damned busy that notifying them just slipped my mind. So for the time being, don't worry about that."

For a moment I sit wordless, taking in the blessing of this favor. Then I say, "Mr Camilo, I don't know how to thank you, you have been a real friend to me. And I'm sure as hell not going to tell them."

"Don't look at me either," Camilo says with a sardonic grin. "And the best of luck to you, Jake, and you know that I mean it."

And just like that I'm released from the clutch of the Law. All vestiges of my weed-smuggling disaster are erased and I am free to roam the world again. It's a great liberating feeling, something I've kept bottled up inside for some time now. Adios to Draconian restrictions!

In the mood to celebrate, I drive over to the old Silverlake hills neighborhood to look up my former acid-tripping partner, Jonathon Bender. To my surprise Bender is no longer living in the hidden cul-de-sac apartment that Evan and I once took sanctuary in from the LA narcs. The place is occupied by a defensive chick with a shaved head who eyes me skeptically, me in my black Russian wool cap and rudraksha beads. But she relaxes a bit when I tell her that I used to live in the same far-out pad.

"Oh, I know who you're looking for, that odd skinny man, kind of twitchy? I heard that he moved out into the Valley somewhere to live with a bossy fat woman."

Say what? Bender moved out of the womb of LA and living with a girlfriend, an actual flesh and blood female? Laughing to myself, I go to a corner payphone and make a couple calls to some mutual friends. It turns out that the bent one is living out on Van Nuys Boulevard with a strange chick who doesn't approve of most of his friends. Intrigued, his telephone number scrawled on a matchbook, I ring him up. He answers in his guarded, tight voice, then flusters to hear my voice.

"Oh my fucking god, Jake! I've been thinking about you, I swear I have! What's happening?"

I tell him I'd like to come and visit, that I have some interesting news. "Something you definitely might want to get involved in, Bender. Some major changes."

Bender hesitates, then says, "uh, sure man, that'd be cool. When did you wanna come? I kind of live out in Nowhereville at the moment. I had to give up that Silverlake pad you turned me onto, my girlfriend didn't feel safe there."

"That doesn't matter, whatever. I'd like to come now if that's all right, or later today. There's some fantastic things about to happen I want to tell you about."

"Okay, yeah," Bender says. "Yeah, you can come on out, my chick tends to be a little phobic of surprises, but she's at work. Come on out. I'll make us some green gunpowder tea."

Bender rattles off his address in his harried voice, then I drive over to the SRF cafe on Sunset near Vermont and indulge in a delicious vegetarian lunch. It's an inner city oasis, the cafe and bookstore, the meditation chapel surrounded by rose bushes and tall palms. But for some reason the chapel is locked today and the affable brother Mokshananda nowhere around.

After scarfing up a spicy lentil-leek curry, I drive on over the hill on 101 and into the prosaic San Fernando valley. Smog covers everything, an odious eye-stinging haze, ocean breezes don't always dip in here. Bender lives in a typical apartment complex with a few dreary bushes and sculpted rocks. But my old friend doesn't answer the door with any verve, his face is pinched and moody. There is a prim, plump woman sitting behind him who greets me with critical eyes. She doesn't even get up from the ebony table that seems loaded with flavored rice snacks alongside the steaming Zen teapot. I say plump but no, she is obese and in stern command of herself, in contrast to his fidgeting personality. I wonder fleetingly how it must be when they have sex together, or do they have sex? As long as I've known Bender he's been involved in one awkward trip after another.

"I'm pleased to meet you," I tell her, smiling, "it's been awhile since I've seen Jonathon."

"Likewise, I'm sure," she says with a blink, not smiling.

Their walls are covered with Asiatic ink-brush drawings and calligraphy, the furniture is ultra-modern, tan and black, probably hers, alleviated by two or three verdant house plants. I glance around for a place to sit and Jonathon introduces this woman as "his fiance," saying to me as though scripted, "I can honestly say, Jake, that we are really very happy. It's a new world for me."

Aiyee, whatever you say, dude, murmuring my congratulations, I try to put some enthusiasm in my voice. But the vibes of this pad are anything but insouciant and free. There is not a single thing out of place, all the artifacts and Japanese vases, the sliding glass doors, the pristine cream carpet, even the faux bamboo walls have spotless inviolable sheen. This is a house without fingerprints. Everything is ironed and buttoned and although no rules are posted, it's obvious there's an inflexible program operating here. But best not to ask unless you want the chapter and verse.

I decide to not mention my release from probation, don't smudge the atmosphere. I suspect that this insecure, controlling woman knows all there is to know about me, anyway, Bender loves to gossip, he has told her all about my outlaw past. Instead, I ease into a description of the avant garde schools I want to set up as the nexus of a new-age self-awareness revolution. In fact, with my partner Torgelananda the Paramahansa Yogananda disciple, I want to establish the first school right here in Los Angeles, dig it, and I need some visionary founding members to make it happen. Together we can change this insanely violent and fucked-over world, that's what it's all about.

Bender at once seems acutely interested. That eagerness to try something worthwhile, that spark in him comes alive in his face. "Yeah, man, that's a beautiful idea and why not? You've got all that advanced training and gurus are popping up all over town. There's like a new guru almost every week, people are hungry for these new spiritual paths."

But his plump inamorata squashes him. Glancing over at her, adorned in a yellow polka-dot sack dress, Bender falls silent. Assuming control with a prim frown, the shrew says, oh I forget her name, it slipped from my mind when I left their apartment as something to not be retained, she says to me, "let me be honest. I've heard quite a few things about your unusual adventures and pursuits.

But Jonathon and I aren't into things like that anymore. We're into zen, just a simple zen is our thing, it doesn't go with that exotic metaphysical stuff. Plus he feels balanced now, probably in a way you've never seen him, isn't that right, baby? He's past all that Lsd nonsense and we're balanced in this lifestyle, balanced together. I don't think we're the people for what you have in mind."

Bender mumbles some inanity, trying to make light of her curt dismissal. Does he remember the long talks we shared about the brilliant zen interpretations of Alan Watts? Where does this chick get off running these assumptions about me? Jonathon snorts his frenetic laugh, holding his hands up like paws. But it's clear as an ink drawing that this unsmiling Cleopatra is the boss here and Bender is her waxen-faced slave. He probably does the dishes and folds her voluminous panties, too.

There's not much more to say and no reason at all to stay. Jonathon musters the nerve to walk me to my car. "She's stressed out lately," he apologizes, "she works as an accountant and her boss is a really bitch. But I'm interested in what your proposal, Jake. It's like an evolution of all our former ideas, and I dig it, I dig it. And don't worry, I'll talk to her, she'll come around."

"I don' know about that, man," I say, "you're girlfriend seems anything but open. Not just to me but to anything spontaneous at all. And why was she even there? I thought you said she was at work?"

"When I called her and told her you that you were in town, she insisted on coming to meet you."

"You called her and told her I was coming over for an impromptu visit?"

"You said you had important news," Bender says defensively, "and we tell each other everything that's going on. And like she said, we're trying to learn zen meditation together."

"Man, you've been trying to learn meditation ever since I met you. It's not something you learn, like scrabble, it's an intuitive practice. But I'm glad you found someone to be with, Jonathon. I hope that all works out for you."

"Thanks, Jake, thanks," he says, giving me a lame shake, "and keep me in the know on this project, okay? I'm really interested."

"I will, my friend, I'll be in touch."

But driving away I know that he won't get involved, his lover-girl won't let him and he'll just hang on the fringes. His own self-doubt blacks is ability to commit, which is why he never set off on that 1966 journey to Oaxaca with Bones Osgood and me. What Bender is looking for, what he has always sought is someone to protect him from the unpredictable. He doesn't mind being restricted as long as he has a protector that in effect becomes his controller. Years ago I refused that role with him, but now he's found a dominatrix who'll gladly keep him in line.

Driving back over the Topanga hills and into Hollywierd I cruise down Sunset toward Vermont. I stop at the Siam restaurant and feast on a big spicy bowl of shrimp pot Thai. Then I find an old hotel a few blocks from the SRF cafe and chapel and take a cheap room for the night. It's a smoggy afternoon, the streets are hot and congested, I need some shelter. Tomorrow I'll go over to the LACC campus and find my friend Aaron Gold, who's devouring the art history, philosophy and psych classes like I used to do. Aaron will give me the low-down on where our old metaphysical comrades happen to be.

In the evening I walk over to the SRF center and find the chapel open and empty. I go inside and go into meditation in which I lose track of time, questioning the ambitious sense of self that claims to be me. I must go deeply through the layers of myself, there is no other way. When I walk back up Sunset to the flop-house hotel the street lights are haloed in a nimbus of mist. The room is sparse, television on the blink, just enough space on the frayed maroon carpet to do my Hatha exercises. The curry spices are roiling around in my guts, spewing hot farts toward the open window. My room is on the third floor of this old brick, ivy-covered building, street noises ricochet down the side alley. These walls have little if any insulation, no, and around midnight I awake to the shenanigans of the drunk couple next door, their salacious squeals and ribald laughter, the moaning of whiskey over the rocks. It's pointless to complain, this is what you get for for eight bucks a night. Insomnia seeps in, casting restless neon images in my mind, and I pass the dark lone hours in drifting meditation.

FROWNING UNDER HIS mop of curly hair, Aaron Gold tells me, "it's not the same since when you lived here, a lot of hip people are scattering away. You know how paranoid this LA scene gets, I don't have to tell you. But things have gotten worse since the assassinations, really edgy. That beautiful mystical psychedelic vibe isn't as strong as before. I don't mean me myself, I mean in general. Anti-war demonstrations are on the quad almost every day, people are becoming much more militant."

"I don't doubt it," I reply, sipping some insipid herbal tea, in a head and tea shop about a block off campus. The wall are hung with hippie accouterments and a striking red and black poster of Che Guevara glaring into the distance, his black beret taut with rage. "This criminal war of our so-called government, the ruthless draft, the insane slaughter. Human beings are nothing mote than cattle to these fucking bastards. And right, when they gunned down Martin Luther and Bobby Kennedy that was crushing but it enraged us. That let us know where we stand."

"So, you don't buy into the rogue gunman theory?" Aaron says wryly.

"Oh fucking please. It's the same shadow group of Machiavellian control freaks that killed JFK. And now with this asshole Nixon getting elected president it's only going to get worse. He's a born liar and so slimy that he slithers. He makes our governor Reagan look like a choir boy."

"Yeah Jake, I agree. Nixon's a hardcore right-winger, not even his boss Eisenhower trusted him. He might try to turn the whole country into a police state and that dude Kissinger will definitely escalate the war. At some point people are going to have to stand up and revolt."

"Aaron, we're going to have to bring it down. By metaphysical or ordinary means, this sham government has to come down. The politicians can't be trusted to do what's right anymore, they don't represent the people, maybe they never could be trusted. Most of them are in the hip pocket of the big military-industrial money, shameless greedy prevaricators sending a whole generation to its death with pious faces. No, they should all be hung in public. Kenneth Patchen said it, Ginsburg howled it, Dylan sang it. The reality is we are at war with our own government in the streets of America, but the news media won't dare call it for what it is. Lawless hippie dopers and renegade blacks, hah, people must rise against such outrageous bullshit."

"Right on, my man," Aaron laughs, touching my fingers with his. "Yeah, the cowardly news media, that's what freaked Ray Vargas out, the intentional distortion of who we actually are. You know Ray, how mellow he is, sometimes like a black Bodhisattva, you know? Once he got over the shock of Martin Luther King's murder, he just up and split outta here. He's convinced the cities are about to disintegrate into killing zones and race riots, fighting between the people and the cops. He doesn't trust the cops of course, but who does?"

"No one, not anymore. Ray split you say, but to where?"

"That's the mysterious thing, I'm not quite sure. He heard about this hippie commune up north of San Francisco, back in the hills, a utopia where anyone is welcome and you come and just do your own thing. He loved the idea of that. But I don't know where it is exactly."

"Damn. I'd like to talk to him about these esoteric self-awareness centers. I think Ray would be a natural and if he's up there even better. We want to get going in San Francisco too."

"Oh, he'd definitely trip on your ideas, Jake, definitely he would. And you know you can count me in 100%. Soon as school's over I gonna come up there and visit you and this Sorenson, he sounds like a far-out dude. I mean Yogananda, man? Paramahansa Yogananda was the best."

"That's beautiful, brother, I absolutely want you involved. But we need to bring Ray in too, that cosmic enthusiasm of his. How do you suppose I can find directions to that commune?"

"I'll tell you who probably knows – Lon Caheres. He and Ray lived together in that apartment where we all used to meet together, they always stayed close. That's where we met, remember? You and your brother Evan were laying Gurdjieff on us and it blew our minds. Then we'd bring out the bongos and congas and all trip together, those were great days."

"Yeah, those were beautiful times, really beautiful scenes."

"For me unforgettable, Jake, and if anyone knows where Ray's hiding out Lon would know. And I know where Lon lives."

"All right, brother man, lay that info on me and I'll go visit him tomorrow."

"You got it. But one thing you need to be hip to, Lon's different now. I mean he's the same righteous cat, but he's changed."

"Well, he always was kind of edgy because of his Nam experience, but how do you mean?"

"Like let's just say he's become a lot more radical. He was getting into Malcolm X's teachings and Martin Luther's murder pushed him right over the edge."

"Fuck, I can dig tat, totally. I really want to see him."

"He'll see you bro', I know he will. He always loved talking reality with you."

FACING LON CAHERES in his kitchenette apartment south of Olympic, I sit in a wicker chair with some peacock feathers attached to the back and fanning over my head. At first I thought this must be some kind of throne and was reluctant to sit in it, but Lon insisted. He sits across from me in an easy chair in his cramped studio with its pull-down bed and a dinette table with two chairs. There's an Underwood typewriter on that table, under a dusty window with a pale curtain. The only poster on these faded walls is the defiant Black Power fist in stark black and white. A stack of books rests on the floor beside his bed and on the top book is a blue cup with a yellow hibiscus floating in it.

We're drinking some kind of instant Colombian coffee which isn't all that bad. One can hear intermittent voices through the walls in a Hindi or Urdu dialect. Lon sips the acrid brew, regarding me, with warmth in his intelligent eyes. His lean handsome face has a chiseled aspect to it.

"I've thought about you sometimes," he says, "about what you're doing these days. Ray and I always figured that you would keep investigating, that nothing would hold you back. I remember those sessions we had with you and Evan and the other cats, we were like a private club. Those days helped put my head back together after Nam. You turned the light on for Ray and me, with Gurdjieff and Ouspensky and the Indian mystics. And I tell you, true y man, that was life-changing."

"I think for all of us that's true, Lon," I nod, "we had a rare vibe going. I'm glad you're still working with that method of self-knowing, just like I am. No limits, my friend, no limits, the limits are all mind-made. And these schools I want to set up are modeled after that Fourth Way concept. But you still taking classes over at LACC? Aaron said he hadn't seen you around in awhile."

"Yeah, a couple of night classes over there, Marxism and existential philosophy. And I'm still working with those primary concepts, they strengthen me. Got a couple Gurdjieff books right over there. But lately I've been tripping on this philosopher, Krishnamurti, I mean, Jake, this man talks my language. You've got to ruthlessly question everything, you have to be your own authentic teacher, there can be no outside authority. Are you hip to this Indian cat?"

"Oh definitely, I've done some reading into Jiddu Krishnamurti and I agree, he's revolutionary. That man is such a radical image-breaker that he scares people, he shatters those hallowed traditions to pieces. His thinking is hard to follow at times, like G's, but I dig I – he gives such insight into the convolutions of the human mind that it blows your mind. But I still consider myself an initiate of Paramahansa Yogananda, at least for now."

Lon rubs his chin and says, "I can't really get into the guru trip like you and your brother did. Don't get me wrong, I respect it, but all that ritualized devotion is not for me. And let me come clean with you, Jake, because from day one you've been a real friend to me. But over this past year I've gone through some tumultuous movements in my identity."

"I can dig changes, Lon. But how exactly do you mean?"

"Changes? Yeah, without any doubt," Lon laughs curtly. "Although I think of it more as personal evolution. I'm not at ease with this fucked-up racist society, and I don't think the Civil Rights Act is going to give black people that much more of a chance. They throw you a bone and kill your truth-talking leader, like a pacifier to stop rocking the political boat."

"But hey man, it's still a step in the right direction and it's significant. Look at all the people who went under for that!"

"Oh I know, my brother, believe me, you know I know. But be honest, Jake, how long? Be in my skin. How long before those new laws have any real effect? Laws are just written rules, all they do is stave off real change. You honestly believe that civil rights act gonna change attitudes? Shit, it won't and you know it won't. No, like you kept saying about the rotten fucking war, we got to take it to the streets to overwhelm it. And that's what's needed, now, for justice, and that can't be disputed. King was murdered in plain daylight, dig it, and so was your good man Robert Kennedy. After all the shit I went through in Vietnam, to barely come out alive, or come home and be treated like a second-class citizen? No. Jake, no more can that be tolerated, no more."

"I hear you, Lon," I say humbly, "and I understand. I'm not the passive type myself."

"Oh I know that, so dig what I'm saying. You are the truest white dude I've ever known. You come from a real place inside and I love you for that. But you see the symbol of that fist up on the wall? That's my symbol now, you're talking to a black militant now, not a mystic like Ray who I love with my blood but I've gone over. My rage has carried me over, Jake, and I'm about to join up with the Black Panthers."

"Man, that's a powerful step but I understand it. I absolutely believe we've got to take radical steps to bring honest change into this rotten system I do. But we've got to stay united, it's so important that we stay united. What was it that Voltaire said, Voltaire so fucking brilliant? But for sure watered-down, idealistic bullshit isn't going to get the job done. Those rapacious bastards aren't going to give up power for any cause, no way, that's obvious. One way and another we must take that power from them."

Lon Caheres reaches over and clasps my hand, holding my eyes with intense feeling. "You are my friend and I am yours," he says. "That's not gonna change."

"Likewise, for always," I say fervently. Leaning forward, we share a strong soul-shake.

"You know what? Ray and I always thought you would start some mystical commune, like what you're talking about. And I am interested, but you got to realize that's my life now, I'm living it to the hilt. One thing Nam taught me, being out on patrol in the night, pay attention to every sound and leaf, you dig? Every fluttering leaf. But now I know who my actual enemy is."

"Yeah man, with total respect I dig that. And we will be talking, Lon. I'll let you know how this trip plays out. Maybe you'll want to come in and take part at some point."

"I'll consider it, yes, I will. But you need to be talking to Ray, man. Ray will really trip on this idea. He has huge admiration for the way your mind works, and I think you know that."

"Okay, but where is he anyway? Aaron said he was off living in the hills north of the San Francisco. Wherever he's living, I'll go there."

"Yeah," Lon laughs, his old conga laugh. "The crazy bastard ran off with this hippie chick and a dog to some nature commune, cute little white girl. He wrote me a letter, sounds like he's living in a tree. It's out there west of Santa Rosa, I'll give you the directions."

"Far out, Lon, that would be righteous. I want to see our brother Ray."

"But Jake, the last few months before he split Ray got really way out. He and this girl were studying this strange book called the Urantia Bible. Ray would read to me in his, you know, voice, very passionate about these teachings. But to me it sounded like pure science fiction. It's like they flipped out on some kind of fairy tale. You ever heard of that Urantia book?"

"No man, never," I say with a grin, imaging Ray, "never heard of it in my life. What's it about?"

"Well, according to Ray's interpretation, people will go through a religious metamorphosis and will become super-conscious half-animals in the coming days. People who evolve will be able to rap in animal talk and be able to swim like fishes and even fly."

"All right then, wow," I start to laugh. "No Lon, never heard of that cult. Guess I'm gonna go up yonder though and find out."

Chapter 22

B ACK IN ATASCADERO, a place so humdrum that a cat might die of boredom here, Sorenson hands me an unopened letter with an enigmatic expression. Random surprises keep showing up like a joker cavorting through my life.

"I think it's something about your brother," he says, without embellishment.

The letter is from my mother, postmarked New Orleans. I open it and read, and the prescient monk is right again. My mother informs me in her chatty way that Even has turned up in New Orleans, with Shandy and her squabbling kids. They traversed the country in the turtle-like turquoise Ford, now having radiator problems, and almost out of money. Shandy intends to call her mom in LA and hit her up for some bread. Evan looks haggard and seems desperate to escape the situation. I smile with pleasure to learn of his plight with his come-hither Lilith, laughing softly to myself. But my brother wants to stay down south and help out our parents. It seems that our father is experiencing bad spells trying to get his breath, emphysema worsening, making him resort to the oxygen tank for hours every day. This is somber news, something that dad never mentions in his clear, philosophical letters. Fate is implacable, it's what happens, the tumbling dice are indifferent.

To be honest, I don't really mind anymore. I am freer than I have been in a long time. The smuggling bust and it's rueful consequences, all that shit's behind me now. My relationship with with life is buoyant and and beautiful. I don't feel obligated to do any particular thing, and the key is the fact that the Selective Service doesn't have a clue as to my regained freedom. They can't slot me into their murderous carnage in southeast Asia. They are guilty of the most heinous crimes against humanity and the precious earth, and all of them, all the connivers, liars and treasonous contrivers behind this profit-driven misery-making will be brought to reckoning.

But enough of that for now, fuck that. For by God and ragged glory, I am a free man, I can hit the road any time the wind moves me. Ray Vargas has answered my vibrant typewritten letter with a handwritten one of his own filled with warm brotherhood. Ray includes a scrawled map of how to reach Wheeler's Sheep Ridge commune in western Sonoma County. He pencils in the warning, "the last stretch of road is bad coming in, so have a spare just in case. Or ditch the car in Occidental and hike on over the ridge, mi casa is su casa! Don't go down the ocean slope to Bodega Bay, if you wind up there you missed the gate."

Ah beautiful. Everything that happens, happens now. Whatever, wherever, we are only happening now. The rest is just imagination and memory, only our doubts and fears get in our way. I give notice at Pablo's Laundry Dry Cleaning in SLO, and ten days later hand in my truck keys to those good people. Then, stuffing my surplus army pack with road gear, my old Oaxaca pack, telling Torgie that I'm off on a mission, I throw the pack in my yellow Lark and light out on 101, a wild paean of freedom in my chest. It all can be done, I have no doubt that we can somehow do it.

North of Gilroy, the highway slows into a two-lane meander through farming villages and odd stoplights. I stop at St Martin's winery for a tasting of five or six of their delicious wines with triple cream brie, then motor exuberantly through green hills toward San Jose. Angling off on the mountainous Pacific highway I cruise up the peninsula and into the city shining in cool, gray fog. Beloved city, San Francisco. I make my way through the hilly maze of streets, the fog opens up in patches of sunshine and Golden Gate park beckons as I pass by, meadows of hippie glory, festooned, long-hair people are everywhere. I follow a crawl of cars through a tunnel and around a curve in the dark green cypresses and come out at spires of the magnificent bridge.

The orange spires of the Golden Gate tower into the blue sky over the windy straits of the bay, white sails flash on the water. The traffic going over into the Marin headlands is light. I cross over the bridge with pure elation rising in my chest, freedom, freedom, freedom for the wandering nomad. I drive past the Sausalito marinas and into the north bay hill and ranch country, through postcard towns, then veer off 101 going west to Sebastopol and beyond into the coastal hills. I come upon the little village of Occidental sheltered in green fields and tall redwoods. Immersed in a reverie of solitude, I could drive these secret backroads all day long, but Occidental is the crossroads. I gas up at the towns only pump and consult Ray's scrawled map, then take a pitted road into the surrounding hills, through hollows of oak and redwood and across slopes of wind-bent cypress, winding my way onto the high ridges that overlook the vast Pacific. The old pavement is rough and broken, not any kind of tourist route. Every so often I notice a hand-drawn sign nailed to a post— "Wheeler's Ranch, up ahead, keep going. Open Land, Welcome."

There, high on the brow of the land, I come to a gate beside the pot-holed road and another hand-made sign, saying, "Wheeler's Sheep Ranch Commune, for the Benefit Of All, by

Decree of Open Land Manifesto." There are a few old pickups and cars parked in a clearing by the sagging fence. I leave my Studebaker and walk onto the land along a tire path through the weeds in the misty sunlit air, the olive pack slung on my shoulder. I walk with a sense of wonder.

For behold, back in the trees and cypress thickets there are random dwellings of different shapes, little shacks of weathered clapboard, tee pees, whimsical tree houses, canvas wall tents, rustic A-frames covered with tarps. Dogs bark, a few people working their gardens, doing their poetic thing, the gypsy children of free land and fog and sunshine. Bells and chimes hang in the trees, tinkling in vagrant breezes. No one pays much attention to me, the comings and goings of apparent strangers common place here.

I stop and ask a comely young woman with matted hair where I can find Ray Vargas. She's cradling an infant and at first I don't realize she is breast-feeding. She wreathes me in her smile. "Oh you must be Ray's friend," she says, "I think he told us about you. They're down there, in that grove of trees. Just follow that little path."

I take the rough footpath down the slope for about a hundred yards or so. In a tangled cluster of cypresses I find a dugout walled with driftwood timber and covered with canvas tarps. A skinny black and gray dog about knee-high comes out of the dugout and starts barking at me, followed by Ray in vagabond clothes. Seeing me, he breaks into his broad smile, crying, "brother, brother, it's been too long! Jake, I've been on the lookout for you!"

"Way too long," I laugh, spreading my arms, "wow, Ray, man."

We embrace like old comrades. Ray smells of wood smoke and patchouli, his dark hair sprouted into a wild afro. Seeing our camaraderie, the dog begins to bound around with excited barks, approaching me.

"Stop that barking, Poochy," Ray admonishes gently, "you calm down right now. This is my friend Jake, Jake's a wayshower. He's one of us, he's family. Hush up now."

Poochy comes closer, sniffing my knee, my extended hand. I rub between his ears, Poochy wags his tail, then goes over and lies down in the dirt by a log to watch us.

We get to catching up right away, sitting on stumps beside a fire pit scrapped out of the rocky ground. I drop my pack, fishing out some notes along with a copy of Gurdjieff's "Meetings With Remarkable Men," earmarked at places where he describes the mysterious powers of sound. It's like taking up a conversation that we just left off yesterday, intense, charged with emotional thoughts, although we haven't seen each other in over a year. On a plank resting on stacked stones there's a glass jar holding some yellow wildflowers, along with three Redtail Hawk feathers.

"Wait a minute," Ray says, "I want to show you my new bible." He ducks into the cypress dugout and reappears with a massive book in his hand in blue hardcover. Moving his stump closer to mine, Ray begins to show me the mysterious Urantia Book.

"Yes, my brother Jake, dig, the Urantia Religion," he says fervently, "I'm really into this trip now, totally. This incredible book has 2000 pages that were celestially transmitted, hundreds of sections covering all aspects of the cosmos and our supernatural creators, yes, yes, all the planetary systems and types of beings, Jake, it is so far out, with revelations about the family of man and how the trees and animals and races entwine and our ultimate destinies. yes, it's mind-blowing. There's over 700 pages on the life of Jesus alone, his unknown history, sort of along the lines of the

Aquarian Gospel only deeper. He's the super-master, Jesus of Nazareth, the true leader of us all."

Taking in this flood of esoteric gab, I ask, "Ray, you say celestially transmitted? What does that mean? Who wrote this book?"

"Right, right, dig, it happened back in the 1930's in Chicago. Celestial beings transmitted the book through the sleeping consciousness of this doctor, who would wake up and write everything down. It didn't happen overnight, of course, it took a few years to psychically transmit and organize all the knowledge. The revelation of the miraculous, Jake, this is it, this is the real deal!"

"So this huge book was channeled to someone in a trance, like a religious epiphany, only ongoing for years?" I'm trying to keep the innate skepticism out of my voice, I love this free-spirited man. "But there was no master lineage involved? It just occurred out of the blue?"

"Yes, yes, more along the lines of the sleeping prophet Cayce I would say, and JC, Jesus is the master link, the only one actually needed. Miracles will be made manifest in human form, this is the new religion for the new earth. So please Jake, you turned me on to ideas that were like a light switch in my brain, it was amazing. Give yourself the chance to check this book out. It goes even beyond where Gurdjieff left off, you will see."

"I'll do it, Ray, I will do so," I reassure him, although my intuition already whispers that it's mainly extrapolated and exaggerated make-believe. The mind is capable of the most exalted nonsense. There are no new religions per se, only the reformulation of ancient concepts that people desperately want to believe to secure some form of immortality. For a minute I hold the heavy book, leafing the pages, then I ask Ray, "these people here with you on Wheeler's Ranch, how many are there? Are they all following these Urantia teachings?"

Ray waves his hands in the air, grinning madly. "No, no man, a few of them are like us, but not everybody, not yet anyway." Ray Vargas laughs into the air, his dark brown skin shining with delight. "That's the beauty of this place, everybody does their own thing. But we all cooperate to make it happen, at least most of us do. There's maybe 60 or 70 freaks staying here, its a free zone, you can come live with us. People come and go, some of them just wander in and out. It's open and easy, there aren't many re-strictions from the owner, Bill Wheeler. He's a beautiful cat, Jake, a generous soul. He's made it so that anyone is welcome, you could move in tomorrow if you want. Oh it's primitive, hell yes, it's primitive, nothing fancy, and we all make it together. There's all kind of folks living on the land here, all kinds of unusual domiciles, and lately we're getting an influx of other hippies coming over from Morning Glory."

"What's Morning Glory? Is that another commune like this one?"

"Yes, yes, exactly. It's a few hills over and a little more sophis-ticated than this one. But Sonoma County is shutting them down for bogus health and building violations, real paranoid political shit. Dig my brother, they're bringing in bulldozers and knocking down people's shelters, chasing them away. They're threatening to do that here too, to come and burn us out, but Wheeler's fighting them in court with his lawyer."

"Fuck, that's crazy Reagan-instigated shit, bro. They're trying to turn the whole goddamn country into a police state. But how do you make it out here, Ray? You've got to have some kind of bread coming in. How do you make money out here in the boondocks?"

"Well," Ray laughs, clapping his hands, "almost any way we

can, you know, you know. We all try to help each other make it, except not everyone does. We've got some bad eggs around, yeah, some of the wanderers just come in and make trouble. We've had some meetings about it, Wheeler might have to banish certain personalities, I'm not saying who. But most of us here are committed, man, we love this free way of living. So we make money and bring in groceries and beer however we can, only no boosting stores because that'd just bring the heat. Sometimes we pick the apples in the orchards over at Sebastopol, a not all the ranchers are hostile. Some of them are friendly and we pick up odd jobs doing the grunt work. Sometimes someone gets money in the mail or scores a temp job in town. Like you always joked, you can always make it if you use your wits."

"I love that, I really do," I tell him. "And it's true, there's always a way to make your way in this world without becoming one of the pigeons."

We lean closer, reigniting our friendship. Late afternoon is coming on, the sunshine is waning, shoals of fog drift in over the hills from the nearby sea. I dig an old sweater out of my road pack and pull it on, Ray puts on a worn sweatshirt. He shows me their dugout, sort of a walled cave bored into the gnarled cypress thicket with a plank floor, a double mattress, a small table with the legs sawed down, with a canvas tarp roof, home sweet home. It's dim inside and probably home to various bugs, too, but the place has a woman's touch. Indian tapestries cover the low walls, a few books and Oracle posters, and a photo of Meher Baba. It's a cramped space, barely big enough for two people and a friendly mutt.

The girl shows up in the pale afternoon light with a sack of vegetables. She's short and slim, smiling, a brown braid down her back and lively, affectionate eyes. "Hi, I'm Nina," she says, "and I know who you are. Ray always talks about you when he goes deep. Welcome to our little Nirvana, I've got us some dinner here."

"Thanks a whole lot," I say, returning her smile. "I love this scene. just like old times."

Ray walks me around and introduces me to the other residents, some friendly, some rather guarded, for I'm the stranger here and ironically I could be the law scoping them out. But I get a brave and honest vibe from these beautiful people, involved as they are in a radical social experiment and dealing with unusual challenges. Most of them have made a conscious commitment to making a free-land open utopia, a hippie solution to what Henry Miller called, "America's air-conditioned nightmare."

Back at the dugout, I see that their crude setup is pretty well organized. Under a tarp-covered shed made of coastal driftwood, there's a stack of drying deadwood from the wind-bent cypresses. Two covered tin buckets filled with good water from the ranch's hand pumps, one for drinking and one for washing. Ray tells me there's a community bath shaped like a tall pine box on the hill, where everyone gets to take a warm, wood-fired shower once a week.

"We're not filthy savages copulating in the bushes," Ray states, "like the local media tries to make out. No man, we keep our scene together and our minds and bodies are clean."

Down the slope a way from the dugout he shows me the hand-dug hole where they shit. It's a narrow trench with heaps of dirt to throw in after with a folding army shovel. Toilet paper spools on tied-together sticks pushed in the ground and covered with plastic.

"When it gets too stinky I just cover it over with dirt and dig another one," Ray shrugs, "like the Indians used to do, right? Except I guess they used leaves to wipe their asses."

Wheeler's Ridge grows chilly in the evening, nothing like the warm, dry heat of Atascadero. Nina makes twilight dinner over a smokey wood fire in fire-blackened pots. Local carrots, onions garlic, and boiled brown rice seasoned with sea salt and curry powder. She serves us on enamel plates with slices of wheat-berry bread and crunch peanut butter, with steaming mugs of Asian tea. Good camp chow that keeps the chill off.

"As you can see we're mostly vegetarians," she says from across the fire-pit, "because we don't have much choice. If we buy meat or bacon we have to cook right away and eat it all, it won't keep. So we wolf up on a lot of beans for protein and spare the animals."

"I dig it," I tell her, "it's fine with me. Once I lived like this in the mountains of southern Mexico, just rice, some beans, quash, corn, whatever the Indians grew in the ground. We lived in a stone hut above a pipe in the rock wall where water gushed out, pure water. It was a beautiful trip and I love what you're doing here."

They clean things up together, Ray and his girl, an affectionate team, using a little soap and some rags, then Nina goes into the dugout and lights a pair of candle lanterns. Ray murmurs that there's room enough for all of us, including Poochy, who lies over in the cypress roots scratching and biting his fur. It's cozy in there, he confides, it's our private den, we can all snuggle together in the night. But I demure, spreading my ground tarp on a flat space and unroll my old brown sleeping bag.

Stars light up in the windows of sky, like a glittering necklace thrown against an ocean of ink. Orion rises above the dark trees, shimmering in the moonless sky above the fog. My brother Ray Vargas and I huddle near the fire, feeding it sticks and twigs as we nurture our ancient bond.

"So tell me Ray, who else up on this land is into the Urantia trip? Other than you and Nina?"

"Not many of us," he says, "just four or five seekers. Like I said, everyone more or less does their own thing. There's some yogis up here too, and there's a couple Hari Krishna's staying on the ranch. It's not like I'm trying to convert anybody, but this big book has become my path, tit strikes the right chord for Nina and me. You and I used to talk about restoring the earth to it's natural glory, to reconnect with essential nature, and I think the whole map is right here in this book. They say that Jimi Hendrix carries the Urantia Book with him wherever he goes and that The Grateful Dead trip on it. It's real knowledge, Jake, beautiful beautiful knowledge."

"I totally dig where you're coming from, Ray, far out man, and far in." I sit the low-burning fire with a dry branch, musing. "And what about psychedelics on this commune? Out in all this natural beauty there's got to be some mystical trippers, right?"

"Oh there are, my brother," Ray flashes his smile, "oh yes, yes indeed. We're all into the organic life. There's a couple of savvy mushroom hunters living among us, they show us the ones to eat for food and the ones that are cosmic. Magic runs wild in these lost foggy hills. During these summer months the Datura super-psychedelic thorn apple grows in the pastures, green bushy plants with white trumpet flowers. I've partaken of that bitter tea, that visionary elixir, Jake, oh Jesus Lord, I can't begin to tell you the things I've seen—incredible and beautiful and scary too, tripping for two days, the most incredible journey, mind-blowing and real, so incredibly real."

I break the dry branches into pieces, nodding to the cadence of my friend's voice. I understand, I myself have voyaged deeply into those primordial psychedelic landscapes. The burning embers flare up, flames crackle, lighting our shadowed faces. Ray's deep eyes are oceanic with love. "The body is just a chrysalis," he says gently, "for another reality to show itself, for the soul who yearns to be immortal, yes, you know my brother, you used to tell us."

In the cool morning we're up after sunrise, the mists furling through the cypress trees. I share their breakfast of oatmeal and raisins, red apples, and honey-sweet coffee. I pass a couple hours dragging in dead firewood with Ray while we reminisce about our friends. Wandering on this primitive commune makes me feel nostalgic for something I once very much wanted. Things change, time changes it. Before the sun is high I'm driving back through the redwood hills and fields toward Sebastopol, then down 101 toward the Golden Gate. Ray Vargas expresses a powerful interest in my envisioned self-awareness schools, eager to bring the new celestial kingdom on earth. But it's hard to say how he'll fit into the picture with his Urantia obsessions. My brother Ray's off into his own strange and mythical trip now, just as I was a few years ago in the Sierra Madre of Oaxaca. The dream is deep and life-changing, always, and it takes constant attention to realize who and you are – to touch the truth and to be that truth, is everything.

Chapter 23

THE TRICKSTER PAST gives you a second look sometimes, a kind of deja vu, as if asking, are you still interested? How strange the way our paths twine and snake back together in unexpected ways, whether by accident or design is a sheer guess. Quien sabe? as my Mexicano friends might say. You pay your dues, you take your chances, I could have been a blues man but took another way that turned into myself.

Back on the sere central coast, I cut loose everything that seems unnecessary to my intentions. It's not the first time, it's become a way of life. I sell the yellow Studebaker for a few hundred bucks, tucking the bankroll down my tall square-toed boots. American nomad, I am, about to hit the road again encumbered only by what I carry and as free as a wind-riding hawk. I buy a broad-brimmed leather hat to shade my face and gather a handful of maps and a few select books. Travel light, move with purpose, and let nothing interfere.

My rent on the oak-shaded duplex up, I shift back into the Center of Light with Torgelananda for a few weeks. I'm biding my time until Aaron Gold finishes his classes and shows up from Los Angeles. The mad reverend monk is generous as always, refusing to let me pay rent, buying us lamb chops and jugs of red wine, not trying to foist any moldering "power food" on me. In the nooks and crannies of the Quonset hut I store away those valuable things that I cannot carry – a box of Yogananda's home study discourses, some extra clothes, my scribbled poetry and meandering prose, along with a small library ranging from Tagore to Kerouac to Rumi, Mark Twain to Patanjali, James Baldwin to Leo Tolstoy to Albert Camus. I imagine a rambling old mansion around San Francisco to be the eventual home for these artifacts of existential experience.

One afternoon Torgie studies me thoughtfully, as I read about Gurdjieff's 28 types of human beings. I feel him looking at me and try to ignore the summons, then left my eyes.

"Let me just point out," he says, his eyes beaming with a preternatural shine, "that his is a momentous work we're involved in and there's no guarantees. So remember, if everything falls apart, you can always tell their fortunes. You've got that unique gift."

"What? Say again?"

"Oh, I see the donations pouring in, don't worry. But this Tarot card thing of yours, that's something you should expand on. It gives you a mystical aura and magnifies your influence."

"Mr Sorenson, no, no, I'm not sure about that at all. I mean, I'm just playing with those cards. It's a form of entertainment, you know, similar to astrology, interesting, but some crucial part has been left out. I can't claim any reliability with Tarot readings, my interpretations are too hit and miss. I'm even tempted to say that stuff gets made up out of imagination just to enthrall people."

"Hell, that doesn't matter. In a way that's the point, you can just make it up. Wrap a fancy turban around your head and hang out a shingle down in Laguna Beach or up in Berkeley. Before long people will flock in to get a reading from you. Charge at least 25 bucks a head."

I stammer a laugh, thinking he must be joking. "But that would be bullshit, I can't give an accurate reading. That would be flying under false pretenses, reverend, no way."

"That don't matter in the least," Torgie reiterates, doubling down. "Don't get hung up splitting moral hairs." He drops his voice into a whisper, saying, "The only thing that matters is they believe whatever you tell them. Then they see you as their leader. Then they'll follow you and the donations will come rolling in. You can persuade them with those fancy Tarot cards"

Momentarily stunned, I mutter, "I don't think so, reverend, no, I don't think so. Look man, that's outrageous and I've got to be real. I'm not into all this hocus-pocus and make-believe. For me, it's got to be authentic and verifiable or I'm not doing it."

"Well, one day you'll see you don't have to be so fastidious," Torgie shrugs nonchalantly. "You just have to lead them in the right direction, but don't worry, we'll get there."

The day following this bizarre exchange it turns weirder yet. I'm upstairs in the COL sanctuary above the country abattoir sorting through years of hand-written journals. Some of these multi-faceted musings are from my acid days. I hear Sorenson stomping around out in the corridor, talking to some unknown person. They come through the kitchen door and Torgie calls out, "hey Jake, come see who the wind blew in, you'll never guess."

I hear that other familiar voice—but no, it can't be. Arising from my pallet by the dusty window, I pass through the beaded curtain and receive a transfiguring shock. Standing there, wide-eyed himself, is my once-upon-a-time pot smuggling partner Bones Osgood.

"Pretty sure this is an old friend of yours," the reverend says, clearly amused. "When I drove up he was standing in the parking lot, staring at old man Mallet's butcher shop in disbelief."

Bones proffers a wan smile, saying, "Whew, man, that was pretty strange all right. For a minute I figured I must've gotten Bender's directions all wrong."

We clasp hands warily, Bones and I, a lot of water under the bridge. "So Bender told you where to find me? Hey man, deja vu all over again."

"Tell me about it. Bender always been the gadfly connector, right? He was in a health food store with this fat chick who was bossing him around. She told me she was a Capricorn, so it all kinda fit."

There's a swarthy woman with Bones, holding a baby in her arms. The child is in cloth diapers, chortling as she pats its back. She's younger than bones, in her mid-twenties with long black hair and a complexion right out of rural Mexico. She smiles shyly, speaking in an east LA accent. The baby starts to cry and she walks it back out into the corridor.

"Well, my friend, it's been awhile," I say to Bones, "what's happening these days?" He looks much the same, somewhat older, with a rueful cast to his face. He shows the year of prison time he had to endure, hard time that I avoided through luck of the draw. But Bones doesn't seem to be holding grudges, and it's clear the Mexicana and infant belong to him. In his lanky jeans, muslin shirt and a string of silver beads round his neck, he's living in unabashed hippie style.

"Same old, same old," Bones smiles, nodding toward the young woman with the baby standing in the door, "along with the brand new and fresh."

Bones chats for awhile with Sorenson and me, the peculiar astrological aspects, the bad scene for freaks down in LA, the monstrous war that keeps getting worse, then the woman interrupts, saying they need to go to the farmacia and get medicine for the restless child.

"Su pequena tummy esta molestando," she says, then in English, "he has an allergy of some kind. He can't seem to sleep right."

I walk them downstairs to their car, a huge old Buick station wagon crammed with their gypsy belongings. I mention Wheeler's Ridge to Bones and he says he's heard of Morning Glory, that he might check that scene out. He laments again how hard it's getting to be to live without kowtowing to authority. There is a subtle strain between us, but we're trying to find ease.

I'm leaning beside his window, looking at him and his Mexican wife, who's soothing their child. She knows there is a complicated history between us, she gives me an empathetic glance: "We're just passing through, I don't mean to cause any hassles."

Bones says in a wry tone, "you've been holed up here all this time, studying metaphysics with that gordito yogi preacher? Seems like pretty dull scene, man, how do you stand it?"

"Yeah," I laugh, "it's been pretty dull at times. But you have to make your own scene, anyway. Evan and I came up here to start an organic commune, then we met him. He's one of Yogananda's direct disciple. Things happen that you never foresaw, right? Now I've been cut loose from probation and I'll be hitting the road again soon. It's a new trip for me, Bones, new day. And Sorenson's been a good friend, we've been able to go deep into the mystical teachings."

Bones nods his head, thinking his own thoughts rather than listening. His inability to listen was what got us busted down at the Tecate borderline, but that's old faded news.

"Yeah, I hear that," he says, as much for his wife's benefit as mine, "but sooner or later you got to do your own thing, you know? You've got to do your thing, not somebody else's."

The infant starts crying again, the girl rocks and whispers to her baby. I give her a sympathetic look, then shift my eyes back to Bones. Our faces are 18 inches apart, we share a telepathic moment, two old friends who know each other's ways quite well.

"I guess you could say it's all about wish and intention," I say to him.

"How do you mean? Nobody else should decide that for you."

"I agree. It's been my my intention to find out what's real and what's not. Beyond that, there's not much to tell. Except that's what I've been doing up here for the past couple years."

Bones gives a shrug and almost frowns, this impasse has always been between us, the shadow between our otherwise natural agreement. Then he flashes me his amiable smile, saying, "cool Jake, and dig. I've got a few pounds of primo Michoacan weed under the blankets back there. Super excellent. I'll be more than glad to cut you a good price."

Surprised, smiling, I shake my head. "No, Bones, no, thanks anyway. I only smoke once in awhile nowadays and I don't keep it around. I'm just beyond all that."

I wave in the sunlit air as they pull out of the gravel lot, tires crunching. Bones turns north on Camino Real to who knows where. My old partner hasn't changed much, still on parole and still dealing weed, with a young wife and baby at his side. He's a kind and beautiful dude, Bones is, but the law doesn't give a fuck about that. One false step and your back in the slammer, the land of doom. Feeling conflicted by this encounter, I walk slowly back upstairs. Torgie sits there in his fat man's underwear, spectacles on his nose, reading a mail-order catalog of Catholic books.

He swivels in his oak rocker and says, "he's an unusual character and quite fortified in his point of view. Stubborn even, you might say. What was that incense on his clothes?"

"Incense? Ah no, Mr Sorenson," I reply with a crooked grin. "That was la mota you were smelling. Marijuana."

"Hah, gotha, I didn't know. Maybe that's why his brain patterns seemed a bit muddled to me. Still, he has that intelligent face, that spiritual demeanor."

"Oh, Bones is evolved, no question about that. We traveled a long ways together across Mexico. It was like wandering with a tripped-out Taoist."

"I noticed something flare up in your aura, a burst of dark intense green. You seem to be harboring some hard feelings toward him?"

"Hard feelings? Hmm, that could be, but not really. The smuggling bust, the break down between us, that was a bad deal and he never really owned up to it. But I can honestly say I'm not hung up on that anymore. I just don't want to mix what used to be with what's happening now. They're different worlds and Bones is still living in the old one."

Sorenson nods, pushing his glasses up his nose. "Yep, I under-stand what you're saying," he says, "those burnt bridges don't cut us much slack."

DURING THE LONG summer days my friend Aaron Gold comes up the coast from LA, traveling by bus. His school days at LACC are finished. I pick him up at the Greyhound station in San Luis, in the reverend's truck, and take him the long way back over the hills. We drive out to the coast at Los Osos, across the sand dunes and back bay into the fishing port of Morro Bay. After a cup of coffee in view of the mammoth surf boulder famous in these parts, we wind up through the Santa Lucia range on narrow highway 41 and back into Atascadero.

It's late afternoon, the sun falling in the wide blue sky over the Pacific. I veer off on a gravel road to a remote spot on rugged bluffs west of town, a panoramic view of the distant ocean coast. The clear afternoon light is translucent, sunset washes the sky over the vast curving sea in indescribable colors, birds in the sky birds on the wing. After a few minutes of quiet awe, Aaron glances at me and says, "I guess I see why you're not too keen on coming back too New York City with me."

"Not right now, my friend," I smile, "I won't be leaving the west coast anytime soon. For me, this is where it's at."

We pass a congenial time at the Center of Light in deep talks with reverend Sorenson about the consciousness movement arising from coast to coast in America. He regales us with his wonderful Yogananda stories, the master's life-like lithograph gazing benignly from the wall. Aaron seems intensely interested in Sorenson's insights into yoga metaphysics and commits to studying with him when he returns from the east coast. Even though I know how wacky Sorenson can be, I have no qualms. I want my young friend involved in the development of our seal-awareness schools, things are coming together.

I sit off to one side on a padded milk can with headphones on my head while they talk mysticism, plugged into the reverend's reel to reel tape recorder. I'm listening to a rock album I recorded from 33rpm, a San Francisco group called Quicksilver Messenger Service that really lights me up. My hair is growing long again, I'm cultivating a Viva-Zapata mustache. I have $750 dollars tucked down into my leather boots, a bankroll for the open road. That gypsy road is calling me again, singing in my blood, a new vision of a new world and I'm feeling immensely optimistic.

And then it's finally time to go, whatever happens happens now. The sun rises in the wild blue sky, birdsong fills oak trees. Shaking hands with the gracious reverend, Aaron and I sling our packs and light out north on 101. It's just a matter of sticking our thumbs out on the on-ramp, hitch-hiking has become a way of life up and down the California coast. Three freaks in a VW bus swerve to the shoulder and beckon us aboard. Jefferson Airplane booms on the 8-track, someone passes round a joint, we're riding high heading for the fabled city on the bay. Sunlight falls across the dry green hills of Paso Robles and the infinite sky enfolds us like a sheltering hymn.

Hours later, Aaron and I part company in San Jose, hugging as brothers at a crossing of roads. He's going a little farther up 101to the SF international airport and from there a TWA flight to NYC. I'm going westward toward the ocean, up the spectacular highway over the peninsula mountains into the shining city on its seven hills. Aaron holds my forearms with intense feeling, saying, "I'll be back in November, Jake, I'm all in brother, count me in. I want to get the initiations from reverend Sorenson and help you get those schools up and going."

Later that afternoon in patches of insouciant sunshine and fog, with no specific direction known, I find myself standing under a big-headed dachshund wearing a bow tie and chef's hat on Market street. I'm feeling hungry but I resist the smell of those greasy hot dogs. My surplus army pack is on the curb at my feet and I've got my thumb out.

To my surprise, a blue VW bug pulls over and I am looking into the face of a beautiful young woman. She gives me a tentative smile and gestures to me. I think she might be in need of directions; so I step off the curb and bend to the passenger window. She's lovely enough to steal your rouge's breath, lustrous auburn hair and soft hazel eyes. This chick's wearing a purple paisley mini-dress with cream stockings covering her shapely legs. Dear fucking God, ah me.

"Well, I must say," she says bravely, "you're impossible to miss under that Doggie Diner sign, I'm on my way across the bridge into Marin on a little adventure. Would that be of any help to you?"

I smile, oh I smile and declare, "oh yes, yes you bet it would," as lucky stars explode in my back-brain. I heft my gear into the backseat and get in. "Wow, looks like your ready for a road trip," she says a bit nervously, "that's an impressive pack."

"Yeah," I say, finding my natural voice, "it's been clear to Oaxaca and back. And right now, I'm doing some traveling with a definite purpose in mind."

"Oh do tell me, please," she brightens, "I'd love to hear. I've been feeling sort of stuck lately and I could use some inspiration."

Her name is Meghan Drum, an Irish-American girl with a melodious voice and sea-shell ears, to call her pretty would make a pauper of words. Her skin like fresh cream, long auburn hair, amber eyes flecked with gold, young high breasts that defy gravity, and a sweet curvaceous body that makes me swallow and so I begin to talk, not too much, just enough to get things going.

She gives me a sidelong glance and says, "I have to tell you this is so strange, me picking you up like this, and I don't even drive. I borrowed this car just for today and you're the only hitch-hiker I've ever picked up. But I saw you there and it was like a magnet pulled me right over." Laughing self-consciously, she says, "I guess I didn't realize I could be this daring."

Trying not to sound insanely pleased, I observe, "well, that's interesting. Because I've never done any long-distance hitchhiking before, this is my first time. I've always gone off and away by either car or motorcycle, but I just wanted to cut loose and it the road. Maybe this is what they call being in sync."

"Oh wow," Meghan enthuses, missing a shift, "that would be pretty incredible. I could really use some luck right now. I feel like

I've gotten myself into this weird rut and I don't quite know how to get out."

"Hmm, I hear you, like a psychological cul-de-sac. Me too, and more than once. But there are ways that always get you free. I think sometimes we just have to look with new eyes."

"New eyes? But is that really possible?" she says with as we motor past GG Park. "I get that intellectually but I just haven't been able to do it yet, you know? Memories and doubts keep getting in the way, or maybe I'm a little afraid. It's as though I'm lacking a technique or something. I've been studying acting techniques and I know how important they are."

"Oh without a doubt its doable, and a real esoteric technique can be a tremendous boost. We have choices. Why stumble around in confusion when you can leap free?"

Meghan looks at me with wide amber eyes, and murmurs, "really, why indeed?"

"I have a rancher uncle up in Montana who used to tell me, Son, being in a rut's not so bad, it's a damned sight better than being in a grave. Because a rut's open at both ends."

She lets loose a melodic laugh, almost like singing. "Wow, I've never thought of that! The way out is already there, if you just look at it the right way. You know something? Talking to you I already feel better. Hey, are you feeling a little hungry? Here, look in that bag and there's a canteen of chenin blanc on the backseat."

She hands me a paper sack full of dates, dried apples and blanched salted almonds, the mellow wine is like a blessing. We approach the towering orange spires and the bridge toll booth. Wind conjures the whitecaps in the straits, a few sailboats are on the water, the sky a vast ravishing breath of Monet blue.

Meghan opens up and and tells me about herself in her bright, voice. She is 22 years old, lives in Berkeley, takes a few psyche and art classes at the university, She is an aspiring stage actress, acting with a Shakespearean theater group and with a improvisational group that stages avant garde plays around the east bay, she sings, she dances. I listen to her in a sense of wonder, next to this lovely, ambitious chick I am a lazy dog. Then she blurts out that her personal life has become a disaster, her love life bringing her down.

"That's why I took this impromptu trip today," she confesses, "I wanted to work things out in my mind, you know, get some perspective on a treacherous scene. Just too much of the obviously wrong person, silly me. I've been going cold turkey on that situation and it's been kind of hard. Not that I want to go back – no, no way – but we know lots of the same people and he's lied about me. For this past month I've stayed mostly to myself and it's been lonely. I don't really have a close friend that I can actually say I trust."

She glances over at me with vulnerable amber eyes. "Am I making any sense or do I sound like a babbling raccoon?"

"No," I say gently, "you're making really good sense to me. If betrayal was involved I know that taste, and it's rotten. That can sure as hell leave you feeling stranded and alone."

"Yes, that's exactly how I feel. But I want to get past it, I want to put it behind me!"

"Right on. Then just stop thinking about it, Meghan, refuse to give it any more attention. That's a Vedanta technique and it works."

"Hey," she says in a shy excitement, "what are you doing this afternoon? I mean, are you on any kind of schedule?"

"Me?" I laugh, "no, not at all. All I'm doing is riding along with you, wherever that takes us. No plans beyond this moment."

"Oh wow, that's wild. Okay look, I'm going to drive to the top of Mt Tamalpais, I've never been up there before. Want to come with me?"

Scarcely believing my incredible luck, I smile and say, "I think I'd love to. I've never been up there myself, I hear the views are fantastic. Yeah, let's do it."

O holy spirit of life! How do you account for such an encounter, so unscripted, so flawless, a grace note out of nowhere? The ride through the green wooded lanes and hills of Marin county is illumined in sunshine, the vast blue sky a perfect robin's egg. The VW chugs up the slopes of Mt Tamalpais, Meghan grinding the gears but doing all right. We feel ebullient and happy, we have deep, strong interests in common—Bengali love poetry, Tibetan mandalas, minor chords of Celtic folk music, he passion for experimental theater mirrors my passion of existential thought.

"I'm just trying to become more of who I really am," she says, "it's not as though that's easy. People are always saying get real, be real, but they don't really understand. It's like we're all walking around in this semi-conscious daze, you know? The ego games that everyone plays, me too, like De Ropp talks about in his wonderful book. Oh, you know all about this stuff, don't you?"

I tell her that I've studied it deeply, I confide my studies in Gurdjieff a mysticism and initiation into the Kriya self-realization techniques. There are no coincidences, everything is connected to everything else, a super-conscious unified cause and it all happens now, not then, nor when, only now, and in some unseen way we design it ourselves, making us our own creators.

Listening to me, Meghan's face flushes with utmost interest. "Oh man, that is for sure, that's gotta be true, things can't just be dumb accident, it's just too far out."

Passionate now, inspired, I describe the purpose of my travels, to bring together an elite group of people who establish a network of self-awareness schools that positively changes society. "Oh my god," Meghan says in a low-octave voice, "I saw a card reader a couple weeks ago who told me something like that is in my future. She said I was going to meet an unusual man who would show me a new way of learning that would make a huge difference in my life. Jake, I'm not exaggerating, this id blowing my mind."

"Yeah? Well, ditto on that, Meghan," I laugh softly, "believe me, the feeling is mutual. Seems like we're on the same wave length."

The winding road up the green mountain slope carries us into bird's eye perceptions. Mt Tam rises 2000 feet above the surrounding countryside, any direction you look is magical. The Pacific spreads to the western horizon like an shining blue plane glass, a silver curtain of fog in the far distance. Around the road curves we take in the verdant Marin woodlands, the panorama of the bay, the far hills of Berkeley and Oakland, the spires of the famous bridge, and the fabled city itself gleaming in the sunlight. We climb to the top of the road in the chugging VW, then get out and climb some rocks and claim it all, this moment, claim this transparent day.

Somehow time has stopped for us, suspended its movement. There is nobody else around, only she and Ion in the chrysalis of something too beautiful to capture. We find a secluded spot among the boulders, the top of the world, out of the breeze, and Meghan sits down close to me.

"I really want to to tell you something," she confides. "I've never been with anyone before that's made me feel things so suddenly and intensely. I don't know how to put it. Being here with you makes me feel like laughing and crying all at once. What is it?"

"What isn't it?" I wonder, my words dissolving like incense.

"All I know is that when I stepped out this morning, I never imagined a meeting so beautiful or being here now, with you."

She moves closer and nudges her face into the hollow of my neck, inhaling my scent. "You smell like wildflowers," she murmurs. "Did you know that?"

I draw her closer, feeling the urgency of her, her plangent heart, the soft crown of her head on my mouth. She tilts her face up and our lips touch and taste, our breath commingles.

"Oh my god look," I say, suffused in rapture, gesturing with my finger into the indescribable, "Meghan, look at that."

Spread below us is a quilt of silver fog unfurling across the north bay and the golden gate headlands. In the eastern sky above the Oakland hills a full moon rises in clear daylight, while on the western horizon the sun sinks in a molten blaze into a reef of sea fog. San Francisco gleams in holy lingering light as if made of mirrors. She finds my hand, our finger entwine. I don't know what that sun and moon portend or what it might mean, but whatever it is momentous.

She presses herself closer, our bodies fervent now, almost breathless, she says to me, "I know we were supposed to meet, Jake, I know we were. Everything about this day is so amazing, such serendipity. Such accidents aren't allowed, right? You've got something I need, I feel it in you, and I'm not afraid."

Knowing her now, knowing I can live in her amber-brown eyes and rise, breathing her in, there is no space for doubt. She is the one I have been looking for, she seeking me, the soul of bright morning. She is meant to be with me and nothing can be denied us. Holding her close and seeing past her sunlit hair at the panorama of earth and sea, I know something deeper than words, beyond clarity, irrefutable. I am all that I behold, I am beloved, I am that.

Down beside the blue waves
I walked looking
and I saw you
as only you can always be.
I wonder now
in my limitless mystery
if you will speak to me
as a dog to his boy,
as a woman whispers to her lover,
as a bird jumping in salt sprays.
For years I have incessantly
babbled out yarns,
wondering inwardly
how far it would be?
I carried around many things
forgetting you almost at will,
yet you stayed with me constantly.
Once I thought
you would be but a season,
you were only a mortal season.
For there is the ice that melts,
there is the ember that dies out,
the new leaf breaks from the snow
and later vanishes.
I could not think you would remain.
I thought perhaps, like the others,

you would come and go,

your trail would lead away,

yet your trail has been one with me.

An unspoken reality,

you are

always with me.

—South Big Sur Coast, circa 1970

www.ingramcontent.com/pod-product-compliance
Lightning Source LLC
Chambersburg PA
CBHW070114120726
47909CB00002B/596